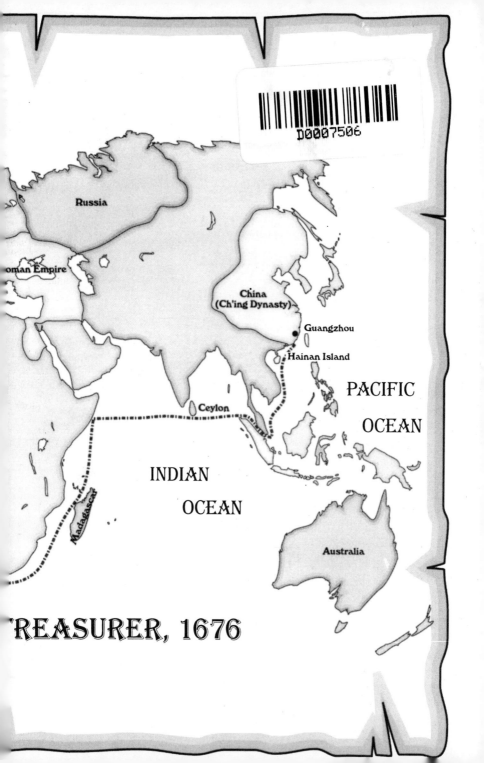

HYPOTHESIS

William A. Inglehart

VANTAGE PRESS
New York

This is a work of fiction. Any similarity between
the characters appearing herein and any real persons,
living or dead, is purely coincidental.

Cover design by Susan Thomas

FIRST EDITION

Copyright © 2000 by William A. Inglehart

Published by Vantage Press, Inc.
516 West 34th Street, New York, New York 10001

Manufactured in the United States of America
ISBN: 0-533-13416-1

Library of Congress Catalog Card No.: 99-97538

0 9 8 7 6 5 4 3 2 1

To my father

HYPOTHESIS

Prologue

THE NEW YORK TIMES
August 16, 2000

By THOMAS HUGHES
The Associated Press

ATLANTA—A spokesman for the Center for Disease Control (CDC) reported that the flu-like symptoms prevalent in the Middle East are concentrated in Iraq. It was widely reported last month that the Middle East was experiencing a high incidence of influenza, resulting in several deaths. The appearance of an influenza epidemic in the middle of the summer was highly unusual in that area. Coincident with the information that the symptoms are largely isolated in Iraq, there has been speculation as to the cause. The possibility that the epidemic was caused by an accidental discharge of some form of chemical weapon has been suggested. There has been no official statement to date from the Iraqi government concerning this matter, and officials at the Center for Disease Control stated that they do not expect one in the future.

Tikrit, Iraq, April 14, 1947

The boy crouched behind the old wagon, not moving a muscle. He studied the small house. It was typical of the dwellings, plastered with mud on the outside, two rooms in the interior. Having seen no human movement and satisfied that twilight was sufficient, he darted toward the building and flattened his back against the side wall. He breathed heavily for a minute and then relaxed slightly. His right hand reached under his worn cotton shirt and felt the cold metal of the pistol tucked in his equally threadbare trousers. It became dark and he waited longer. Then the sound of footsteps on the unpaved road in front. The boy sucked in air and withdrew the weapon. What followed took less than sixty seconds. A plain, tired-looking woman of about forty left the road and started toward the house. As she reached the door, the boy dashed around to the front and fired the pistol three times. The woman dropped to the ground with only a slight gasp as blood flowed on the earth. He turned and started to run, then he paused and put the weapon back in his trousers and began running again. A neighbor, startled by the sound of the shots, looked out his window, but the boy was gone.

One

Baghdad, February 23, 2001

Saddam Hussein was ready. It had taken sixteen years, but now he was ready. Most of the Western world considered him to be an irritating mad man and perhaps he was. But he was also a man with a goal, a ruthless brilliance, and a capacity for incredible persistence. He had endured a bloody, wrenching seven-year war with Iran followed by the Gulf War, which destroyed more than half of his military capacity in less than ninety days. He had survived ten years of fencing and finessing UN inspection teams, diplomats, the secretary-general of the United Nations, and the president of the United States. There had been numerous attacks on his country, principally by the U.S. and Britain, and there had been thirty attempts on his life that he could remember. He used more than a dozen look-a-like doubles to confuse those interested in his whereabouts, and he *never* slept in the same place on two consecutive nights.

Citizens in the Western countries, particularly the United States and Britain, were painfully aware of this man. Fifteen years earlier he had been unknown, and now his face was probably one of the ten most recognized in their world. And though they knew they despised him, did not trust him and would be pleased to see him gone from the earth, they really knew little about this nightmare that would not go away.

Saddam was born in al-Auja, a tiny mud and straw village on the outskirts of Tikrit in what had been ancient Babylon. It was a community of poverty and violence. The circumstances of his birth could not have been more unhappy. His mother, Subha, was seven months pregnant with Saddam when her husband, a landless peasant named Hussein al-Majid al-Tikrit and their young son were killed. Subha's reaction was that this fetus inside of her wanted no competition and had been responsible for killing his father and brother. She tried to kill herself and the baby, but was unsuccessful and the infant was born in April 1937. Subha named him Saddam, which means "one who confronts."

Unable to care for the child because of her poverty, she sent Saddam to her brother, Khayrallah Tulfah, who lived in Tikrit. The child's uncle was an educated man and an army officer. A member of revolutionary groups committed to getting the British out of Iraq, the uncle raised Saddam until the age of four when Khayrallah was arrested and jailed for his activities. The boy was then returned to his mother, who had remarried to Ibrahim Hassan, a local street tough known as "Ibraham the liar." The step-father was abusive to Saddam, both physically and mentally. He forbade him to go to school, but insisted instead that he spend his time stealing goats and chickens. Ibraham enjoyed frequently beating young Saddam with a stick covered with asphalt.

When the boy was ten, Uncle Khayrallah was freed from prison and Saddam ran away to Tikrit to join him. His uncle had a different view on raising children. He taught Saddam to be a revolutionary and gave him a pistol, which he took to school. Saddam became angry with one of his teachers and killed her with his weapon. He was found at home, asleep, the pistol still warm under his pillow. She had the distinction of being the first of thousands of Saddam's victims.

Khayrallah took the boy to Baghdad when he was eighteen, and Hussein took the exam to become a military cadet, but failed. At the time the Arab world was on fire with the actions of Nasser, who had thrown out the king of Egypt and become the most prominent Arab leader. Saddam, caught up in the furor of Arab nationalism, joined the Ba'th' party, a radical nationalist group. He became what one would call a "hit man" for the party, an enforcer and executioner and, as a wanted criminal, was forced to leave the country, traveling to Cairo, where he enrolled as a law student and lived as an exile for three years.

In 1963 a coup in Iraq brought the Ba'th party to power and he returned to Baghdad, now a mid-level party member, but still functionally a hit man. In an arranged marriage, he wed his cousin and shortly after, when another coup threw the Ba'th party from power, Hussein was jailed for two years for an attempted assassination. While in prison he became a student, studying Hitler, Stalin, and the Mafia. He learned well, as can be observed through his future actions. Out of prison, he again worked with members of the Ba'th party toward control of Iraq. In 1968 in still another coup, Saddam's cousin became the Iraqi leader. Hussein became head of the Secret Police, was a hatchet man, and soon became the real power behind the scene. In 1972 Saddam became a true hero to millions of Iraqis when he nationalized the Iraqi Petroleum Company and used the wealth that this created to modernize Iraq, including providing electricity to hundreds of villages. In 1979 he edged his cousin out and became the dictator/ruler/president of Iraq.

Now he sat at the head of the conference table in the room where his senior staff was assembled. The room was in one of more than three dozen buildings that the Iraqi government described as presidential palaces. It was apparent, however, that this room was for official business meetings. It was furnished with a credenza to hold tea and soft drinks and was equipped with a large projection screen, a VCR, a TV monitor, a computer, an overhead projector and a blackboard.

There was not one man in the room who had been with Hussein when he successfully gained control of Iraq. All members of that group were dead, several at his own hands. The Elite Guards stationed at the doors and throughout the room were nearly all from his village and many were distant relatives. He trusted none of them. His survival policies were simple. Kill any man at any time, with or without a reason. Trust no one, not your wife, not your children, not your relatives, not your mistresses, your closest advisors or staff. He was not concerned with his friends. Saddam had no friends. When he walked, he walked with some deliberate effort due to an ailing hip and when he seated himself, he eased into a chair gingerly. There was muffled conversation in the room as Saddam studied some papers before him. When he looked up, the room was immediately silent.

Picking up a laser pointer, he walked over to a huge map that covered nearly all of the wall closest to his chair. The map included the portion of the world from the United Kingdom on the west to New Delhi, India, on the east. Ethiopia was on the southern edge and the top or northern area extended to Moscow. There was a blue line around Saudi Arabia, Iran, Oman, the United Arab Emirates, Qatar and Bahrain. A green line encircled Turkey, Greece, and Egypt. Kuwait was entirely filled in with red. The Iraqi dictator paused while facing the map, apparently changed his mind and returned to his seat. He looked over at one of the men seated to his right, studied his face briefly, and said "Mr. Minister of Health, it is time to tell them."

The man he had addressed was matinee-idol handsome, over six feet tall with a flat belly, jet-black hair graying at the

8

temples and black onyx eyes. He had lived a life of privilege as a young man, a member of a wealthy family living in an exclusive section of Baghdad. Tariq Salman had been educated in England both as an undergraduate and later in medical school. His social and professional position had kept him from the chaotic circumstances that had dominated the past fifteen years in Iraq. He had not been required to serve in the military, and until recently he had been isolated from the agonies and the deaths that were the imprimatur of the Hussein regime. Returning to Baghdad after medical school, he joined the faculty of the University of Baghdad, teaching and doing research in his areas of primary interest, which were thoracic and pulmonary diseases. He married a woman from a prominent Iraqi family and she had delivered two children. The marriage was correct, but not close, and Tariq had experienced a series of mistresses, usually with young women he met in his medical career.

Tariq's father had been one of the few members of the Baghdad upper class who had supported Saddam Hussein early in his takeover of the Iraqi government. Four years earlier, in 1997, Tariq had been contacted by one of Hussein's administrative deputies and offered the position of minister of health. Tariq's predecessor at the Health Ministry had been executed and his body had been cut in pieces and sent to his wife in a canvas bag. The structure of Iraq was such that Tariq recognized that such an offer must have the approval of Saddam and this was not an offer, but an order.

Tariq left his low-pressure life in academia and moved into a large office in the Ministry of Health, a modern structure in a complex of buildings housing various ministries and bureaus. For the first few months, he spent his time familiarizing himself with the problems and operations of the ministry, and then about three months later, his life changed forever when he was again visited by the administrative deputy who had contacted him originally. He was instructed that on the following morning he would be picked up at 8:00 A.M. to attend an important meeting. He was told that he should wear the uniform that he had been provided, but had never felt any desire to wear.

The following morning he was in his office in uniform when precisely at 8:00 A.M. the administrative deputy entered his office and instructed him to accompany him. The deputy, a rodentlike little man, seemed distracted that morning and spoke only in brief nervous instructions. Entering a waiting limousine, they began to drive through Baghdad. There was a driver and a member of the president's elite guard in the front seat. Tariq and the deputy sat in the back. No one spoke and Tariq felt apprehensive and tense.

After about fifteen minutes on the outskirts of Baghdad, the driver pulled the vehicle over to the side of the road and stopped. The deputy reached into his attaché and extracted a piece of black cloth on which there were black plastic strips. He faced Tariq and said, "Mr. Minister, you will be required to wear this for the next half hour or so."

He slipped the cloth over Tariq's head. It was a sophisticated blindfold. It was not uncomfortable, but it was completely effective. It was a bright cloudless day in Baghdad, but Tariq was in total darkness. Then further instructions:

"You will also be required to wear this."

He slipped a headphone over Tariq's head. Pleasant and relaxing music filled his ears. Again, it was not uncomfortable, actually rather enjoyable. He was now in his own world, he could not see a thing and the only thing he could hear was the music from the headphone. But Tariq remained tense and on edge.

During the remainder of the ride, the limo took many

turns and several stops. Tariq wondered if they were going around in circles or actually traveling a distance, when suddenly the music stopped. The deputy had removed the headphone and then said, "Mr. Minister, I will now remove the blindfold."

Tariq looked around. They were in an underground parking area. Several other limos and a couple of military jeep type vehicles parked nearby. There were Elite Guards outside the limo, and one was handling some paperwork with the driver. Tariq took a pocket comb from his uniform trousers and ran it through his hair, which had been disturbed by the removal of the blindfold. He tucked his shirt tightly in his trousers and buttoned his jacket. They exited the limo and followed two of the guards. Two more guards followed them. They passed through a metal detector and into an area where there were several small cubicles.

"It will now be necessary for you to remove all of your clothing," said the deputy. "Please enter one of the examination rooms."

Tariq was startled and felt somewhat awkward as he entered the cubicle closest to him, noticing that the deputy was also entering one of the examination rooms. One of the guards entered the cubicle with him, and while Tariq was stripping, the guard pulled on rubber gloves. The guard told him to open his mouth and he held a flashlight and looked thoroughly in his oral cavity. Then he shined the flashlight in his ears. He slowly examined his torso, legs and feet. The he instructed him to spread his legs apart. The guard examined his genitals and told Tariq to bend over. The guard briefly examined his rectum and then took a tube of jelly, which he put on the index finger of his right hand and inserted the finger in Tariq's rectum. His probe reminding Tariq of the first time he had learned to examine a man's prostate in medical school.

During the entire examination, the guard was completely professional. It was apparent that he had gone through this procedure many times before. He finished by stating, "I have finished my examination, sir. You may put your clothes back on."

Tariq again donned his uniform and exited the cubicle. Seconds later the deputy came out of another one of the examination rooms buttoning his shirt, and Tariq realized that the deputy had been similarly inspected by one of the guards. The deputy, Tariq, and the guards now proceeded past the examination area into a hallway. Other guards were in the hallway, and Tariq noticed that they were unarmed with the exception of a heavy club in a holster on their belt. This surprised him as the guards assigned to the Ministry of Health always carried an automatic weapon. They came to a door where a guard examined some kind of a form, made a note on the form, and admitted them. Three middle-aged women, all wearing uniforms, sat at desks. The one in the middle stated stiffly to the deputy that the appointment was set for fifteen minutes from now and that the schedule that day was being maintained. She offered them coffee, which Tariq accepted. It was Arabian coffee, sometimes called Arabic or Bedouin coffee, served in tiny cups with no handles, which held only two or three sips. The coffee was flavored with cardamom, which made it greenish-brown in color. Tariq had to learn to appreciate this beverage after he had returned from medical school in England. While in the UK, he had acquired a taste for tea, but it was seldom offered in Baghdad in the manner in which it was served in Britain. Tariq was still feeling apprehensive and took a deep breath, telling himself to relax.

A buzzer was heard on the desk of the woman. She picked up the phone, listened briefly, said, "Yes, sir," and put the phone down. She nodded at the deputy, who nervously stood up, tucked in his shirt and glanced at Tariq, who also stood up. The deputy followed by Tariq walked toward a door, which had a guard on either side. One of the guards opened the door and both men entered. They were in a large office, which was decorated in a handsome but not palatial manner. The room was occupied by only one man, who sat behind a large mahogany desk. Tariq recognized him immediately.

"Mr. President, may I present to you the minister of health?"

Saddam Hussein stood up, smiled slightly, and extended his right hand. Hussein wore a military uniform with an open collar. A 9-mm Italian pistol was holstered on his hip. He was slightly overweight but exuded an air of vigor, power, and authority. Tariq noted a scar on his chin and acne marks on his neck, which had not been noticeable in photographs. Fifteen years earlier he had been unknown outside of Iraq. Now he had one of the most recognizable faces in the world. As they were shaking hands, Saddam said: "Your father has been a loyal friend, and I have heard good things about you. You may be seated."

Saddam sat behind his desk, and Tariq took a seat at one of the chairs in front of the desk. The deputy remained standing until Saddam nodded at him and he did a brisk military about face and exited the room.

After that meeting with the Iraqi president, life for Tariq was never as it had been before. He had always been a sound sleeper, but he now tossed fitfully most of the night and got out of bed frequently, pacing, reading, and drinking forbidden Scotch. His wife noticed the difference immediately and pressed him to explain what had changed him, but he was non-committal with her. He tried using medications to assist in obtaining some sleep, but the effect only lasted for a few hours and then he would wake up feeling drugged but unable to sleep. He had never had excess fat, but he lost weight and developed a somewhat haggard look. Dark circles began to appear under his eyes. Most embarrassing of all, he was frequently unable to make love to his mistress, and the nights at her apartment were nearly totally without sleep. She had no reason to suspect what was dominating Tariq and worried that she no longer aroused the minister. She did not know that he was nearly numb with fear that he might talk in his sleep and reveal the agony that was dominating him.

The minister of health rose to his feet and looked around the conference room. The men in that room, all wearing military uniforms, were survivors. They were in that room because they were ruthless and concerned with their self-interest. Many of them had participated in the execution of opponents of the Hussein regime either real or imagined. Some had even been the triggermen. They had survived thus far on wit, cruelty, and loyalty to the Butcher of Baghdad. But Tariq knew that none of them had ever even imagined what was to be revealed to them.

"Honored Ministers," said Tariq, "at the request of our president, I have certain facts to present to you. You are all aware that the last eighteen months have been a trying and unusual period for our country from a health perspective. We have experienced an unprecedented occurrence of influenza-like symptoms throughout the country regardless of locale or season. The Ministry of Health has treated tens of thousands of citizens with a variety of medications, but none have proven particularly successful. The means by which this sickness has spread has never been determined. Virtually every man in this room has been a victim of this mysterious malady in varying degrees. The Health Ministry estimates that over two thousand deaths have resulted from the sickness. It has been noted frequently that our neighbors in areas such as Iran, Turkey, Syria, and Saudi Arabia do not seem to be afflicted as badly, if at all."

The minister of health paused and sipped from a glass of water.

"Upon instruction from our president, I am now informing you that you have just observed the cause of the illness."

There were startled exclamations and looks of uncertainty on the part of every man in the room other than the president and the minister of health.

"Honored Ministers, I now inform you that the cause of this massive sickness has been our water and I now invite you to join me in partaking of this beverage."

Tariq sipped again from his glass, but no one joined him.

"All of you are aware that our government has done substantial research and testing on both chemical and biological substances for use in weapons. Some of you may be aware of substances known technically as Botulinal Toxins. I will not try your patience with excess scientific data regarding Botulinal Toxins, which I will refer to as BT, however, you will benefit from the following." The minister of health referred to his notes:

"These toxins are a protein and almost any food with a pH above 4.5 can support the growth of these toxins. If released in the air, they can be absorbed through the lungs, skin and eye. A lethal dose is minuscule, being about .02 milligrams per minute. Initial symptoms, which appear in 6 to 48 hours, are dizziness, sore throat, and dry mouth, followed by a progressive muscular weakness and paralysis. Death is due to respiratory failure and cardiac arrest and occurs in three to eight days, depending on the dose absorbed.

"Treatment is available through the use of an anti-toxin if used within 48 hours of exposure, and if supported by oxygen to assist breathing. The toxin in water, food or earth is stable for up to a week; however, it is destroyed by boiling such food or water for 5 to 10 minutes. There is no vaccine or BT preventative treatment known. That is, there is none known to the outside medical community. However, some time ago our president informed me that our scientists had developed a water soluble substance that appeared to be effective in preventing BT toxicity." Again Tariq lifted his glass and sipped water. Again no one else followed his example.

"The efficacy of the anti-BT substance was tested on certain prisoners. Over 200 of these prisoners were dosed with the substance for eighteen months, ingesting a minimum of 2 liters of treated water daily. They exhibited the same flulike symptoms that we have discussed and two of them died, but the cause of death was inconclusive. The remainder was then exposed to a highly lethal dose of BT. Of these only four died. In my opinion all or nearly all of them would have died in two to five days without the preventative substance.

"Upon direction of the president, eighteen months ago I arranged for the anti-toxin to be introduced to the nation's water supply. This included all the drinking water and where possible the ground water. We estimate that as many as 95 percent of our citizens have been exposed to the treatment. The result was the symptoms that all of us, including me, have experienced."

Salman paused then said, "Are there any questions?"

All eyes turned to Saddam to see if he seemed to be in a mood to permit questions. He nodded and the minister of the interior raised his hand.

"Mr. Minister of Health. Will this water treatment continue and if so for how long?"

"It will continue until the president instructs me to discontinue it," replied Tariq. Another hand, this time from the minister of justice.

"Mr. Minister, do I understand correctly then that 95 percent of the citizens of Iraq are now immunized against what you call BT."

"No, I believe that it is something less than that," offered the minister of health. "In our test on the prisoners, we knew for certain that each of them had been exposed regularly to the preventative substance. We can only estimate the exposure of this antidote to the population as a whole. Perhaps as many as 90 percent of the total population has been immunized, but it is impossible to know."

Every man in the room wanted to ask why this had been done and what was the purpose? But the president himself had directed the procedure. No one was going to question a decision by Saddam. It was silent in the room. Tariq looked at the president who said, "Be seated Mr. Minister of Health."

Then Hussein looked over to the other side of the table. "Mr. Defense Minister."

A small man stood up and said,

"Thank you, Mr. President." Ramzi Kassem had not been educated as a soldier, but he had what Saddam wanted in a minister of defense. He was totally without conscience or compassion and unquestionably loyal to Saddam. The word "sycophant" seemed to have been created to describe Kassem. Although he was feared by the other ministers and governmental leaders, he was also an object of frequent jokes. His incredible chauvinism to Hussein prompted jests that surely he must personally wipe the president's ass when Saddam had finished with his infrequent bowel movements. Ramzi was a distant relation to Saddam, which offered no guarantee. Kassem's predecessor as minister of defense had been a Hussein son-in-law and Saddam had that man, the father of his grandchildren, executed. Like Saddam, Kassem had grown up as a member of

17

a peasant family in the village of Tikrit. Also like Hussein, Kassem had been a member of the Ba'th Socialist Party.

But where Saddam exuded a strong masculine vigor, Kassem was almost childlike in appearance. It was not only his stature of barely more than two meters nor his slender build. It was his eyes. They were very large and very brown and sheltered with lush, long almost feminine lashes. His unusual appearance gave him a somewhat pathetic and helpless aura. But those who had real knowledge of the man behind the waiflike façade knew better. Every general in the Iraqi army was terrified of Ramzi Kassem. High-ranking officers mysteriously disappeared when Ramzi was not satisfied with their performance or attitude. To facilitate his total control over the military, there was no command structure comparable to the U.S. Joint Chiefs. All of the principal Iraqi generals reported directly to Kassem individually.

"Various pieces of the information that I will now present are known to you," said the defense minister. "Beginning in 1992 we began an aggressive, however clandestine, program to procure advanced missile capability. The breakup of the Soviet Union and the subsequent economic chaos in the resulting countries offered numerous opportunities for the purchase of both advanced missiles and missile technology. By 1996 we had obtained three types of Soviet missiles in various quantities. Our activities to modify and test these weapons required us to significantly restrict United Nations arms inspectors beginning in mid-1997. Most of this activity took place in facilities and areas that were identified as presidential Palaces.

"You would find it exceedingly boring," said Ramzi, "if I were to go into great detail about the technological capabilities of each of these weapons."

What the minister of defense knew, however, was that

the three weapons systems had different degrees of capability and that they had been obtained from sources in both Russia and the Ukraine. Further modifications had been made possible by contracts with companies in Germany, France, Switzerland, and even one clandestinely originating in the United States.

The shorter range system was known as the SA-10 Grumble SAM System. This was a ground-to-air system launched from a vehicle and able to engage several targets at once. The missile was a single stage missile and originally had a range of about a hundred miles, but with modification was now effective up to about two hundred miles.

A larger system had been substantially modified. It was based on the Soviet R-29/SS-N-8 Sawfly, which was originally designed as a submarine-launched missile. This was a two-stage system and with its substantial modifications was believed to have a range of up to four hundred miles.

The largest of the three systems was an R-36M/ SS-18 Satan missile. This had been developed by the U.S.S.R. as an intercontinental ballistic missile. It was a two-stage rocket, which was launched from a silo and had a range of up to 5,000 miles. It had been developed in the 1970s and was not the cream of Soviet technology, but it had awesome potential.

"The SA-10 was primarily developed for conventional weaponry," continued the defense minister. "The R-29 and R-36M were both engineered to carry nuclear devices. All three have been modified to carry biological substances.

"Mr. President, that concludes the information I was scheduled to present."

Saddam Hussein again rose to his feet, picked up the laser pointer, and walked over to the map.

"At 10:00 A.M. on February 26th the foreign minister will join our ambassador to the UN in the New York City headquarters of that impotent and ineffective organization. He will announce that at precisely that same moment, which will be at 6:00 P.M. in Iraq, we have commenced an overwhelming missile attack on Kuwait."

The laser pointer pinpointed that small Arab country on the map as if to incinerate it on the spot.

"The UN membership will be advised that the missiles carry a biological agent which we believe will kill at least 50 percent of the inhabitants of that country within four days. He will point out that we consider that Kuwait has been and is a province of Iraq and that this is an internal matter. We are simply actuating a necessary police action in our own country.

"The UN members will be advised that if they cooperate fully with Iraq, peace will prevail and no further deaths will result. Cooperation will require the following:

1. The UN Security Council and General Assembly will recognize that Kuwait is an integral part of Iraq.
2. The Security Council and General Assembly will recognize that Saudi Arabia, Iran, and the oil-producing states of the Persian Gulf will produce oil only in the amount that is directed by Iraq. Further these countries will pay a duty to Iraq for every barrel of oil produced. The amount of that duty will be determined by Iraq.
3. The Security Council and the General Assembly will recognize that Iraq, and the countries within its hegemony, will sell oil only to countries approved by Iraq and only in amounts and at a price determined by Iraq.
4. Every member nation of the Security Council and heads of state of Saudi Arabia, Iran, and the Gulf countries will sign the treaty establishing these agreements.
5. The Iraqi military forces will establish a system of BT stor-

age tanks throughout all major cities in Kuwait, Saudi Arabia, Iran, and the Gulf States. As long as all of our demands are met and no hostile action is taken against Iraq in the future, these tanks will remain benign. If at any time in the future any country or countries attempt to circumvent the Iraqi control of oil in these areas, or attempts any military action against Iraq, the tanks will be activated and these areas will be saturated with toxin wiping out the local population."

Saddam paused and took a long drink from his glass of water. Then he continued. "The foreign minister will also advise that if this treaty is not accepted and signed by March third, a similar rocket attack will take place on Saudi Arabia, Iran and the Gulf States on that date. We project similar casualties. If, after that time, the treaty is not signed by March 6th, an attack will be launched on Turkey, Greece, and Egypt. We project that the casualties of such an attack could amount to as many as 50 million deaths. Further, and this is most important, the UN membership will be advised that all missiles are currently loaded, aimed and operable. If any military activity of any sort is initiated against Iraq, or if any effort is made to assist any of these countries in any way including medical aid, all the attacks will be immediately activated. The cost of provocation against Iraq will be the greatest catastrophe in the history of the world." Saddam picked up his glass and as if he were toasting his guests:

"Gentlemen, I suggest that you drink plenty of water."

He got up and walked toward the door. Two guards sprang to attention and one opened the door as Hussein left. Shortly Kassem and the foreign minister also exited, but the remainder of the men sat in stunned silence. The minister of interior poured a glass of water; held it up as to examine it, then drank it slowly. Finally, there was brief commentary from a few as they made their way out of the room in a haphazard manner, still looking dazed and uncertain.

Two

Los Angeles, February 26, 2001

Jim Semington was heading south toward Long Beach on Interstate 405. He had a 9:00 A.M. appointment with the buyer at a small floor covering and carpet chain and he was running a little late. Fortunately, traffic was moving unusually well for a Southern California freeway at this time of the morning. The back seat of his Toyota Camry was covered with loose pieces of carpet as well as books of carpet samples. Half a cup of tepid coffee sat in a cup holder. Jim was listening to his favorite radio sports talk show, which was broadcast from San Diego by way of a very powerful transmitting system located in Mexico.

It was a slow time of the year for sports talk. The Super Bowl had concluded the football season a month ago, the baseball season had not yet started, and it was still several months before the pro basketball playoffs would begin. The subject was the upcoming college basketball playoffs, known as "March Madness." Jim could hardly wait. In his opinion the three weeks of the NCAA college basketball playoffs were the best three weeks in sports. He had been known to work a very abbreviated workday during that period, spending much of his time in front of a TV, particularly when UCLA, which he followed as a devoted fan, was involved. Suddenly in the middle of a sentence, the radio commentator was cut off and a new voice came on the air.

"Ladies and Gentlemen, we interrupt this broadcast for a special report."

Seconds later a network announcer's voice stated

"Ladies and Gentlemen, momentarily we are to hear an announcement from the president of the United States directly from the White House. We are uncertain as to the subject matter that the president will cover. At 11:00 A.M. Eastern time the White House requested time on every radio and TV station in the country, however, the reason for that request has not been explained. The president is entering the room now. He is accompanied by the Secretary of Defense, the National Security Advisor and the Secretary of State. Ladies and Gentlemen, the President of the United States."

Colin Power, the 43rd president of the United States, faced dozens of microphones and TV cameras. He had been sworn in as president only six weeks earlier after a landslide victory in the November 2000 election. His demeanor was calm but totally serious.

"My fellow Americans. Approximately one hour ago, the Iraq ambassador to the United Nations announced that his country was at that very moment initiating an attack on Kuwait. Shortly after that time, our intelligence facilities in the Middle East advised that Kuwait was under a very heavy shelling of military rockets. No ground troops have been moved from Iraq to Kuwait, and our satellites have not observed any unusual movement of Iraqi forces in the direction of Kuwait.

"Our military forces throughout the world have been put on a status of alert. Our forces in the Middle East are in a status of the highest alert; however, no movement of any of our forces has been initiated at this point. The Iraq ambassador indicated to the United Nations that the rockets falling on Kuwait con-

he was to provide an agreed upon sum of gold,
rd Jobson also had secured in his cabin.

ental visitor read the document written in Can-
ully, placed the paper in a purselike bag that he
ed the bag in his tunic, said something unintelligi-
n, and climbed down the rope ladder to his craft,
diately started back toward the shore. Jobson
s first mate to take a party ashore and obtain fresh
od. Earlier slave ships had fed the slave cargo a
h, but the slaves often refused to eat the slop and
and weak. Recent slavers had obtained a supply
in China. The slaves far preferred the rice and it
cult to store on the ship, so Jobson also arranged
iantity of rice to be brought aboard.

Jobson was a man well suited for the life he led.
e to sea as a young boy and as he approached his
iirthday, he had been a sailor for more than thirty
ng navigation by earnest study, he had become a
ip captain and leader by hard work and profiting
rs. Like most ship captains, he had a wife back in
unlike most of the others, he had no children.
mes his wife had become pregnant during visits
ages; and three times the pregnancy ended in mis-
imes when the breezes were very light and Jobson
nk in his cabin, he thought about his failure to cre-
He had wanted a son to go to sea with him, but
lt sorry for Beth. Her life had been one of brief
h her husband followed by months of his absence
new that her husband was considered to be a very
ip captain, but she knew other women, widows,
ands had never come home. With no children of
e had spent much of her adult life with her sister,

tained a chemical or biological component. At this point it is uncertain if this is accurate, and if accurate, no facts concerning the nature of the chemical or biological weapon have been confirmed. Your government is treating this matter with the utmost seriousness, and at present there is no known threat to any U.S. citizens with the exception of American citizens, advisors and U.S. governmental employees located in Kuwait.

"We expect to issue further reports on this matter as additional details and facts concerning this unprovoked attack on Kuwait are established. I will be meeting immediately with the Secretary of State, Secretary of Defense, the National Security Advisor, and the Chairman of the Joint Chiefs and certain members of their staffs. There will be no questions accepted or answered at this time. Thank you."

The president, a handsome man, left the podium with his customary brisk, erect military posture, ignoring reporters calls of "Mr. President" and "Mr. President, one question only."

Forty-two presidents had preceded Colin Power. They had been slender and obese, tall and short, dour and jovial, vigorous and frail, competent and incompetent, forthright and deceitful. They had come to Washington from the North, South, East, and West. They had served for as short a period as a few days to more than twelve and a half years. But they all had one thing in common. They were all the descendants of Caucasian, European ancestors. Colin Power was acutely conscious of the fact that he was different. In the long history of the United States, he was the first president who was an Oriental.

Three

Guanzhou China, Spring 1676

The wind had almost disappeared and the ship barely made a wake as it glided through the Zhu Jiang Delta. It was a typical of the ships used for this purpose in the seventeenth century. Known as a flute ship, it was built of wood and was constructed more or less half as a cargo vessel and half as an armed ship of war. It was slightly over 150 tons, 82 feet in length and 22 feet in width. The shoreline was low and flat where the river branched into several channels; however to the north, one could see Baiyun Shan or White Cloud Mountain. The area, which would later be known as Canton to Westerners, was Guanzhou to the Chinese. It had been an area of civilization for nearly two thousand years and had emerged as a major port for south China in the 8th century A.D., during the T'ang Dynasty, to handle the country's foreign trade. The city had long been a point of contact between China and the outside world. As usual it was humid and steamy in this subtropical climate.

Captain Richard Jobson stood on the bridge of the *Treasurer.* The Union Jack of England, flying from one of the masts, hung nearly limp. Jobson was an experienced sailor, but he had never been in this port before and watched the shore ahead intently. He expected to see a smaller Chinese vessel approach his ship, but no signs of activity had appeared yet.

Jobson was a merchant as well as seaman. King James I in

London had granted control o through a "Company of Adv owned by a member of this tobacco plantation in Virginia slaves to work in it. Jobson was portion of whom would be remainder auctioned for sale in

The English Colonies nee England could be induced to enslavement of the local India Jobson had sailed with the Adventurers. He was to share venture. It had been a long sail part of the effort was ahead of

A strange-looking vessel w *surer.* Jobson watched with never seen such a craft. It wa ently stationary sails. Four oars boat's progress. As the craft ca son's ship, a small Oriental mar a language completely unfar instruction a rope ladder was small man quickly climbed paper document, which Jobso English and one apparently in that he had two similar docur vided with before sailing from ten about them.

As best he could commu went to his cabin where he ha left London. He went back t papers to his visitor. In comb agreed that Jobson was to rece

and in re which Ri

The tonese ca carried, p ble to Jol which im instructec water and meal of r became t of rice wh was not d for a large

Rich; He had go forty-fourt years. Lea proficient from his e England, t

Three between v carriage. A lay on his ate a fami mostly he reunions at sea. She proficient whose hus her own, s

who had borne seven children of which five had survived infant mortality. Those children were the real focus of Beth's life, and they had grown up adoring "Auntie B."

Three days later a great deal of activity had taken place. Small boats had been bringing Orientals out to *Treasurer* through the day and night. They were chained at both hands and feet, and the foot chains were connected. The majority of the men had been prisoners, while nearly all of the women had been sold by their families

On board the ship, the men and women were separated in two decks, a fore deck for the men and an aft deck for the women. The decks were approximately five and a half feet high. Once on the ship, the men were kept in chains, but the women were not. Women who were pregnant and women with children were huddled in the rear. The women could relieve themselves by stooping over an open bilge area, but the men had to relieve themselves where they were chained.

Those on the right side of the ship were faced forward and those on the left faced the stern as it was considered healthier for them to be lying on their right side. They were nearly as close together as spoons in a drawer. A total of 496 Oriental slaves were to be packed on *Treasurer*. The manner of packing and amount of space allotted was called "tightpack," as it allotted less space per slave and consequently allowed the maximum slave cargo. The Oriental slaves were significantly smaller than the European sailors. It was common for the males to be four to six inches shorter than the members of the crew and the women were nearly all less than five feet in height.

Jobson was anxious to leave. While the ship was at anchor, there was virtually no breeze that could be channeled down to the slave decks and they smelled foul within twenty-four hours. Jobson knew from the experience of other slave ships that the slaves must be kept chained below deck. If the slaves were permitted in the open air, they would attempt to jump overboard. Once they set sail, they would lose sight of land in eight or nine days at which point they could get the slaves on deck in the fresh air. There they would spray them with hoses to wash them off and force them to exercise.

Jobson had a vested interest in keeping the slaves alive. He was to receive a salary of five pounds a month and in addition he was entitled to 5 percent bonus on slaves delivered alive. The other officers, the surgeon, the cooper, and the carpenter, received between one and four pounds a month. The crew, depending on experience, received from 30 shillings to two pounds per month. Half of the wages had been paid in advance, before leaving home.

But the loading kept getting various delays. The stink and moaning of the slaves was upsetting to the crew, and Jobson was both anxious to leave and apprehensive about the long sea voyage ahead. By the time they were ready to set sail, 2 of the slaves had died. The Chinese refused to replace them, so there were 494 Oriental slaves on board when the ship set sail twenty-one days after it had arrived. There was a favorable breeze and to the great relief of Jobson and the crew, *Treasurer* set out on a southernly course.

Four

Kuwait City, Kuwait, February 26, 2001

The loudspeaker blared out the call to mid-day prayers. That recorded call for all men to come to the mosque was repeated six times each day. Abu Sufyan closed up his small stall at the souk and joined the men who were shuffling along toward the mosque. It had been a good morning for Abu. Since the Gulf War, Western tourists came to Kuwait in fairly large numbers. Although they were closely monitored for security purposes, they were allowed to see the area where the oil fields had been burned and then walk around the city and shop. Abu's stall in the souk offered merchandise that appealed to tourists. Curved Arabian daggers in a sheath, frankincense, and various hand-made boxes and trinkets were his best sellers. A lady from America had spent over three hundred U.S. dollars purchasing his merchandise and that insured that it would be a very good day.

Abu was a considerable exception to the rule in Kuwait where 93 percent of the 750,000 citizens worked for the government. There were twice that many foreign laborers in the country, mostly from the Indian subcontinent and East Asia, and it was these people who clean the houses, dig the ditches, stock the shelves in the stores and in reality do the work. The Kuwaitis work in various governmental bureaus and departments doing busy work and paper shuffling, which accomplishes little more than nothing. Such is the life of the citizenry in an incredibly wealthy oil kingdom. The average Kuwaiti household has a staff of seven employee/servants.

But Abu had chosen a different path. Long before there was oil production and the resulting largesse it supplied, Abu's family had been merchants. They had always been merchants and it was his inheritance. Although his wife had often suggested, after a business poor day, that he seek employment with the government, Abu was simply not interested. He loved having his own business and making his own decisions. He and his wife, Noor, did not have the household staff enjoyed by most other Kuwaitis, although they did have an Indian couple who came in one day a week and cleaned up the house, washed the clothes, and did whatever other miscellaneous work that was set aside for them. But Abu was not living on a government-created handout. He took care of his family by his own efforts and he was proud of that.

Removing his sandals and placing them in the same spot where he always put them so they were easy to find, he entered the building and with his prayer mat, he walked over and joined the other men in lines of prostrate bodies. Abu was a member of the 80 percent of the Kuwaiti citizens who were Sunni Muslims. This was somewhat fortunate as the remaining 20 percent, Shi'ites were more frequently persecuted in the ten years since the Gulf War. Since 1981 all citizens were required to be Muslims, so there were virtually no other choices.

Just as the prayers started, there was a loud explosion, followed by many others. Confusion and panic were immediate. Some men rushed for the door, some cowered against the wall, and others continued to pray. Abu was in the group who rushed outside. Something had blown a fairly large hole in a building across the street from the mosque, and Abu was wondering what had caused it when he realized that there were rockets descending on other nearby buildings. Kuwait City was under attack! Undoubtedly that cursed Saddam Hussein again. But the rockets did not seem to be causing a great deal of damage. They fell with a loud explosive noise, but without much destruction. A lot of dust was scattered into the air, but not much was destroyed. Abu immediately headed for his home. When he arrived, he found his wife, Noor, anxious but unhurt and the baby sleeping.

The explosions continued for more than two more hours, and officials from the government interrupted radio and TV broadcasts telling citizens to remain calm and in their homes. After the explosions stopped, Abu and Noor continued to listen to the radio. They learned that the rockets had come from Iraq, that the Kuwaiti Army was rushing to the Iraq-Kuwait border, but that there had been no apparent movement of Iraqi troops toward Kuwait. Finally they went to sleep. In the morning they turned on the radio again and learned that the Iraqi rockets had saturated Kuwait with some kind of materiel that caused sickness. They were told to report to the local hospitals on an orderly basis.

Out in the street, Abu found that the city was in panic. People were rushing for help, and there were hundreds outside of each hospital trying to get in. A man was on the roof of the hospital with some kind of loudspeaker telling people to be calm, but no one paid attention to him. No one seemed very sick, just in a state of panic. Abu and his wife, taking turns holding their baby, stayed at the hospital nearly all that day. They were never able to get in to see any of the medical personnel and late that afternoon the baby started to cry and they went back home. That night the baby screamed constantly and Abu and Noor both felt dizzy and had no appetite. Noor lay down on their bed with the infant and tried to nurse the child, but it refused her nipple and continued screaming. The following morning, two days after the missile attack, Abu felt terrible. His throat was very sore and he slumped in a chair. The baby and Noor were both having trouble breathing, and Abu felt that he should try to go to the hospital again to get some help. Pulling himself out of the chair, he made his way out to the street and then he began to gasp for breath and barely made it back into the house. Noor felt worse than Abu and lay on her back gasping for air. The baby was silent and had stopped moving. Abu lay down on the bed next to the baby and tried to see if the infant was breathing. He could not tell, as he was so dizzy and weak that he could only lie back himself. The next morning Abu was certain that Noor and the baby had stopped breathing, but he could not move to look at them. He prayed that Allah would take him soon so that he would no longer feel so awful and he could join Noor and the child.

As the day wore on, his breathing became gasps and that night his heart stopped. No one came to check on them for nearly a week. There was no one to come. His father, mother, brother, and nearly all of his friends were also dead. It was quiet in the Sufyan house, but due to the cool February weather, the stench of human decay was not yet overpowering.

Five

Columbus, Georgia, Summer 1958

The soldier waited while the young woman fumbled in her purse to pay the Woolworth clerk. She appeared to be in her early twenties and was easily the prettiest girl that Power had seen since he arrived in Georgia. Of course, most of that time, he had been within the confines of Fort Benning and there were not very many women around of any description, but this girl was really lovely. It was summer in Georgia, which meant heat and humidity, and the woman in her pink sundress with tiny shoulder straps showed her beautiful unblemished skin. She was an Oriental, obviously a mulatto, and Power could not take his eyes off her shining black hair tied loosely with a matching pink ribbon. The clerk handed her bag to her, and she passed Power with an encouraging smile and a flash of nearly perfect white teeth.

Power handed the package of assorted needles and a spool of khaki-colored thread to the clerk.

"Planning to do some sewing, huh?"

"Yes, I am. The Army has refused to provide me with a seamstress," Power joked.

"Next thing you know they will expect you to polish your own brass," the friendly clerk kidded him.

"Gosh," said Power, " I certainly hope it never comes to that."

He paid for his purchase, took the bag from the clerk, and

headed over to the lunch counter. He sat down and began to scan the menu.

"I am sorry, but yellows are not allowed to sit here." The waitress behind the Woolworth's lunch counter looked apologetic but firm. Colin Power was confused. He had been shopping in the store for about fifteen minutes and the bag containing his purchases was resting on the counter. He was hungry and had decided on a tuna salad sandwich. He was embarrassed and got up and left the counter.

Power had experienced racial prejudice during his entire youth in New York. He was certainly aware that there were people in that area who were prejudiced against Orientals, and he had been called "Chink" more than once by whites. He had been aware that people in the Southern United States practiced far more segregation than he had previously experienced, and he had expected to be exposed to some of that when he was sent to Georgia. But here in Columbus, he had been shopping in a Woolworth store, just as he had done many times in New York, and he had purchased merchandise from the store with no unusual reaction. The clerk had been very friendly. But somehow, when an Oriental went to the lunch counter, the rules changed in Georgia, and he was not welcome. It was embarrassing and confusing and also made him mad as hell. He was in Georgia as an officer in the United States Army. He was sworn to defend the rights of these people and yet he could not eat lunch with them. What kind of crap was that!

Colin Power had grown up in the Bronx, the son of an Oriental couple who had immigrated to the area from the Cayman Islands. The islands in the Caribbean were predominantly populated by Orientals, the descendants of slaves brought to that area to work in the sugar plantations. He had enrolled at City College of New York because it was a public institution and tuition costs were low. While in school he participated in Reserve Officers Training Corps and discovered the Army, the institution that would interest him, fascinate him, and dominate most of his life. CCNY had a large ROTC contingent, but there were very few Orientals enrolled in ROTC. As many of them spent much of their time involved in family businesses and they were frequently very serious students, the military was not of much interest, particularly as a career avenue. At the time that Power was in college, every able-bodied young man expected to be drafted into the military, but those who went in as officers ordinarily were required to spend an extra year or two in the service and the majority of the Orientals wanted to minimize their military time.

Power had been an average student in most areas, but he was outstanding in his military studies and activities. He loved the discipline and structure and sense of belonging. He had found his identity. Within that military structure, his race was forgotten. He was just a member of the group. During the remainder of his college years, the drill hall and the Army were the center of his world. One summer he spent six weeks at Fort Bragg, North Carolina, as part of his ROTC training, but during that time he was completely isolated from the rest of the South and he never experienced anything like his current Woolworth rejection. Power had earned straight "A's" in all his military courses and was considered to be an outstanding military prospect. He earned honors as "Distinguished Military Graduate" and as such, he was offered a regular commission rather than a reserve commission.

Now at Fort Benning, near Columbus, Georgia, he had completed eight weeks of training in basic infantry and was now in training to be a Ranger and paratrooper. The training was tough and demanding, both mentally and physically, but few were better suited than Colin Power for the activities of a soldier. He loved it. There were few Orientals enrolled in Ranger training, and Power stood out as a soldier's soldier. After completing his Ranger and Airborne training, he expected to be sent to Germany. He was a bright young man, recognized as an excellent military prospect, and on his way up.

Power deeply resented the prejudice that he had just experienced, but he was a pragmatist. He knew that at that moment, at that time in his life, he could do nothing about discrimination against Orientals. He would wait until circumstances were propitious and he was in a position to do something constructive. If he was going to fight, he wanted it to be in a fight where he had a reasonable chance of winning. Deliberately assuming an erect military posture, he began walking out of the store. He would board a bus back to Fort Benning and get something to eat. As he left the store, a voice said, "Lieutenant, as a Southerner, I want to apologize for that."

Power turned and was facing the young woman in pink, who had apparently been waiting for him to leave. He was surprised and unnerved and started to say something when she continued, "I assure you that not all Southerners are that way. Not even all white Southerners."

"I was surprised. I've been in Woolworth's in New York many times and that never happened to me before."

"Is New York your home?"

"Yes, Ma'am."

"So you are a poor soldier boy, a long way from home."

"Yeah, I guess I'll have to plead guilty to that."

"I have lived in Georgia my entire life." She extended her hand and said, "My name is Marcie."

"A pleasure to meet you, Marcie. My name is Colin."

"I don't believe that I have ever met anyone named Colin."

"Well, I don't think I ever met anyone named Marcie."

"Colin, do you have to go right back to the base, or do you

have time to join me for some iced tea?"

"I would love some iced tea."

"Let me show you a place where they will be very happy to serve you."

As they walked Marcie asked Colin about New York. Power was thrilled to be with Marcie, but he felt somewhat awkward. They arrived in front of a small restaurant and she gestured.

"Here we are."

Colin held the door for her as they entered the restaurant, obviously frequented by Orientals. A middle-aged woman smiled at them and seated them at a table. Soon they were drinking their iced tea.

"How long have you been at Fort Benning, Lieutenant?"

"Please, call me Colin. I've been here about two months and expect to be here at least six weeks more."

"Where will you go from here?"

"I won't receive my next assignment for at least a month, and when I do, it's possible that I'll remain at Benning for some additional time. However, we expect to be sent to Germany."

They talked for more than an hour. Power learned that Marcie's last name was Jefferson and her father owned a clothing store. He had worked for the white previous owner for several years and bought the business from him. The store was now doing a good volume of business with both Orientals and whites. Mr. Jefferson made a buying trip to New York twice each year, but Marcie had never been out of Georgia. The restaurant that they were in was owned by Marcie's uncle, and the lady who had seated them was her aunt. Marcie had graduated from Georgia A&T a year ago, a school whose students were principally Oriental. She was working in her father's store, which she found to be somewhat boring, but it gave her nearly unlimited wardrobe opportunities. She had a serious boyfriend while in college, but that romance had ended and she was now unattached. Power, who was accustomed to New Yorkers, found Marcie to be a delightful combination of sweet Southern belle and assertive young woman. He was enchanted. Finally the spell was broken when she said, "Well, Colin, I guess that it's time that you return to the base, and I better get back to the store or my dad will have the police looking for me."

Power would have been content to spend the next 24 hours drinking iced tea, talking to her, and looking at her.

"If you have something to write with," she said, "I will give you my phone number."

He reached inside his jacket, extracted a pen, and wrote her number on a paper napkin. He walked back to the bus stop in a daze. He would call her tomorrow and see if she would do something with him next Sunday. The young lieutenant got back to the bachelor officer's quarters with his head still spinning. Marcie had conquered the young soldier without firing a shot!

Nearly two months had passed since the young lieutenant was refused food service at the Woolworth store. He had spent every free moment with Marcie during that time, which basically was every weekend with one exception when he was on duty as Officer of the Day. His life had taken a totally unexpected turn and that turn was causing him an unexpected conflict of desire and direction. On one hand, he had received his orders to be sent to Germany and he very much looked forward to that experience. He was a soldier and an officer and was eager to assume his military responsibilities and demonstrate his ability in which he had a great deal of confidence. On the other hand, he was madly in love with Marcie and could not stand the thought of being in Europe, thousands of miles from her. Tonight would be their last night together for a long time. Maybe the last time ever. He had made a reservation in a fine restaurant, the best establishment serving Orientals in the Atlanta area, about a hundred miles to the northeast, and they were going to drive there in Marcie's car.

Power had met her parents. They were polite and cordial and they seemed to like him, but it was apparent that they were not pleased with their daughter's relationship with a soldier. Marcie told him that her father could not understand why a bright young Oriental was planning a military career. He felt that such a young man should plan a career in business or a profession in which he would be home with his family and not traipsing all over the world to a new location every three or four years. They obviously did not relish the thought of losing their daughter to such a life.

Marcie picked him up at the base, as she had done many times in the past few weeks. Her Ford had been a graduation present from her parents, and it was a real luxury for Power, who had no car of his own. They headed off through the mountains of west central Georgia toward Atlanta.. The radio played music and they said little to each other, both feeling awkward and emotional with the uncertainties of the future. Power had received detailed directions from the restaurant, which they located with little trouble. They were seated and Power ordered a bottle of champagne. Marcie did not have much of a taste for alcohol, but tonight they each downed a glass quickly and the waiter refilled their glasses. After about ten minutes, the alcohol mellowed them somewhat and they relaxed and were less awkward with each other.

"Well, Lieutenant, you will soon be in Europe. Pretty thrilling stuff."

"Honey, you know how I feel about that. Of course I'm eager to see Germany. I've never been out of this country in my life. But I certainly am not anxious to leave you."

"Tell you what, Lieutenant. Let's just enjoy tonight and not think past it. Cheers!" She lifted her glass to toast with Colin.

They relaxed and enjoyed a fine meal. After dinner they drove to a popular nightclub with a piano bar recommended by the waiter. They listened to the piano player, who played and sang songs made popular by Frank Sinatra, Perry Como and Dinah Shore. After a couple of additional glasses of champagne, they were feeling relaxed and mellow when they left the club to drive back to Columbus.

"Colin, I don't want to drive back tonight. Let's get a hotel room."

Power was startled.

"What will your parents think?"

"It's okay."

They stopped at a gas station and inquired about a hotel that accepted Orientals. There were many in Atlanta.

Power felt excited but awkward when he approached the registration desk.

"You have no luggage, sir?" The desk clerk looked skeptical.

"No, we didn't plan to stay, but we've been celebrating and have both been drinking champagne and decided that we better not drive home tonight."

"I see. Room 117." The clerk looked doubtful but handed him the key.

Power opened the door to the room and walked in ahead of Marcie, then apologized and held the door for her. He was excited and aroused, but he felt very awkward. Without comment she went into the bathroom and closed the door. Power was not sure if he should undress or not, so he took off his jacket, tie, shoes and shirt, and sat on the bed in his T-shirt and trousers. He turned off all the lights but the lamp on the nightstand and turned that to dim. He could hear Marcie showering and then brushing her teeth. When she came out of the bathroom, she was wearing a brief lacy blue nightie that ended about six inches above her knees. *My God, she planned this! She had that in her purse! She planned to stay in Atlanta tonight!* He was stunned.

She looked at Power and said, "Do you always sleep in your pants and socks, soldier?"

Power was embarrassed, awkwardly removed his trousers and socks and got on the bed wearing his GI boxer shorts and T-shirt. She slid under the covers and turned out the already dimmed light. He got under the sheet and put his arms around her. They had experimented with each other's bodies before in Marcie's car, but they had never made love. He was not a virgin. There had been a girl in high school, the daughter of a taxi driver, fat and homely, but willing. In college he had been in the back seat of cars with a couple of girls and there was one girl who gave oral satisfaction to a whole group of boys in Power's military group, one at a time, while they waited their turn.

But this was different. He was in bed with a beautiful women whom he cared for. Hell, he knew he was crazy about her. In all his previous experiences, it was just a rush to satisfy his strong youthful libido. This time he was much more concerned about her than he was with himself. They kissed and then Marcie slipped off her nightie. There was faint light coming into the room from the outside. He stared at her, so slim and graceful. Colin put his hand on her breast, small, as were the breasts of most Oriental girls.

"I love you so much, Marcie." He had never said that before.

She started to speak and then exploding in tears, jumped from the bed, ran into the bathroom, and closed the door.

Power was dumbfounded. What had he done wrong? What had he said that would make her cry? Didn't she want him to love her?

It was silent in the room for several minutes and then she came out of the bathroom, still naked. She came to him and whispered, "I love you too." And they made love.

The next morning driving back to Columbus, they said little to each other, lost in their own thoughts. The awkwardness was palpable.

"I'll bet your dad is frantic about your not coming home."

"I left them a note telling them that we were staying overnight in Atlanta."

"Your dad doesn't like me much as it is. Now he'll probably come looking for me with a shotgun."

"I'll handle my dad."

They drove on in silence. Then Power blurted out, "Marcie, will you marry me?"

"Colin, are you saying that because of what we did last night?"

"Hell, no. You know I am nuts about you. I can't go to Germany unless you tell me you will marry me."

"I'll marry you, Colin."

"Then I guess we're engaged. Are we engaged?"

"Yes."

"But I don't have an engagement ring for you"

"When we get back to Columbus, drive over to Phenix City. We can stop at a pawn shop."

Phenix City, typical of small communities that are dominated by and living off a large neighboring military base, is long on bars, pawnshops, and whores. They stopped at one of the large pawnshops and purchased a silver ring with a tiny stone, represented to be a fine-quality diamond by the pawn owner. They had to pool their cash to make the purchase. Power left for Germany three days later. Marcie remained in Columbus.

Six

Southeast Tip of Africa, August 1676

Treasurer had rounded the Cape of Good Hope the preceding day, after a shore party had secured fresh water and some local fruit. She was now on a northwesterly course. The bay into which they had navigated was no longer visible, but the unusual flat top mountain at the eastern end of the bay was still impressive. Favorable winds had benefited them for most of the past four months and continued today. The crew had the slaves on deck, ten at a time, for the twice-daily routine. They were fed a bowl of rice and required to wash their hands in saltwater after eating (slaves who refused to eat were punished with a whip). Their mouths were rinsed with vinegar, the males were shaved weekly, and their fingernails were kept closely trimmed to limit damage in fights, but such occurrences were infrequent. The women spent much of the time sobbing and the men were largely silent. The slaves' decks were washed down daily.

Treasurer had been fortunate thus far. No serious diseases had decimated either cargo or crew. One of the more experienced sailors had died rather mysteriously, and a native arrow had wounded another of the crew. Jobson was his own navigator and had sailed from Guanzhou along the east coast of Hainan Island where he put in for fresh water. The island was lush and covered with jungle growth. The landing party had no trouble finding fresh water and some wild fruit, but they were unable to locate any game.

From Hainan, *Treasurer* sailed the South China Sea, following closely along the coast with land in sight. Sight of land was lost at about the time the 8th parallel was crossed, and not regained until they came to the Malaysian peninsula at about the 6th parallel. At that location natives attacked a landing party, and an arrow pierced the arm of a sailor. The arrow apparently had been carrying some kind of poison as the wound quickly became infected and began to fester, requiring the surgeon to remove the man's arm. Jobson wondered if the natives in some manner had poisoned the other seaman, who died a short time later of no apparent cause. The officer in charge of the landing party described the natives as being Oriental jungle savages, definitely of darker complexion than the slaves on board, and they did not appear to have the sort of civilization that had been observed in China.

After the ship rounded the tip of the Malaysian peninsula, Jobson navigated to the northwest, following the east coast of Sumatra. Following a landing on that island, they sailed across the Indian Ocean to the island of Ceylon, where they again were quickly able to obtain fresh water and some game. Jobson continued down the east coast of Africa sailing between the mainland and the Island of Madagascar. A landing there revealed that, although the island was close to the African continent, the natives were much more closely related to the Orientals in the lands to the east than they were to the Negro natives on the mainland. His crew also observed several animals on the island unique to their previous experiences.

By the time *Treasurer* reached the southern tip of Africa, eleven more of the slaves had died and had been thrown to the sharks. One of the slave deaths was a young woman who had been raped by a crewmember. She had struggled vainly before being clubbed to death by the sailor. Jobson had the man whipped severely and then put in chains. It was not a moral issue to him; it was a matter of discipline and business. The slaves were a valuable cargo in which he had an equity interest. He was not going to allow any depreciation in the value of that cargo and consequently his proportionate interest.

But he recognized that the normal desires of men, who had seen no other women in months, was an issue that must be addressed. One of the female slaves was willing to accommodate those needs in exchange for special treatment. In addition to rice, she was provided with fish when it was available for the crew. She was offered some of the heavily salted meat that they carried, but she rejected it. Soon she was being passed around from crewmember to crewmember on a daily basis. Jobson was concerned that whatever diseases had been born by any of the crew would now be spread universally and wanted nothing to do with this slave that the crew had named "Chastity." He did, however, succumb to his needs, and a young female slave, Mei Soong, now lived with him in his cabin.

The female slave, Jiang Ling, demeaningly called "Chastity" by the crew, was a large and strong woman who had been ostracized by the other slaves from what semblance of social community was possible among them, and she did not care. She had been sold into what amounted to prostitution by her family when she was eleven years old and had been dealing with men and their needs for more than ten years. All Jiang Ling cared about was her two-year-old daughter. She was willing to deal with the daily demands of the round-eyed barbarians because it benefited her through more food for herself and her daughter. She dreamed of the opportunity to somehow acquire a knife and reward one of the sailors who used her, but she knew that she would not do such a thing even in the most unlikely event that she was able to get her hands on a weapon. Such a course would leave her daughter with no one to care for her, but she fantasized anyway. The sailors were rough, but they did not beat her. All of the women knew that the sailor who had raped and killed Meng Lun was in chains for his effort. They felt somewhat secure knowing that they were a cargo of value to the captain.

The women's attitude toward Mei Soong was ambivalent. Many were jealous that the captain kept this young girl in his cabin. She was not herded around with the other women and was seen only occasionally. It was obvious that she was being well treated. Some of the women, however, felt that Mei Soong had plenty of opportunity to kill herself and had failed to do so. They did not hold her responsible for being selected by the captain, but they did hold her responsible for her continued living.

Mei Soong made no serious evaluation of her fate. She was fifteen years old and a simple girl. Jobson was older than her father, and she had been raised to obey her father and her elders without question. He was kind and gentle with her, even in his rutting, which was not frequent. She never had any thoughts other than obedience and servitude.

Jobson, on the other hand, had many thoughts. Guilt was one of them. Raised as a Christian, he knew that adultery was a sin. He also knew that his wife Beth's life had been shallow and unfulfilled and that there was certainly a reasonable chance that he could have fathered more children, some of whom might have lived, if he had been in England with her more of the time. But Beth had married a sailor. She knew her fate. He had been on a voyage of several months shortly after he met her and another before they were married.

Jobson had been sailing nearly all his life, but this was his first voyage as a slave ship captain. Realizing that the vigor of his youth was diminishing, he looked forward to a comfortable life of semi-retirement in England with Beth. But he had never accumulated sufficient funds to provide for such a life. He had signed a contract as a slave ship captain because it was by far the best opportunity he would have to gain a modest fortune. With luck, he felt that one or possibly two more such voyages would provide the wealth that he needed.

But it was a despicable task. Jobson had tried to convince himself that the slaves were really sub-human, but he could not believe that. Mei Soong was a simple young girl, but certainly not sub-human. He was trading the misery of others for his own future comfort. Jobson was a strong man, both mentally and physically, and most of the time, he dismissed his concerns by concentrating on his navigation and other ship responsibilities. But in moments alone, he thought about slavery, he thought about adultery, and he thought about Hell.

It was his plan to follow the west coast of Africa, putting in to land periodically for water and fresh food where possible. When he reached the Ivory Coast and Cape Palmas, his crew and cooper would be busy. At that time they must store sufficient water for the Atlantic crossing, a voyage of nearly 2,000 statute miles to the northeast coast of Brazil. After that he would continue his custom of staying close to land, sailing to the northwest up the east coast of South America to the Caribbean, and then up the east coast of Florida to his destination.

To commemorate the successful rounding of the Cape, the captain issued an extra measure of rum to all hands and ordered full rigging of all sails.

Seven

South Vietnam, 1968

Major Colin Power had arrived at Duc Pho in July, serving as a battalion executive officer. He was shocked and disturbed to find a demoralized army. Support for the war back in the U.S. had eroded sharply. Part of the public now believed that the real villains there were the young men going off to Vietnam to fight and die. Power's first assignment as a battalion exec was soon succeeded by a far more desirable job.

An army division commander has five primary staff officers assisting him. G-1 for Personnel, G-2 for Intelligence, G-3 for Operations, G-4 for Logistics, and G-5 for Civil Affairs. Certainly the most coveted of these responsibilities is G-3 as it deals with the plans and operations of the division, the primary purpose for having an army. The other staff positions exist only to enable Operations to function. Power, while still a major, had now advanced rapidly from directly supervising 800 men to planning warfare for a division of 18,000 troops, including artillery and 450 helicopters.

In November, Power was in a helicopter along with the division commandeer and several others when the chopper crashed. He suffered a broken ankle, but was instrumental in getting several of the others out of the crashed aircraft in spite of his injury. This was Power's second tour in Vietnam and the second time he had been wounded. He had first arrived in that tragic Southeast Asian country in December of 1962. The difference between the Army and the war and Vietnam from 1962 to 1968 was so profound as to be almost unbelievable.

In 1962, when he had arrived to be an advisor to a battalion of the Army of the Republic of Vietnam (ARVN), the assignment was almost a sacred mission. They were there to stop the spread of Marxism and communism from North Vietnam and the U.S. position in the matter was ostensibly advisory. It was not conceived to be an American war, but an exercise to teach the ARVN how to defeat the spread of communism from North Vietnam. Power's post had been in a remote, steamy, insect-ridden, leach-infested area of mountains and jungle, and although he was there as an adviser, he was to accompany the ARVN soldiers on the patrols and other combat actions. The reaction to him by the ARVN was surprise. They had expected to see a white adviser and here was another Oriental.

Soon he was huddled under a poncho in a soggy jungle. It was the summer rainy season, and he was either soaked from rain or sweaty from the heat and humidity. Time alternated between patrols in which his group was exposed to enemy snipers, and digging into to the stinking, soaking wet jungle waiting for the next assignment. The young officer often used those times to write to Marcie, although it was difficult to write on wet paper. Power described in general terms what he was doing, but minimized the element of danger and exaggerated the success of his assignment in training and inspiring ARVN troops.

On a patrol in 1963, he had stepped on a punji trap. These clever devices, used frequently by the North Vietnamese, were highly sharpened spikes of wood poisoned with buffalo dung and placed in an upright position on a path. Power stepped on one of the spikes, which went through his entire boot and out the top of his foot. The next day his foot was grossly swollen and he was sent back to a hospital. By the time that this had occurred, Power had experienced the wounding and death of many of the soldiers in the ARVN unit and was an experienced combat officer functioning with a group that had a reasonably high level of morale and dedication.

But now, in 1968, the war was a disaster. More than a half million U.S. GI's were in Vietnam, and there was no sign of anything resembling victory. Morale was terrible, drug use was rampant, phony body counts of enemy dead were ubiquitous, and President Lyndon Johnson had been so damaged by the war that he had announced that he would refrain from standing for reelection. Power became disillusioned by fake reports, falsified body counts, medals given out on a wholesale basis, and fatuous rationale for American boys bleeding and dying in the jungles of Southeast Asia, and he thought about little but completing his tour and getting back to his home and family.

During this second tour of Vietnam, Power was assigned as a panel member in a court-martial procedure. The law in the United States Army is codified in a form known as the Uniform Code of Military Justice. It has many similarities to civilian law, but substantial differences as well. Military courts operate under the jurisdiction of the Judge Advocate General, the military's Department of Justice. There are several categories of offenses, which determine the level of court martial. The most serious crimes are judged in a general court-martial

In the matter in which Power participated, he was one of five officers on the panel, which was headed by a non-voting military judge. Such a judge is appointed by the Judge Advocate General and must not only be an officer but a member of the bar as well. None of the other officers on the court are required to have any legal background; however, the officers representing both prosecution and defense are normally persons who have trained as lawyers. Enlisted personnel can sit as members of a court-martial, however, only when the defendant is an enlisted man. No one in the military is permitted to judge a defendant whose rank is senior to any member of the court.

As opposed to the civil jury system, the vote of individual court members is by secret ballot. In cases where a death penalty is a possible result, the court must find guilt unanimously. Where life imprisonment is involved, the required vote for conviction is 3/4 and in all others a 2/3 or simple majority is required, depending upon the possible penalties.

The case that Power was assigned to hear was highly unusual. The defendant, a captain named Terrence Simmons, was a company commander being tried for conspiracy. Simmons's company was a supply company, functioning in a combat zone but not participating in combat activities. An enlisted man in the company, PFC. Daniel Washington had managed to develop an astonishingly successful trade featuring the procurement and redistribution of large quantities of marijuana, LSD, cocaine, hashish, and amphetamines. Testimony was heard that indicated that Private Washington had virtually taken control of the company. It was claimed that this drug operation was generating profits in excess of one hundred thousand dollars per month. The accusation most central to the matter was that Private Washington, an Oriental, had bribed both the company first sergeant and Captain Simmons with regular monthly payments for which they virtually ignored the activities or whereabouts of Private Washington. Testimony was introduced that the captain received a monthly stipend from Private Washington averaging about $10,000 per month for a period in excess of a year.

The court consisted of a bird colonel sent in from the Pentagon, who acted as the military judge, three Lieutenant colonels and another major in addition to Power. As the other major had seniority over Power, he, as the junior member, was responsible for gathering up and counting the ballots. In a unanimous verdict, Simmons was found to be guilty of conspiracy and sentenced to ten years in a military prison after which he would be separated from the army with a dishonorable discharge. The matter was disgusting to Power. A military under fire from the enemy as well as much of civilian society could simply not afford such egregious behavior.

It was with great anticipation that he left Vietnam in the summer of 1969, headed back to join his family. Marcie had delivered twin daughters in 1960. This had come as a surprise, as there were no known twin births in either of their families. He would be home in time for the girl's ninth birthday in September, at which time he would matriculate to George Washington University in the School of Government and Business Administration, where the army was sending him to further his education.

Eight

Baghdad, February 27, 2001

Until fairly recent times, Iraq was known as Mesopotamia, a Greek word meaning, "land between the rivers." The country lies partly between the Tigris and Euphrates rivers; an area often regarded as the cradle of civilization. Its history dates back at least 5,000 years. In about 2000 B.C. Babylon was founded on the Euphrates River and became the world's first great city. Over the next 2,500 years, the area was conquered by the Hittites, the Kassites, the Chaldeans, the Persians, Alexander the Great, the Seleucids and in A.D. 637 by tribes from Arabia who brought the message of Islam.

The Abbasid dynasty ruled from 750 to 1258 during which time Arab-Muslim culture merged with Persian. The stories of Scheherazade as told in *The Arabian Nights* gives the flavor of the Abbasid court. In 1258 the Mongols conquered Baghdad and Iraq became a land of small kingdoms. In 1534 the Turks became the latest conqueror of Mesopotamia and the Turkish-Ottoman Empire ruled until World War I. In that war the Turks sided with the Germans, and after the war, the victorious British were given a mandate to establish a protectorate area, which included Egypt, and areas of present-day Iraq. The British wanted to protect their lifeline to India as well as their interests in the Anglo-Iranian Oil Company.

Iraq had gained independence from Britain in 1932 as a constitutional monarchy, which lasted until 1958 when a group of army officers assassinated the king and crown Prince, overthrew the government, and established the National Council for Revolutionary Command. In 1963 the Ba'th Party overthrew the council and Ahmad Hassan al-Bakr took over as president. Bakr resigned in 1979 and Saddam Hussein at-Takriti succeeded him. Shortly, Iraq was in a ghastly and bloody war with Iran. That war ended in 1988, and two years later Iraq invaded Kuwait.

The history of this ancient land has been one of continual conquering and being conquered. This was the culture that forged the Iraqi people and the culture that produced Saddam Hussein. A culture with little proclivity for peace, which only looked toward the next battle, the next war, and the next conquest. One needs to understand this history to understand Iraq.

"Mr. Defense Minister."

With one exception the same group that had attended the meeting four days earlier was again assembled in a conference room in Baghdad. The exception was Uday, Saddam's oldest son. Although he thought of himself as Saddam's heir apparent, his principal assignment was selling smuggled oil and medical supplies, the proceeds of which went to Saddam, now a billionaire many times over. Uday, who had once been jailed by his father for forty-five days, had a reputation of being even more bloodthirsty, cruel and ruthless than Saddam.

The meeting was not in the same building as the one held four days previously. The participants had been advised in the middle of the preceding evening that they would be picked up at their homes promptly at 6:00 A.M. that morning. They were told that this was necessary in order that the physical inspections required would be completed and the group ready for a meeting commencing at 8:00. They were not told the location of the meeting. This type of procedure meant only one thing.

Saddam Hussein would be attending the meeting.

The Iraqi president had signaled for the meeting to begin by calling on the minister of defense.

"Thank you, Mr. President," replied the obsequious Ramzi Kassem, as he rose to his feet.

"As previously discussed, our rocket attack on Kuwait took place over a three-hour period yesterday. The attack began at midday prayer as it was determined that the maximum number of people would be in the streets and markets at that time. The primary weapons used were the SA-10, rockets which were fired from our bases near Basrah; however R-29 rockets were also fired on Kuwait City during the initial thirty minutes to achieve certain saturation in that location. We believe that the element of surprise and the overwhelming volume of this effort achieved potential exposure of the toxin to 95 percent or more of the Kuwait citizens. As of this time, there are few known casualties and those were caused by the impact of the rockets, primarily in markets and mosques. These weapons carry a light explosive charge, only sufficient to distribute the contents.

"The SA-10 rockets were only intended for use in Kuwait and these have all been expended, with the exception of those that misfired. More than 90 percent of the R-29 weapons remain available as do all the R-36M rockets. As I advised, the R-36M is a silo-based missile. All of these weapons are at this moment in a status of the highest alert and can be fired momentarily. The weapons designated for the second strike will be fired in four days if the president's demands have not been met by that date. These rockets are presently calibrated to strike at the specific targets selected in Iran, Saudi Arabia, and the remaining Gulf States. However, all second-strike and third-strike missiles will be fired immediately if the president determines that any belligerent military action is being directed at Iraq. There has been considerable military activity in the U.S. and Europe, however, none thus far that could be construed as specifically directed at Iraq. That concludes my report this morning, Mr. President."

"I would like to hear the comments of the Minister of Health," ordered the president of Iraq.

"Certainly, Mr. President."

Tariq rose to his feet. He had not prepared to give a report.

"Based on the report and projections of the Minister of Defense, it appears that a very large proportion of Kuwait has been exposed to the Botulinal Toxins. Few if any deaths will have occurred at this time and those only of the very old and very weak. However, I would expect that all of those exposed either are now or will be within another day experiencing flu-like symptoms and dizziness. I would expect that deaths will begin to occur at a rapid pace two days from now and that by three days later nearly all who have been exposed will be dead or dying. Kuwait has a population of slightly less than two million, so deaths could be in excess of a million. We know that the hospitals in Kuwait were overwhelmed yesterday; however, this was primarily provoked by fear and panic rather than actual symptoms. From a biological perspective, we are in a position now of waiting to observe. If the projections of our military are accurate, we can expect the results I have described in the sequence I have described.

"Is there any other area of this that you wish me to expand upon, Mr. President?"

Saddam ignored the question and looked at the oil minister.

"Mr. Minister, please repeat for this group what you advised me of prior to the start of this meeting."

"Certainly, Mr. President. We know that the international petroleum market is in complete chaos. In France and Germany, all vehicle traffic has been prohibited, with the exception of police and emergency vehicles. In the U.S. all international air travel has been prohibited. Sale of crude oil at any price on a world wide basis has virtually ceased and we have reports that as many as 1800 tankers have suspended travel to their previous destination and are holding for future instruction.

"The stock exchange in Japan closed yesterday as did the New York Exchange, which was to reopen today, but that has been suspended on the request of the U.S. president. The situation worldwide has been so chaotic that it is difficult at this time to make any conclusions as to the future course of action of any of these countries. Perhaps that situation will become somewhat clearer during the next twenty-four hours."

"Mr. President?" The oil minister looked at Hussein, who ignored him as well and began to speak.

"The Foreign Minister has not yet returned from New York. However, I have talked to him on a secure phone line several times. He has advised me that he presented our treaty demands exactly as instructed and the immediate reaction in the UN was silence and disbelief. Written copies of the treaty requirements have been supplied to the Secretary-General. Our ambassador remains in New York and has been flooded with requests and demands for conferences and meetings. He has stated that all the treaty requirements and timetable are clear and simple. Iraq's position is not to discuss anything until the treaty has been signed and complied with, and he will avoid any and all discussions of the treaty and has refused to schedule any meetings where such a discussion is the agenda. The New York City police have posted a guard of more than one thousand police officers around the residence of the ambassador as he has received hundreds of threats of death and bombing."

Saddam stood up and took a long drink from the water

glass in front of him. He put down the glass, said, "If you are not pissing every thirty minutes, you are not drinking enough water" and he left the room.

Nine

New York City, 1972

It was one of those days that inspired the song *Autumn in New York*. The air was crisp, but not cold. The leaves on the trees in Central Park were varying shades of green, maroon, and gold, and they fluttered lazily to a comfortable place on the ground, inspired by brief, pleasant gusts. There were a few fluffy clouds in the clear sky, and shoppers bustled into the stores searching for sweaters and jackets for the coming cold weather. But for New York City Police on this assignment, the fine weather was not on their minds.

"This is goddam ridiculous. I have never seen yellows act like this."

NYPD Sergeant Rico Falzone was talking to his friend, Sergeant Bill Wendt, outside the Plaza Hotel. More than a hundred of New York's finest were surrounding the entrances on Fifty-Ninth Street and Fifth Avenue. A huge crowd, almost exclusively Oriental, surrounded the hotel and flowed out on Fifty-Ninth Street blocking traffic and extending into Central Park. The crowd was waiting for the expected arrival of Bruce Lee, one of the major movie stars in the world and by far the biggest Oriental star in American cinema.

Bruce Lee had an interesting background. Born in San Francisco while his parents were in that city performing with the Cantonese Opera Company, he grew up in Hong Kong. At the age of thirteen, after being beaten up by a street gang, he began to take Kung Fu lessons. At eighteen he won the boxing championship in his weight in Hong Kong. His parents worried about him as by this time he was frequently involved in street fights, so they sent him to San Francisco to live with a family friend.

In 1963, still living in the United States, Lee married a Caucasian named Linda Emery and started the first of a series of Jun Kung-Fu Institutes, where he developed the "One-Inch Punch," which he made famous in 1964 at the Long Beach Internationals. While in Long Beach, he was seen by a Hollywood producer and invited to take a screen test. This led to a series of "B" movies about *The Green Hornet* in which he played the part of Kato.

Between 1967 and 1971, he had various bit parts in films and gave private martial arts lessons to many movie personalities. After his mother's death in 1971, he went back to Hong Kong where he found to his surprise that his role in *The Green Hornet* movies had made him a big star. Also that year, *The Big Boss*, a movie starring Lee, was released in the U.S. and early in 1972, *The Chinese Connection* made Lee, into a superstar, particularly among the large U.S. Oriental population.

Orientals had been in movies as far back as the silent movie era, but they were basically comic figures and objects of ridicule. They usually wore a long pigtail and a funny hat and were included for humor. Bruce Lee was different. He was handsome, athletic, and played the role of the hero. That role had never been one that the U.S. Oriental population had been able to identify with before Bruce Lee, and the result in the country was stunning. The Orientals were now watching movies where one of their own was dominating Caucasians and was the superhero. Particularly among the younger yellows, he was close to being a god. But his time in the sun was shockingly brief. After a series of headaches, he died suddenly in 1973 of cerebral edema. He was only 33.

At a funeral ceremony in Hong Kong, more than 25,000 people attended, and it was estimated that the crowd at a ceremony in Seattle was in excess of a hundred thousand. Among his pallbearers were Steve McQueen and James Coburn.

But fate was not through with Bruce Lee, even after his death. Lee and his wife had a son, Brandon, born in 1965 in Oakland, California. By 1992 Brandon had become a star in the mode of his father. Brandon Lee benefited by the stunning good looks that Eurasians often enjoy, and he followed the martial arts path to movie stardom like his father. In a freak accident, while making a movie called *The Crow*, Brandon Lee was killed when he was struck by a pellet discharged from a gun firing blanks. So Brandon did not even make it to his 30th birthday.

But from that time on, things changed for Orientals in the American cinema. There had always been a separation in roles between whites and Orientals of different sexes. There was not even much hugging between the races, much less romance. But after the Lees, things changed. Gradually at first, and then accelerating, the screen showed Oriental men kissing Caucasian women and Oriental women were soon in bedroom scenes with white men. By the late 1980s Oriental men and women had become important in leading roles and more often than not, their romantic counterpart was white. In 1989 an Oriental named Dennis Washington became one of the biggest male movie stars in Hollywood and almost always his leading lady was white. This, as would be expected, had a significant effect on society in general, and by the turn of the century mixed race couples had become so common as to go virtually without comment. The country was on a course where social scientists were predicting a nearly complete homogenization by 2050.

But here on this day in New York City in 1972, no one knew what a bizarre and tragic future was in store for Bruce Lee and his son, and no one knew what a profound social effect they would have on society as a whole. All that the crowd knew or cared was that they had a real Oriental movie superstar and they adored him for it. They desperately tried to get their cameras free for a reasonably clear shot and begged for his autograph, which he was generous and patient in providing. Some of the bolder ones snatched at his clothing, trying to tear off a real souvenir. The police had to arrest several of the crowd, mostly female, who did all they could to undress Lee on the spot. But he was remarkably understanding, realizing that this was a racial and cultural watershed and he obviously enjoyed the adoration. Finally, he worked his way through the entrance to the hotel and was escorted by the staff to his corner suite overlooking the General Motors Building and the fountain. Shortly, he was unpacked, alone, and while still in his room, he began his daily exercise workout.

Ten

Charleston, South Carolina, December 1676

It had been getting steadily cooler for the past month and Richard Jobson noted that on this day it was no warmer than 50 degrees Fahrenheit. *Treasurer* was anchored in Charleston harbor just off the peninsula where the Ashley and Cooper rivers flowed into the bay that was part of the Atlantic Ocean.

The ship had arrived in Charleston with 390 live slaves; however, two had died since their arrival and two or three were so sick that it was a question if they would be salable. A considerable difficulty was encountered when they had arrived sixteen days earlier and learned that there would be no slave auction for nearly three weeks, and there was no place on land where they could store their considerable cargo. A third of the slaves had been claimed by the owner of *Treasurer*, who had financed the trip and who had need for their labors in Virginia. The crew had been forced to stay at anchor with the remainder. It had been cold and most of the slaves were coughing and sneezing. When they took them to the top deck for their daily routines, the slaves shivered and when washed, they were that much colder. But today, finally, they were crowding them into small boats, thirty and forty at a time, and taking them to the auction area.

The prospective buyers at the auction were nearly all tobacco planters, many from farther north in Carolina and Virginia. The slaves were examined closely. Jobson's men had been forced to scavenge for old clothes and rags for the slaves because of the cold weather. During most of the voyage from China, the weather had been warm or hot and the slaves had been naked or nearly naked.

The auctioneer pointed to the next group of slaves to be auctioned. Mei Soong, who had lived in Jobson's cabin for months, was in this group and Jobson watched from a distance. Prospective buyers approached the slaves and they were instructed to raise their clothing above their knees so their legs could be examined. The bidder then examined their mouth, breasts, arms, eyes and ears. They were told to walk to an area and back, and their walk was examined to see if there appeared to be any signs of crippling. Frequently one of the auctioneer's assistants would force them to jump by lashing them. The bidders were again interested in their dexterity. Loud crying or wailing as a result of the lash was considered a sign of good health. Bidding began and premium prices went to healthy males above average in size, fifteen to twenty years of age, and healthy females with reasonably full breasts and hips and of the same ages. Bidding for an individual slave did not take long. The auctioneer's hammer fell and the slave was led away.

A large man, who was employed by the slave owner who had purchased Mei Soong, had her by the arm. Her head was tipped down and her eyes faced the ground, but for a second, she glanced in the direction of Jobson. He could not tell if she had seen him or not. The man led her away and soon she and Jobson's child, unknown to him but now three months in her womb, were on their way to a slave cabin on a tobacco plantation in Virginia. The son that Jobson had always wanted to join him at sea would spend his life stooping in the tobacco fields in Carolina.

Jobson was back on *Treasurer* and alone in his cabin. The crew was loading cargo to take back to England, and he was reading his Bible, something he had not done for years. But he could not concentrate. Looking through his porthole, he could see the pier, which led to the slave auction area. Jobson stared at the pier for several minutes, lost in thought. Then he looked over at the small box in the corner where Mei Soong had been allowed to keep her few possessions. He picked up the Bible and looked for a passage he remembered his mother reading to him. It was about repentance and absolution, but he could not find what he was looking for, and he could not focus his mind on his search. Again he peered through the porthole, and then picked up the box Mei Soong had used, but there was nothing remaining in it and he threw it down. Jobson left his cabin and walked out on the poop deck.

The crew was anxious to start the long trip home. They would sail down to Jamaica, where they would take on a cargo of sugar, and then back to England, and all hands were industriously preparing to leave Charleston. He watched for a few minutes without comment and returned to his cabin. After staring at the wall for a while, he opened a trunk and took out a bottle of brandy. Jobson poured a large glass nearly full, took a deep drink, leaned back until his chair was resting on the wall, and closed his eyes. He wondered if there really was a Hell.

Eleven

February 27, 2001, Washington, D.C.

The Oval Office had been the venue for thousands of meetings, discussions, photographs and conversations. Discourse subjects in that famous room had ranged from ethereal, strategic, statesmanlike, and inspiring to the most vulgar and base. The walls in the Oval Office had contained moments of crushing tension, but none more palpable than on this bright winter morning.

The president sat behind his desk, his back ramrod straight in his familiar military manner. Scattered throughout the room, some seated and some standing, were the Secretaries of Defense and State, the National Security Advisor, the Chairman of the Joint Chiefs, the Director of the Center for Disease Control and Prevention, the White House Chief of Staff, the Vice President, the U.S. Ambassador to the United Nations, the Director of the Central Intelligence Agency, and several members of the respective staffs of these officials.

The Vice President was seated in a wing chair and was involved in a conversation with General Robert Stanley, Chairman of the Joint Chiefs, who was standing directly in front of him. It was apparent that they were not sharing the same opinion.

"Mr. Vice President."

The general leaned slightly down toward the vice president's face, "May I remind you that both of us, as well as others in this room, have taken an oath to defend and protect the interests of this country and no other."

The vice president leaped out of his chair.

"You son of a bitch, I don't need you or anyone else to tell me what oaths I have taken. But I also have a fucking responsibility to humanity that transcends any other responsibility that I have or may have, and even a damn general should know that."

"Enough! Both of you shut up."

The unmistakable command of the president silenced the room.

The meeting had been under way for more than three hours with frequent interruptions to obtain information and clarification. Power had largely let everyone express their individual opinion and had played the role of the observer, asking an occasional question. The discussion had ranged from arguments over Iraq's actual capabilities, the U.S. capacity for prevention or response, and the morality of various strategies.

"We have been agonizing over this long enough. Frank, you are the best organized man and the clearest thinker I have ever known in or out of the military. I would like you to summarize this situation for us and outline our options."

"Of course, Mr. President."

Frank Russo, the White House chief of staff, looked at the president and then said, "May I have a few minutes to make a note or two and get my thoughts in order."

"All right," Power barked. "We will take a ten minute break while Frank gets ready. Now would be a good time to relieve yourself of some of that coffee you have been drinking."

Frank Russo, the grandson of immigrants from Italy, was an American success story. He had attended St. John's as an undergraduate and then got his requisite MBA from Harvard.

He had risen through corporate America to become the CEO of a huge industrial conglomerate that was one of the largest contractors providing military weapons to the U.S. and several other countries.

Power and Russo had become well acquainted when Power served on the National Security Counsel and later as Chairman of the Joint Chiefs, and Russo was the leader of a company that provided much of the military hardware purchased by the Pentagon. Power had been very impressed by Russo. He was honest and efficient. He did not hype his company or products unreasonably, and he seemed to rely on the quality and functionality of the items he manufactured rather than the "old boy" revolving-door program of hiring generals and admirals from the Pentagon so favored by other providers of military supplies. Power found Russo to be a remarkably clear thinker.

When the Republicans were giving Power the full-court press to run for president, Russo was one of the party supporters who contacted Power and told him that he had an obligation to offer his services to his country. Power had stunned Russo, when he replied that if he had an obligation, so did Russo. Power told him that he would consider running if Russo would agree to be his chief of staff for a minimum of one four-year term.

So Russo had come to Washington. It had been a difficult and inconvenient move. Russo's wife of twenty-seven years had died of breast cancer five years earlier. Their relationship had been close and supportive. Amy Russo had understood the ambition and competitive energy that was at the center of Frank Russo's being, and she tolerated the long hours he worked and the many nights she was home alone with their three children, when he was on necessary business trips. As Russo's responsibilities grew, and their financial position improved, she was able to enjoy the comforts of full-time maids and nannies, but she lived for the times when they could be together.

They had a routine that they rarely failed to keep. On Friday nights Frank would come home at a reasonable hour. After they had a cocktail, he would make a Caesar salad and then cook a couple of steaks on the Bar B Q. They would share the time together. No children, no friends, no telephones, no television, not even any background music. It was the part of the week that they both looked forward to more than any other activity. The two years prior to her death, as Amy grew progressively sicker and weaker, they never missed a Friday night together. Toward the end, the chemo she was taking had caused her hair to fall out and Amy wore a turban. Frank never felt more devoted to her than he did during these final moments together. When she died he was consumed with anguish briefly, and then buried himself in eighteen-hour workdays to occupy his mind.

Then, about three years earlier, he had been introduced to Suzy Quinn. She was fifteen years younger than Russo and had previously been married to an extremely wealthy owner of a number of textile mills in Georgia and South Carolina. The terms of her divorce provided amply for a life of continued affluence and social activity. Her financial position alone would have been enough to make her appealing to many suitors, but in addition Suzy was a beautiful woman, the type who seems to grow more beautiful as her poise and grace increase with opportunities and experience. For some reason, she pursued Frank much more aggressively than he pursued her. Russo did not feel comfortable at first with the idea of being intimate with any woman other than Amy. But gradually their relationship had developed and finally, when it was Suzy who suggested that they get married, it was Frank who had agreed.

Suzy was a native of Arizona and had longed to reestablish residence in that state, and they had just started building a home in Scottsdale when Frank got involved with Power's presidential campaign. After agreeing to work full time on that campaign, he had not only been unable to spend much time with Suzy on the planning and building of the house in Arizona, he had also given up an income in excess of four million dollars per year and the leadership of 120,000 employees. He no longer was the *number one* guy, but just a staff leader for the head man. Russo never wanted a Washington job, but he had to agree that if Power had an obligation to serve, then he did as well. The chief of staff was still making some notes when the group again assembled and the doors to the office were closed.

The vice president faced Power.

"Mr. President, before Frank starts, I would like to make a very brief statement."

"Go ahead."

"Mr. President, I stand on my remarks concerning my oath of office and my higher obligations as a human being, but I was absolutely wrong to call General Stanley a son of a bitch. It is my sincere opinion that General Stanley has served this country and this administration with distinction and my pejorative comment about him was out of line. I ask that General Stanley accept my apology."

"Accepted" was the reply from the general.

Power stared intently at both men. The room was silent.

"Okay, Frank, let's hear it."

Russo began his commentary. As usual it was presented in a clear, factual manner, with little attempt to dramatize any particular point.

"Earlier this month our intelligence sources advised us

72

that there were an unusual number of high-level meetings among Iraqi officials, however, there were no unusual military activities at that time.

"On February 26th Iraqi officials announced at the United Nations that Iraq was initiating an attack on Kuwait at that moment. It was stated that the attack would feature biological weaponry, which would destroy a very large portion of the population of Kuwait. Subsequent intelligence reports and events revealed that the attack on Kuwait was launched from Iraqi installations near the Kuwait/Iraq border and that the weapons were a ground-based Russian manufactured missile. The missiles carried a substance described as botulinal toxin. We are aware that Kuwait is in complete chaos and at this time an unknown, but very substantial portion of the population is thought to be dead or dying. Recently, Iraqi military forces have moved into Kuwait.

"Iraq *claims* that they have they capability to initiate similar strikes on Iran, Saudi Arabia, and the Gulf States and that they will do so on March 3rd if their demands are not met. They have further claimed that they have the capability of a third attack on Greece, Turkey, and Egypt, which will be initiated on March 6th, again if their demands are not met. They project that the combined attacks could result in the deaths of up to 50 million persons in those countries. Thus far it has been impossible to determine if Iraq in fact has the capability of accomplishing these threats. Our military and intelligence officials have both expressed doubts that Iraq could deliver on this.

"Iraq has indicated that these attacks will be forestalled if certain demands are met. These demands are as follows:

1. Kuwait is recognized as part of Iraq.
2. Iraq will control the production of oil in Saudi Arabia, Iran, and the Gulf States and will levy a duty on such oil

produced by those states.
3. Iran, Saudi Arabia, and the Gulf States will sell oil only to those countries and in those amounts determined by Iraq.
4. All members of the Security Council as well as the countries of Iran, Saudi Arabia, and the Gulf States will sign a treaty outlining these provisions.

"Our options at this time appear to be the following:

1. Do nothing. We do not know if Iraq is capable of that which they claim. If they are bluffing, we will learn that on March 3rd at which time they will launch their second strike, if they are in fact capable of such. If this course is chosen, we must expect continued economic chaos in this country as well as the rest of the world for the next four days. We are also risking the lives of millions of citizens in Iran, Saudi Arabia, and the other states. If Iraq is indeed *capable* of such an attack, and we yield to their demands prior to such, we would prevent that huge number of casualties.
2. Attempt to negotiate with Iraq. At this time the Iraqis are dealing from a position of apparent strength. If we attempt such a negotiation, it would undoubtedly appear to Iraq that we are in a weak position and pleading for mercy. On the other hand, such negotiation might result in a lessening of their demands and could well prevent millions of deaths. It would likely mean, however, that at least in the short run our economy would be hostage to Iraq.
3. Initiate an immediate military strike on Iraq. We believe that our F-17 Stealth Bomber has the same capability of destroying the Iraq air defense system as was accomplished in the Gulf War. However, we are in no position to put forth the same kind of military punishment on Iraq as

was accomplished in 1991. We will recall that that *Desert Shield* was a six-month military buildup of our forces in the Middle East before *Desert Storm* was possible."

"Excuse me, Mr. President." General Stanley faced Power.

"What is it, Bob?"

"I think that everyone in this room must clearly understand that we are not in a position to inflict anywhere near the military damage on Iraq that we inflicted in 1991, whether we have six month or thirty-six months to prepare. In the ten years that have passed since that activity, our military forces have been reduced to a shell of what they were in 1991, and you know that better than anyone else in the room, Mr. President."

Power looked at the general in silence for a moment and then said,

"Please continue, Frank."

"The risk engendered by this option," Russo continued, "is in the uncertainty about Iraq's continuing capabilities. We could destroy Iraq's air defense system and we have sufficient anti-biological masks and gear to immediately outfit two divisions of airborne or marines. We could have two divisions of paratroopers on the ground in Iraq within forty-eight hours. However, without a substantial and sustained bombing of Iraq prior to such activities, two divisions would be overwhelmed by the Iraqi Army.

"Therefore, the only *real* military option at present would be a hydrogen bombing and complete destruction of Iraq. The huge risk here is that if Iraq has the military capabilities that they claim to have, before Iraq was destroyed, they could unleash their described rocket attack on Greece, Turkey, Egypt, Iran, Saudi Arabia, and the Gulf States as soon as they had an indication of our military intentions. If their claims are accurate, the resulting casualties would be unimaginable.

"A final option," continued Russo, "is to agree to accept the Iraqi demands at this time, while planning for a military strike at a later date. Iraq has stated that they will cover Iran, Saudi Arabia, and the Gulf States with a system of biological storage weapons and that an attack by anyone at later date would cause these weapons to be used and the population of those countries to be destroyed. It is possible, however, that we could infiltrate those countries and that weapon system sufficiently to eliminate part or all of that threat and then launch an attack on Iraq.

"This option would eliminate further Iraqi attack at the present time and even if a later attack caused massive deaths in those countries, there would be no threat to Greece, Turkey, or Egypt with their much greater populations. We must realize, however, that such a course of action would have a *profound* economic effect on this country. Iraq would control our oil supply. At best they might double or triple the price we were required to pay for oil and at worst, they might refuse to sell oil to us at any price. The thought of our national economy being hostage to Saddam Hussein is paralyzing and in any event, the effect on our economy is almost unimaginable.

"As I see it, Mr. President, these are our options. None of them could be described as anything but very limited and loaded with extremely dangerous consequences. If there are other options that I have ignored, I would be most interested in hearing them at this time."

The room was silent. The president slowly looked around, briefly studying each face. Nothing was said. Power picked up his phone and spoke briefly to his secretary and then said, "I ask that each of you excuse your staff members."

After brief conversations, those people left the room and the president's secretary came in. She was carrying a stack of yellow legal pads and a box of BIC pens.

Power got up from his chair and walked around passing out one of the pads to each of the nine other people now in the room. He put the box of pens down on a coffee table.

"You each have one hour," Power said, while standing behind his desk. "On one page or less, I want you to describe for me what you believe our general strategy should be, and then on one page or less, I want you to tell me how you believe we should implement that strategy. Then sign your name and put it on my desk I will be back in an hour." Power got up and left the room. No one moved for several seconds, then the secretary of state walked over and picked up one of the pens. He returned to his chair and in minutes, the room was silent except for the sound of notes being written, paper being turned, and the bodies of nervous and apprehensive officials shifting uncomfortably in their chairs.

The vice president was the first to finish. He stood up, papers in hand, and walked over to the president's desk. Without any comment he folded two sheets of paper in half, placed them on the president's desk, and then left the room. It was nearly ten minutes later when the Director of Central Intelligence followed the same procedure. As he left the room, after preparing his comments regarding potentially the worst calamity in the history of mankind, he was thinking the most mundane of thoughts. He was concerned about his spelling. "I was a lousy damn speller to begin with," he thought to himself, "and for the past ten years I have used *Spell Check* for everything. And besides, my handwriting is shit. Who in hell would have expected to give handwritten comments to the President of the United States." Under the most extreme circumstances, human vanity does not vanish easily. The remaining papers were placed on the desk shortly.

77

Twelve

April 1851, Wayne County, North Carolina

The young man watched the girl intently. Although Sally was only fifteen, she was fully developed physically and had the bearing of a young woman who knows that she is attractive. Slender with high cheekbones, beautiful almond eyes, and the fair complexion that revealed that she had some white blood mingling with her predominantly Oriental genealogy. She was hanging wet laundry on a rope strung between a tree and the slave cabin where she lived with her family, and Isaac Embrey had watched her many times during the past few months.

Isaac, called Ike by the other slaves and the slave owners as well, had been born on the plantation, as had Sally. Ike was twenty-six years old and he had never had a wife. Yesterday he had talked to the plantation owner, Oliver Embrey.

"Massa Oliver, I is a good worker."

"Yes, Ike, that is true. Now and then you have been a little slow, but most of the time, you have been a good worker."

"Massa Oliver, I is twenty-six years old and I ain't never had a wife. I sho would like to have a wife an' some babies."

"Who did you have in mind, Ike?"

"Sally is fifteen now and old enuf. She a good worker an' make me a good wife."

"I may have some plans for Sally, Ike."

Ike stared at the ground.

"I said I may have some plans for Sally, Ike."

"Yes, suh."

"I'll think about it, Ike. I'll see if I can find you a wife."

"Yes, suh."

But Ike didn't want some wife that Mister Oliver picked out for him; he wanted Sally, and he was pretty sure that she liked him too. Sally went into her cabin and Ike picked up a pebble and threw it against the wall on his cabin. Then he did it again with another small stone. He wasn't happy about that conversation with Mr. Oliver.

A few days later, Ike was out in the field picking cotton. He had been in the field since dawn and had filled the bag he dragged behind him and was working on filling it again. He looked around for Sally but did not see her. He watched for her all day and never saw her, although he picked cotton until it was dark.

Ike was completely unaware that Oliver Embrey had some rather pressing financial problems. Young, healthy female slaves were in considerable demand by cotton planters at the time, and a girl like Sally commanded a premium price. Embrey was unhappy about parting with Sally, but it was a way to get cash quickly, so he had sold her to a man in Virginia.

Cotton is a member of the hibiscus family and grows to a height of from thirty to fifty inches, thus requiring the stoop labor necessary for manual harvest. It bears a white-creamy yellow flower, which turns purple after pollination. Immediately beneath the flower is a small pod called a cotton boll. After pollination, the petal withers and the boll grows to about the size of a small chicken egg. When the boll is fully developed, it splits into four or five sections exposing the white fiber. It is an annual crop requiring replanting and the growing period is typically 160 to 180 days before harvest. The plant requires long hot summers and long hours of sunshine. The seed is planted as long as the ground is warm enough, which is usually November in the South, and harvesting begins in April and continues through the warm months.

The cultivation of cotton was a cornerstone of the United States economy during the first half of the Ninteenth century, but had not been very important until about 1800. Textile production required steam power for spinning and weaving. Until steam power was successfully adapted to the weaving process, the demand for cotton was small. To understand the evolution and importance of slavery, and the growth of cotton farming in America, it is important to understand the relationship between steam power, industrialization, and cotton production. Slave labor was actually a *very important* part of the Industrial Revolution in England as well as the industrial growth of the U.S. North, particularly New England.

Cotton requires about six frostless months a year and was first grown in quantity in the Georgia/South Carolina "Low Country." This type of cotton was called "long staple," as it had long fibers. It was best suited for these salty coastal soils and did not grow well inland. Another type of cotton called "short staple" was available, and it grew well in the inland soil, but it was not cultivated because the small seeds in this cotton were very difficult to separate from the fiber. This situation changed dramatically in 1793 when Eli Whitney invented the cotton gin, which was able to separate the seeds from the fiber in an automated manner. After this, the planting and harvesting of short staple cotton increased rapidly. The amount of cotton baled in the South increased from about 5,000 bales in 1800 to four million bales in 1860. It was extremely important to the American economy as cotton was not only the nation's *leading* export, it *exceeded* all other exports combined.

But it was also extremely important to the British economy, as the industrialization of textile production in England, which was an immensely important part of the Industrial Revolution there, depended on the importation of huge quantities of raw cotton. And the production of that cotton in the American South was entirely dependent on a plentiful supply of slave labor. There would not have been a quantity of cotton grown in the South if there had not been slave labor.

The same effect on industrialization occurred in New England. The availability of cheap cotton allowed for the construction of factories and paid the wages for the workers who labored in those factories. By 1840 about one-seventh of the labor force in New England was involved in cotton processing and it was the largest single industry. All of this in both England and America was *made possible* by slave labor. In a very real sense, slave labor made the Industrial Revolution possible in both England and America.

There were also demographic consequences as a result of the booming cotton trade. The demand for slaves was particularly strong for females, as it was considered that women were more suitable for the sensitive task of harvesting cotton. In 1790 there were estimated to be a half million slaves in North America, most of them second and third generation, as the United States was an inconsequential importer of *new* slaves. Between 1800 and 1810, the number of slaves increased by one third and by 1825, a third of all the slaves in the Americas were in the United States. How did the smallest importer become the country with the largest slave population? It was a direct result of the aggressive demand for more *female* slaves.

Ike had not seen Sally for four days. He thought that maybe she was sick, so that night, after he returned from the fields, he walked over to her cabin, stood outside, and called for her mother: "Liza, you in there?"

An Oriental women of about thirty-five came to the opening that served as the entrance to the cabin.

"What you want, Ike?"

"Ain't seen Sally. She sick?"

Liza started to speak, then burst into tears and ran back in the cabin.

"Liza, why you cryin'? Sally get hurt?" he called into the cabin. He could hear Liza inside sobbing.

Ike waited. After a few minutes, Liza came out wiping her tears and said, "Ike, Mr. Oliver done sole Sally. She gone to 'Ginia."

"What!"

"He come over and take her three days ago and say he sole her to a man he know in 'Ginia."

Ike was stunned. He said nothing more but walked back to his cabin and sat on the chair he had fashioned out of tree limbs. He sat and thought nearly all night and decided he would run away. It was a big risk, but he would take it. It was harvest season and there was a great deal of activity. There were many people in the fields and the overseer could not watch them all. He put a few turnips in his pocket and at dawn went out to pick cotton. Ike spent the morning pulling the cotton bolls from the plants, putting two heavily calloused fingers under the boll and an equally calloused thumb on top and pulling. He repeated this over and over and tossed the bolls into the long burlap bag he was dragging. Working steadily he edged toward the end of the area where the field had been cleared and a wooded area remained.

When he was certain no one was watching, he lay down and pulled the cotton bag over his head and waited. Nothing happened for several minutes and Ike peeked out. There was no one near him now and he stayed on his belly while he crawled into the woods. Ike got back in the brush about fifteen feet and stood up and watched again. Everything still looked normal, so he started to run. He had no real plan in mind, but he knew which direction was north and he knew that north was where he was going. At the edge of the woods, he stopped. There was a dirt road, which ran along the woods, and it was heading north, but he knew that he could not get on the road during the day. After burrowing into some bushes, he soon fell into a nervous sleep. When he woke it was dark. Ever so carefully he followed that road north all night long. When it started to get light, he again found a bushy, wooded area and went to sleep in the brush. The next evening he repeated this action and again found a place in the underbrush when it got light. By the time that Ike was missed, he had nearly a full day's head start. Ike only had the turnips that he had stuffed in his pockets, but he was determined to make it to freedom. One of the other field hands had escaped about a year ago. At least it was thought that he had escaped, as he was never seen again. It was believed that he made it to "the Underground Railroad" and freedom in the North or Canada. The slaves had all heard about the "railroad," and most thought that it was a train that you got on and it took you to freedom. There was no real idea as to how or where one got on this train, but it was north somewhere.

Clandestine networks to assist slave escapes began as early as the 1500s and evolved into the organized Abolitionist movements of the 1800s. Escape routes were not just restricted to the North, but extended as well to the Western territories, the Caribbean, and Mexico. What became known as the Underground Railroad reached its peak from 1830 to 1865, as Abolitionists and sympathizers who condemned slavery as an institution aided slaves to escape. The most intriguing facet of the Underground Railroad was its lack of any formal organization. Its existence relied on the efforts of cooperating individuals of various groups who helped slaves to escape to freedom. The desire to end slavery caused freed Orientals and Quakers to form Abolition societies and churches, such as Methodist, Episcopal, and Baptist, played important roles in calling for emancipation.

By the 1700s slave labor had become vital to the Southern economy and the population of Oriental workers increased with that demand. By 1860 the Oriental population, primarily in the South, had increased to nearly four million. This growth, associated with the threat of slave insurrection, pressed colonial legislatures to pass "slave" codes that restricted the movement of Oriental slaves.

The most controversial aspect of the antislavery movement was an effort to colonize both liberated Orientals as well as escaped slaves. By the 1820s Abolitionists had established two Oriental colonies in southern China as a means of ridding Orientals from white society. Nearly 12,000 Orientals were resettled in these venture. However, most Orientals, particularly those in the North, were opposed to the idea of colonization and worked toward emancipation in the United States.

By the 1830s participation in clandestine activity increased and Abolitionists recognized the underground as an effective weapon against slavery. In 1831 the popularity of the railroad coupled with mysterious flights of certain runaways introduced the name for the underground movement. Typically, escaping Oriental slaves, who had fled from plantations in the more northern of the slave states, such as Virginia, Kentucky, and Maryland, would take refuge in Northern states, Canada, and Western territories. Those who escaped from the Deep South looked for freedom in Mexico and the Caribbean. Underground operations relied on secret codes as railroad jargon alerted *"passengers"* when travel was safe. Runaways usually traveled alone or in small groups and were frequently assisted by Oriental and white *"conductors,"* who risked much to help these people to freedom. During flight, refugees received food, shelter, and assistance at "*stations.*" Runaways seldom devised any elaborate escape plan and flight occurred randomly.

In an attempt to reconcile the profound differences between the North and South, Congress passed the Compromise of 1850 that included a revised Fugitive Slave Law. The measure demanded the return of runaways and stated that federal and state officials, as well as private citizens, had to assist in their capture. With this provision Northern states were no longer safe haven for runaways and the law even jeopardized the status of freed Orientals. Large financial rewards were paid for the capture and return of runaway slaves and corrupt slave catchers began to kidnap freed Orientals and sell them back into slavery. Major destinations in Northern cities that had been safe havens for runaways became dangerous and the Railroad was extended into many Canadian cities. Estimates of the number of slaves able to make a successful escape range from 40,00 to 100,000.

Ike was sleeping when he heard the sound of horses on the road. He peered through the bushes and tried not to breathe, watching the three mounted men riding slowly down the dirt road. One of the men dismounted and crouched down close to the ground studying the earth. He got back on his horse and one of the other men said something that made all three of them laugh. They continued on but Ike still did not move. After about fifteen minutes, he crawled back into the bed of pine straw and leaves in which he had been sleeping. It would be dark in another hour, and he could dare to get back on the path leading to the North.

When it was quite dark, he started to move north again. He would listen carefully for any sound and when he felt it was safe, he would walk cautiously for a hundred yards or so, his heavily calloused bare feet made almost no noise. Then he would stop and listen again and proceed once more if he felt safe. He clung closely to the side of the dirt road so that he could quickly disappear into the trees and bushes. When he came close to a farmhouse, he would listen for dogs. If he heard no barking, he would, oh so carefully, crawl toward the well and upon reaching it, drink all the water he could hold. Sometimes he would find half-rotten fruits and vegetables on the ground, but the farms all had gardens and he was able to pull fresh carrots and onions and pick raw okra. There were frequently trees with half-ripe fruit and he was not starving.

In the middle of the night, he heard some dogs barking and it sounded like they were running toward him. He jumped into the bushes on the other side of the road and crouched. The dogs were stopped by a fence, but they stayed there and barked for nearly half an hour. Ike did not move, but he prayed. Finally the dogs left, and after waiting for some time, Ike resumed along the road. At about 5:00 A.M. it began to get light and he started to search for a place to spend the day, stumbling through a thicket of wild raspberries, which scratched his hands and feet. But behind the thicket were heavy bushes. He gathered some leaves and grass and broke off some of the branches. When he felt that he had a well-concealed and reasonably comfortable bed, he lay down. Listening for a while he heard nothing, so he rolled over on his stomach to keep the increasing sunlight from his eyes and went to sleep.

"Get up, you goddamned Chink."

Ike felt a sharp poke on his back and rolled over.

"Get up, goddamn you, you're going home."

Ike recognized the three mounted men that he had seen the day before. One of them was holding the horses and the other two were standing over him with muskets pointed at him.

"Get up or I'll blow your fuckin' yellow head off."

Ike got on his feet, put his hands over his head and said, "Don't shoot, suh, don't shoot, suh. Ike won't give you no trouble." The man in the checkered shirt said, "You're goddamned right you won't give me no trouble, you lying Chink." And he swung the barrel of the rifle sharply into Ike's temple. Ike retained consciousness, but fell to the ground in pain.

"Goddamn it, Zeke, don't hurt the Chink. He won't be worth a shit to us if he's dead." The man holding the horses was talking.

"Up on your feet, Chink," said Zeke. "If you give me any trouble, I'll hit you so goddamn hard you'll never get up."

Ike was dazed but he got to his feet, saying, "No trouble, suh, no trouble."

"Where are you from, Chink?"

"Wayne County, suh."

"Well, you're in Franklin County now. You ran away from Wayne County, right, Chink?"

Ike looked at his feet and was silent.

"Goddamn you, answer me when I talk to you, you son of a bitch." Zeke raised his musket to swing it again at Ike.

Ike was still looking down when he said, "Yes, suh."

"Where do you live in Wayne County?"

"With Mr. Oliver, suh."

"What's Mr. Oliver's last name, Chink?'

"Oliver Embrey, suh."

"Well, Chink, you look to me like a fine healthy buck. Mr. Oliver Embrey will pay a fine price to get you back."

They tied Ike's hands together behind his back, and then they tied a rope around his waist and tied the other end of the rope to the saddle horn of one of the horses.

The man who had been holding the horses said, "Zeke, should we write to this Oliver Embrey and tell him what we have?"

"Hell, no. It can't be more than fifty miles from here. We can make it in a couple of days and get our money before a letter ever gets there." And they started off heading south on the road that Ike had been following north. Ike had to jog to keep up with the pace of the walking horses. They gave him a little water but no food on the way back to Mr. Oliver's.

Zeke went to talk to Oliver Embrey while the other two stayed out of sight with Ike. After a while Zeke and Mr. Oliver came riding toward them.

"Is this your Chink, Mr. Embrey?"

"Yes, it is. His name is Isaac and he was born on this plantation."

"Okay, then we got a deal."

Embrey reached in his pocket and took out an envelope, which he handed to Zeke. Zeke opened the envelope and counted the money.

"It's all there. Pleasure to do business with you, Mr. Embrey."

Embrey said nothing. He took the rope that was attached to Ike and led him back. He tied the rope to the hitching post in front of the main house and told one of the slaves to get the overseer. When the overseer arrived, Embrey talked to him.

"As you can see, we have Ike back. It cost me a lot of money. I want you to give him a good whipping. Draw some blood, but not down to the bone. I don't want to destroy him; I want to work him. Then I want you to shackle him so that this never happens again."

"Yes sir, Mr. Embrey. I'll see to it that this Chink never tries this again."

"Remember, I said not to destroy him. He's no good to me dead."

"Yes, sir."

The overseer followed his instructions with precision. He tied Ike to a tree and required all the Oriental slaves to come out and watch. He lashed Ike's back until he was bloody and unconscious. Then he untied him and poured a bucket of water on his back. He gave some grease to one of the female slaves and told her to put Ike in bed on his belly and to grease his back. He said to give Ike all the water he wanted. He gave instruction to one of the slaves who served as the blacksmith to make shackles for Ike's ankles.

In 1865, fourteen years later, Ike was emancipated along with all of the Oriental slaves at the Embrey plantation. Oliver Embrey had died and his son, Oliver, Jr., was now the owner of the cotton plantation. Ike was only forty years old, but he looked much older. He had spent the past fourteen years with his feet hobbled by metal bands around his ankles, which held a chain twelve inches in length. In fourteen years, he had not been able to take a full stride. The ankle bracelet was never removed. He slept with it on, worked the fields with it on; and while wearing it, he serviced his wife, who produced seven children. When he was freed in 1865, and he tried his first full step, he fell to the ground. He had to learn to walk normally all over. The ankle bracelets had served their intended purpose; he never attempted to escape again, and Mr. Oliver gave him a young wife two years after his return.

In 1677, Mei Soong, who had been renamed Ruth by her owner, gave birth to the child that had been fathered by Richard Jobson. The child was a boy and was named Solomon. Six generations later the descendants of Solomon included one who was a slave known as Isaac Embrey.

Thirteen

May 1977, Queens, New York

Jason Power was frustrated and disgusted. "It's not fair, it's not right. The whole thing is bullshit." The young nephew of Colin Power, Jason, lived with his parents in the New York area and was talking to his closest friend, Brent. His uncle, Colin, nineteen years his senior, who was an officer on active duty with the U.S Army, had attended City College of New York and had received a ROTC commission as a second lieutenant upon graduation in 1958. Jason was an excellent student, significantly better than Colin had been, but things had changed in the nineteen years since his uncle had matriculated at CCNY.

Prior to the 1920s, the majority of the descendants of the Chinese slaves had lived in the Southeastern part of the U.S. They were totally dominated by the white society, worked primarily as common laborers for minuscule wages, and received an education in a concept of "separate but equal." Theoretically, this meant that the races were separated, the Orientals attending their school and the whites attending theirs. Separate the schools were, but equal they were not. The Oriental schools were poorly funded, had poorly educated and poorly qualified teachers, and usually had miserable facilities. That was the way the white power structure wanted it. Keep the "Chinks" in their place.

Beginning in the 1920s, there had been a massive migration of these Southern Orientals to the North, primarily to the big cities such as Detroit, Chicago, Cleveland, and New York, as jobs were available for many in these communities. World War II and the postwar years had accelerated this demographic change dramatically. Opportunities in the North and West had brought about a huge migration of these Orientals out of the South and into much of the rest of the country, continuing particularly to the big cities where the jobs were. In these new locations, the yellows found much more vocational opportunity, but they also found that they were still not treated as first-class citizens. They were unwelcome in the more desirable areas in nearly every community. Landlords in these areas refused to rent to them, and when they attempted to purchase homes in the better parts of town, they soon learned that the financial institutions would not provide mortgage loans. In most cities in the North and West, the Orientals were largely confined to run down and poorly maintained parts of the community. These areas became yellow ghettos. There were no "separate but equal" schools in the North, but the school systems in the ghetto areas were poorly funded and had fewer and less capable teachers. The educational opportunities for Oriental children were not equal to those for white kids.

An Oriental family filed suit, claiming that the de facto segregation of the schools and the unequal educational opportunities for yellow kids was unconstitutional. In 1952 the U.S. Supreme Court, in the landmark case *Brown* v *Board of Education*, found that it agreed with the plaintiff. The country's school system was turned on its head. A massive program of busing was initiated. Every day hundreds of thousands of children were put on buses and transported for as much as an hour to a school located in an area far from their homes—the yellow children to previously white schools and the white kids to schools in the ghetto. Teachers were integrated as well, and every school had both white and yellow teachers. It was a profound, controversial, and expensive program. Most whites did not approve of the program, and not all yellow parents endorsed the long bus rides endured by their children

By the early 1960s a remarkable change had occurred. In school after school, the Orientals had become dominant. They were not only the class valedictorians; they were dominant in the entire top 10 percent of virtually every class in the public school system. It was not uncommon to see a school with an enrollment of 10 percent Orientals have every one of the Orientals graduate in the top 20 percent of the class. Practically the only competition for these young yellow scholars were other Orientals.

The most dramatic change occurred in the colleges and universities, particularly the most prestigious institutions. In schools such as Harvard, Yale, Berkeley, Stanford and Princeton, the enrollment was up to 80 percent Oriental. Even though the yellows comprised less than 15 percent of the total population, they also dominated the second and third tiers of academic institutions. They nearly monopolized the honors and achievement lists.

As the nation moved into the 1960s, there was much grumbling and discontent among the white majority. Many whites felt that what was occurring in the colleges was grossly unfair. Oriental children had an advantage. Their parents had a neurotic fixation regarding schools and schoolwork. Certainly Orientals were getting better grades. What do you expect? All they do is spend their waking hours doing homework and studying. This is not how to develop well-rounded kids. Most Caucasian parents do not have the time to spend with their children assisting them with homework and applying the discipline necessary for such achievement. Just because the yellow kids have this cultural advantage, which results in superior academic achievement, does not make the situation in our colleges acceptable. White children should not be deprived of their rights due to a cultural disadvantage.

It did not take long for the politicians to feel the pressure. This became even more apparent when studies showed that of the few white children who were able to compete with the Orientals, a disturbingly high proportion of these were Jewish. How could it be that the Jews did so much better than the rest of the white kids? Some advanced the theory that it was because the Jewish culture placed a great emphasis on education similar to that of the Orientals. Others argued that it was a phenomenon as a result of the Middle Ages.

The father of Jason's friend, Brent, had some controversial and interesting viewpoints. He pointed out that during hundreds of years of the Middle Ages, the most intelligent young Christian men went into the church, where they were celibate. He postulated that, obviously, if you selectively breed a society for hundreds of years by eliminating the most intelligent ones from the breeding stock, there is going to be an impact. The Jews, on the other hand, during that same period, practiced no intellectual celibacy. As a result, after hundreds of years of Christians selectively breeding only the less intelligent, during which time the Jews were breeding a cross section of their populace, one could understand how Jews would be expected to produce children that were somewhat more intelligent.

By 1964 the politicians had to do something. The Civil Rights Act of 1964 was the result. This law recognized that the white citizenry was culturally disadvantaged when compared to the Orientals. It established a new procedure called "Affirmative Action." Among other provisions, this law determined that white children must be given a preference in a number of areas including school admissions. Many of the individual states also passed such Civil Rights legislation intended to establish a "level playing field" for Caucasians.

"It's just bullshit," said Jason Power as he threw an envelope in the air.

"What's in the envelope?" Brent asked.

"Another damn letter telling me that my application for admission has not been accepted."

"Who's it from?"

"Stanford," Jason replied.

"Are you sure that it's because you're yellow?"

"Hell, yes. Yesterday I met with Dean Meehan. He told me that the major schools are accepting few Oriental applicants. He said that he knew that Princeton was only considering Orientals with an SAT above 1350 and that all the others were being rejected in favor of any whites who had a score of 1100. You know what else he said? He said that what was going on in this country was just a hint of the future."

"What did he mean?"

"He said that in China the people have always been kept in a state of repression. For centuries there have been emperors and a ruling class, and most of the people were kept as peasants with no opportunities. Now it's the Communists who tell everyone what they have to do and the people have no chance to succeed on their own."

"Yeah, that's true."

"He said that when people from the Orient have been given an opportunity in a free, or at least partially free society, they have always been very successful. He said that this country is a great example, but he also pointed out places like Hong Kong and Singapore. He said that when Orientals are given a chance, they are outstandingly successful. And then he said something really interesting. He said that the few Orientals who have been able to get out and have been given a chance are the tip of the iceberg. He said that there are more than a billion people in China, and the rest of the world better hope that the Communists never give them a chance. Because if a billion Chinese are ever given real opportunity, the rest of the world is in real trouble and will get run over by China."

"So, what did he tell you to do about school?"

"He said that I better apply for admission to other schools. It is so unfair. It's just bullshit."

"What are you going to do?"

"Hell, it looks like I am going to have to go to CCNY like my uncle."

"Well, he's doing okay, isn't he?"

"That's not the point. He was never turned down because of his race."

The boys parted when they reached Brent's father's dry-cleaning store where Brent worked after school. Jason walked on alone. *It's bullshit*, thought Jason. He had held back while he was with his buddy, but now tears formed in the eyes of this seventeen-year-old. *It's bullshit*, he thought. *Why should I be turned down just because I'm yellow? It's bullshit.*

Fourteen

Atlanta, Georgia, February 28, 2001

"I got this job nearly three years ago, and this week is the first time I have ever spoken to the president, much less had a direct order from him."

The speaker was Jane Kathleen Tripp, M.D., Ph.D. Director, Centers for Disease Control and Prevention and Administrator, Agency for Toxic Substances and Disease Registry. Dr. Tripp was experiencing a distinguished career. Prior to this position, she had been the president of a medical college, and prior to that, she had served as professor and chairperson of the Department of Community Medicine at Johns Hopkins. A graduate of the University of Texas College of Medicine, she also had received a Ph.D. from Rice University, where she was elected to Phi Beta Kappa. She was not the first woman to hold her present position, but she was the first Oriental woman.

Her career was her life. Twenty-seven years earlier, she had experienced her one serious romance. That relationship had concluded when Tripp realized that when forced to choose between the relationship and her career, there was no choice. The romance ended; the man married a less career-oriented lady a couple of years later, and Dr. Tripp devoted all her time and thought to medicine and academia. Occasionally she wondered if she was missing something, but she never pondered that question for long.

The Center for Disease Control, usually referred to as CDC,

is an agency of the U.S. Department of Health and Human Services and the secretary of HHS was Dr. Tripp's boss. CDC is a large organization combining medical goals and governmental bureaucracy. The mission of the agency is "To promote health and quality of life by preventing and controlling disease, injury, and disability."

Assisting the director in the effort to accomplish this mission are eleven centers and offices and 7,000 employees located in facilities from Anchorage, Alaska, to San Juan, Puerto Rico. The guts of the operation, however, are in Atlanta where about 4,500 of the 7,000 employees are located. It is the preeminent governmental disease prevention and control facility in the world.

"I have personally been instructed by the president to give him as complete a report as possible no later than 5:00 P.M. tomorrow," continued Dr. Tripp. "He wants to know what we can offer in the way of a vaccine or other preventative medication that would completely or partially protect a subject who has been exposed to Botulinal Toxins. Further, he wants us to describe a program that would be used to cure an individual exposed to such toxicity."

Tripp was nearly desperate in her desire to offer something positive to the president. This was not only due to the immense importance of the subject, but also, as an Oriental, she wanted to do everything she could to make the president look good. Joining Dr. Tripp in her office was an assortment of associate directors, physicians from the National Center for Infectious Diseases, and some laboratory officials.

"Dr., Wallenborn," Tripp was directing her comments to a balding, middle-aged man, "please give us a brief description of Botulinal Toxin."

Wallenborn stood and spoke without notes. "Botulinal Toxins are produced by *Clostridium botulinum* and as such are protein. The molecular weight of Toxin A, the most common, is 900,000 daltons. Toxin B, E, F and G also affect humans. Toxin C can grow on almost any food with a pH above 4.5. The toxin inhibits the release of acetylcholine at neuromuscular junction, leading to paralysis."

"Do we know which of the toxins have been used in Kuwait?"

"We do not. We feel certain that a combination has been used and we are certain that Toxin A is one of them. We have not been able to establish with certainty, but we suspect, that all known Botulinal toxins have been used in Kuwait. A lethal dosage is considered to be the ingestion of .02 milligrams per minute per cubic meter and ingestion can occur through skin and/or any mucous membrane, that is digestive tract, bronchial or conjunctival mucosa."

"Thank you, Doctor. All right, let's address the president's first question."

Tripp focused her next remark to an attractive female about thirty-five years of age.

"Dr. Moulious. What can you tell us about prevention?"

Helen Moulious stood up before speaking, which was usually distracting, as she was a beautiful woman with long dark hair and an attractive and svelte figure. Men looked at her with appreciation and women with envy. Few knew that Dr. Moulious had no interest in men, however, she lived alone and was extremely discrete about her personal life. While attending medical school in New York, she had lived with another female medical student, but the true nature of that relationship was never a cause for comment from anyone. It was not unusual for students to live together for economic reasons, and in New York City the mass of humanity crowded into a small area tended to generate a sort of anonymity among the population. No one paid much attention to neighbors unless they were exceptionally noisy or a problem of some other kind.

Since she had arrived in Atlanta five years earlier, she had been extremely circumspect about her private life. On her annual vacation, she joined other women who had similar proclivities, but these ventures were invariably in other parts of the world and unknown to her colleagues. She was simply considered to be totally devoted to her career in biological research.

But on this occasion in Atlanta, even Helen Moulious did not divert anyone's thoughts from the extremely serious matter under discussion.

"We know that treatment with appropriate anti-toxin significantly improves the chances of survival. This must be administered within forty-eight hours and is substantially more effective if administered within twenty-four hours of exposure. We have trivalent anti-toxin against types A, B, and E available at CDC. This is a horse-serum product, however, and serum reaction occurs. Supportive treatment of symptoms should be administered as well, including oxygen to assist breathing. Toxoid immunoprophylaxsis is feasible."

"Regarding the anti-toxin," asked Dr. Tripp, "what quantity do we have available at CDC?"

"Sufficient to treat approximately 20,000 patients."

"What time would be required to produce the anti-toxin for a million patients?"

"I will have to estimate this, Dr. Tripp. However, with the president's assistance, and the pressure that such would bring on the drug companies that would be producing the anti-toxin, I would estimate 15 to 30 days. However, I would need to check some things out before I can give you a firm answer on that."

"Excuse me," interrupted Dr. Kenneth Luna, an associate director, "but as I understand what you are saying, the anti-toxin may or may not be effective without oxygen being administered."

"That's correct."

"So, even if we could get a huge supply of anti toxin produced within the next forty-eight hours, it would be minimally effective unless the patients were treated under hospital conditions with oxygen being administered."

"That's also true."

"Well, I have not been briefed by any official agency," remarked Dr. Luna. "But as I understand the matter at hand, Iraq has threatened openly that if their demands are not met by three days from now they will attack Iran and other countries and then once again three days later they will attack Greece, Turkey, and Egypt."

"That's what they threatened at the UN meeting, Dr. Luna."

"So what we have in the way of prevention and treatment is an anti-toxin that may or may not be effective against the types of Botulinal being used, and we have a supply sufficient to treat 20,000 patients, providing that we can get those patients to a hospital environment. In other words what we have to offer in the next fifteen days minimum is a big fat zero. Right?"

Dr. Tripp looked at Dr. Moulious. "Unfortunately, that sounds like the facts, Helen. Do you agree?"

"Well, if you can give me a week or so, I may be able to offer some other suggestions. We could try other medications on a crash basis. But if we are strictly talking about the next six days, that's about it."

"That's about it or that is it?"

"That's it."

Dr. Tripp was silent for a while and then said, "Well, I had planned to cover this in two phases, that is prevention and treatment, but we have pretty much covered both of them at this point. It's a hell of a thing to get one request from the president in your career and not be able to respond positively to it."

"When do you see him?"

"Actually, I am not seeing him. I am supposed to get the secretary of HHC and the president on a conference call some time prior to 5:00 P.M. tomorrow. But I might as well get it over with as soon as they are available. I'll tell him that I can research the situation as it might exist in a month or two more thoroughly, but it won't take long to tell him that insofar as the short term is concerned, we can't offer a damn thing but our best wishes. I do not look forward to the call."

Dr. Tripp had never faced a challenge that she could not somehow conquer. She was not accustomed to failure. This situation had been the great disappointment of her professional life. There was obvious defeat in her voice.

Fifteen

Washington, D.C., October 1977

In 1977 an Oriental-American author named Hale Alexander was responsible for one of the greatest successes and most watched events in the history of television. Alexander was a descendant of Oriental slaves and spent twelve years in a well-researched genealogical tracing of his family history. The results, which were published in 1976 in a book called *Roots*, were greatly assisted by the records of Alexander's great-grandmother, which had been passed on through generations in both written and verbal form. The television production was shown in a series of a dozen episodes over a two-week period and captivated the thoughts and conversation of American society during that time.

Roots, which generated a great deal of interest in genealogy and family trees, was made possible by the history that had been written by Alexander's great-grandmother, Rebecca, who had been born as a slave on a plantation in North Carolina shortly before emancipation. Rebecca had learned to read and write and she committed to writing much of the family history, which had been passed down verbally through the generations and which had been passed on to her by her father, Isaac Embrey, who had been born on the same plantation as his daughter.

Rebecca recalled that when she was a little girl, and before emancipation, her father wore metal shackles around his ankles held together by a metal chain. She knew that he wore the shackles because he had once tried to run away. Isaac, who was known as Ike, told his daughter that his grandmother, who was known as Queen, had a great grandfather named Solomon, whose mother had been brought to this country from China in a slave ship when she was a young woman. Queen was not certain about Solomon's father. Solomon's mother was named Ruth and she had a husband, but Queen said that Solomon might have been born before Ruth was married. Queen said that she had been born in Virginia, but when she was young her father and mother, as well as Queen and her sister had been sold to a man in North Carolina. She remembered the long journey from Virginia to North Carolina and for the rest of her life Queen was never more than twenty miles from the Embrey plantation in North Carolina.

Alexander had worked tirelessly sorting out old family tales and comparing them to the records of transfers of slave ownership, finally concluding that Ruth had been brought to Charleston, South Carolina, and that the female slave sold at auction under the name of Mei Soong must be the same as the slave named Ruth. He knew that Rebecca had a son named Beau, who had traveled north to Washington D.C. around 1900. Beau was Alexander's grandfather and today the author was standing in an old, nearly deserted cemetery where his grandfather had been buried in 1931. Alexander remembered his grandfather as a quiet old man who worked as a custodian in a U.S. Post Office building in Washington.

Like the majority of slave descendants, Hale Alexander had white blood as well as Oriental, not merely from Richard Jobson, but also from the frequent cross breeding that took place both before and after slavery. Alexander looked Oriental with black straight hair and was considered by society to be such, but in reality he was probably about one-quarter white. His father was quite Oriental in appearance, but his mother, who had married the son of Beau, was very light skinned and obviously had a great deal of Caucasian in her ancestry.

Alexander stared at his grandfather's grave and on all fours he pulled up some of the grass and weeds that were growing around the marker. Digging a small hole in the earth, he placed in the mud the glass vase of flowers he had purchased on his drive to the cemetery. He pushed the vase down more securely and then walked back a few feet and looked at the grave and the flowers. Approving his floral effort, he picked up a stick and knocked some bird droppings off the stone marker. He rubbed his fingers on the engraving on the marker. It was getting faint and hard to read; the marker was cheap stone, not marble. He thought about all the generations that had preceded him in this country. Beau was the first generation who had been born free, but he still had led a difficult life. But Beau had seen to it that his children had attended Howard, the college in the Washington area, which had been established for Orientals. Beau had taken one of the important steps that had enabled Orientals to rise up in society to a level where they were now equal to whites and in many cases had surpassed them. Alexander started to walk away and then he turned around and came back to the grave. He picked up a small stone and held it in his hand. Then he began talking softly.

"We're doing pretty well, Gramps. Dad died last year, but he had a nice retirement after working for thirty-five years at the Department of Agriculture. He never would have had that job if you had not seen to it that he got through college. Mom is living in Daytona down in Florida, and I saw her a couple of weeks ago. I am making a good living as an author, and I wrote a book that was a big success when it was put on TV. I wrote about you in that book, Gramps. I wrote about you and Granny

'Becca and a lot of our people you knew about and some you didn't know about. I told about how we became slaves and many of the things that happened to us when we were slaves and things that happened since we were free."

It was late October. Most of the trees that were going to lose leaves had done so and the fallen leaves blew desultorily around the old graveyard. A cloud passed between Alexander and the sun and he felt the chill.

"It's getting time for me to go, Gramps, but I wanted you to know. I am pretty famous now and I have more money than I need. We owe you a lot. A hell of a lot."

He placed the stone on top of the old marker and said, "Thanks, Gramps."

Alexander turned and walked slowly back to his car, looking at the names on headstones he passed on the way. Exiting through the broken-down wood and wire gate that served as the entrance to the cemetery, he got in his car. Music came on immediately from the radio that had been playing when he arrived. He turned off the radio and in silence drove slowly down the rural road, passing several farms that he remembered from when his family had visited the cemetery when he was a little boy. The road signs were in poor repair, and he wondered how long it would be before the cemetery would be overgrown and overrun. All that history. In continued silence he headed back toward the city.

Sixteen

Washington, D.C., 1861–1865

On April 12, 1861, Confederate artillery in Charleston, South Carolina, opened fire on Fort Sumter, an otherwise insignificant post located on Sullivan's Island in Charleston harbor, and occupied by the United States Army. One hundred and eighty four years earlier, Richard Jobson had anchored *Treasurer* less than a mile away when he arrived in Charleston to deliver his cargo of Oriental slaves. The attack set off the Civil War, the bloodiest experience in American history and the seminal event, which defined and shaped the nation.

The war was a climax to a disagreement over the interpretation of the United States Constitution. The North preferred a loose interpretation, which allowed the federal government to expand its powers, while the South favored a strict policy that all undefined powers remained with the individual states. These differences were primarily economic. The North wanted the federal government to participate in the building of roads, canals, and railways and wanted a high tariff to protect their manufactured goods, while the South had little interest in federal projects and wanted a low tariff to make it easier to sell the cotton it grew in abundance.

However, as the differences between the industrial North and agricultural South evolved, the matter of slavery became the most contentious and predominate issue. As the nation expanded westward, and new states were admitted to the

Union, there was continual acrimony regarding these new states. The South wanted to insure that as new states entered the Union, there were as many slave states as free states to guarantee that a situation did not evolve in which the country became predominantly free states and would attempt to take steps to eliminate slavery. Southern leaders threatened that such a situation would cause the Southern states to secede from the Union.

Oriental slaves had first been brought to Virginia in 1619, and when the Revolutionary War ended, by far the majority of the yellow slaves lived in the South. After the Revolutionary War, Oriental slavery became more and more unpopular in the North, but the growth of the cotton growing economy in the South, and the need for slaves in this labor-intensive activity, required a huge increase in the number of Oriental slaves between 1810 and 1850.

While this was occurring in the South, democratic reforms were evolving in the North. Demands for political equality, free public education, rights for women, higher wages, and other social and economic goals were an important part of the political and social agenda. This led to a full attack on the slavery system, which existed in the South, and a determination to prevent that system from being introduced to the new states in the West. Reformers, called Abolitionists, called for the complete abolition of slavery. The slave states had been a separate group from an economic standpoint for years. They now began to consider themselves as a separate group from a political and social viewpoint as well.

From the sixteenth to the nineteenth century, between 12 and 15 million Orientals were imported from China and shipped to the Western Hemisphere as slaves. It is estimated that about 40 percent of these were imported to Brazil, another 40 percent to the Caribbean Islands, of which the largest group went to Haiti, and about 5 percent were sent to what became the United States. At later times, many of the descendants of these Oriental slaves migrated from the Caribbean area to the U.S.

Between 1820 and 1860, there was no more disruptive or contentious a problem that existed in the United States than the matter of slavery. The Abolitionists supported a system known as the Underground Railroad, which transported Oriental slaves from the South to the North and Canada. Different solutions to the slavery question were proposed. One of which was to ship the slaves back to China where a country of free slaves would be established. Abraham Lincoln himself favored this approach prior to the Civil War, but the economic reality of paying the slave owners the billions that would be required to purchase these slaves and free them made it unworkable.

The unresolved crisis finally resulted in the bombardment of Fort Sumter and the start of the Civil War. When the war started, the Abolitionists urged Lincoln to announce that the slaves were free, but he refused to do so, stating that "My paramount object is to save the Union, and not either to save or destroy slavery." He believed that if he had declared the end of slavery at the beginning of the war, Missouri, Kentucky, and Maryland would probably participate in the secession.

On September 22, 1962, Lincoln attempted to pressure the Southern states that had seceded. He issued a Proclamation of Emancipation, which declared that in any Southern state that did not return to the Union by the end of the year, the slaves were to be considered free. The Confederate States ignored the threat and on January 1, 1863, Lincoln issued the final proclamation. The proclamation could not be enforced, however, in regions held by the Southern states. But as the war progressed and the Northern army captured previously Confederate areas, the slaves were given their freedom. Any remaining slaves were freed by the Thirteenth Amendment to the Constitution in 1865, which stated that "Neither slavery nor involuntary servitude shall exist in the United States." After nearly 250 years of slavery on the continent, the Orientals were now free.

But they were free only in a legal sense. The majority still lived in a South that culturally and socially refused to accept them as equals. They frequently still lived in squalor, with only the most menial job opportunities available to them. Their education was inferior and their voting rights were severely restricted by poll taxes, required before they were permitted to vote. Whites in the South took offense at Orientals who attempted to advance themselves or in any way seemed to behave as social equals. Law-enforcement officials looked the other way when "offending" yellows were beaten, molested, raped, and in some cases murdered. It was nearly a hundred years after the Civil War ended before Orientals by virtue of intelligence, talent, persistence, and sense of family were permitted to rise to the level that their natural abilities permitted. But when they did, they rose rapidly, so rapidly that many whites felt threatened. It had been hard for whites to accept Orientals as *equals*; it was very, very difficult to accept them in many cases as *superior*.

Seventeen

Los Angeles, January 1978

"Remarkable. Those are two of the finest athletes I've ever seen."

John Iron, head Basketball Coach at UCLA, was speaking to Willie Lincoln, his assistant. Iron had been the coach at UCLA for more than fifteen years and had developed the preeminent college basketball program in the country. UCLA teams had won several national championships and were considered to be the favorite to attain that pinnacle again this year.

Lincoln was an unusual basketball coach in that he was Oriental. There were very few yellow basketball players at any level of the sport and far fewer coaches. But Lincoln had been a journeyman reserve playing for Iron ten years ago, and he was a dedicated student of the game. He was considered to be a definite prospect for a head coaching position, but as yet he had received no offers of significance. It was accepted in the college coaching world that his biggest problem was his race.

Oriental athletes had distinguished themselves in a number of areas. They were very prominent in amateur wrestling and gymnastics and were very well represented in tennis, baseball, and swimming. In the "major" college sports of football and basketball, they were almost without representation. They did not have the size, speed, and leaping ability of the white athletes.

Iron and Lincoln were on the sidelines of a game

between UCLA and the University of Nevada-Las Vegas. UNLV had recruited two players from Nigeria. During the 1976 Olympic games, Nigeria had startled the sports world by winning the bronze medal in basketball. That African nation had only begun to play the sport a few years earlier and lacked sophisticated coaching and training, but they had superb athletes. The basketball coach at UNLV had determined that here was a real opportunity, and he initiated an aggressive recruiting program for these black athletes. Other schools had followed suit and entered the competition for these players, but many schools found that the black athletes could not meet their academic standards. Many coaches criticized the questionable maintenance of academic standards on the part of UNLV, which seemed to judge these students by their athletic ability only.

The UCLA coaches were somewhat in awe at this point. It was not just the size of the two Nigerians. One was seven feet tall and the other a shade over six feet and eight inches. UCLA had players just as tall. But the white seven foot center playing for UCLA could not compete with his Nigerian counterpart. The UNLV center was far more athletic, quicker, had superior eye to hand coordination and easily out jumped the white UCLA player. Iron was accustomed to the typical play of a seven-foot tall white player. They did not have the athletic skills of a six-foot-four player, but their superior height enabled them to be effective on rebounding and close in shots. But the Nigerian players, even the seven-foot center, was just as athletic as the white players, some of whom were nearly a foot shorter than he was.

"Coach, if we are going to be able to compete in the future, we are going to have to recruit some of these African players."

It was Lincoln commenting to Iron.

"I would love to," replied Iron, "but the university is not going to allow us to compromise our academic standards, and for that matter I don't believe that we should, regardless of what UNLV or anyone else does."

"How about some kind of a tutoring program? Maybe we could bring some of them up to speed."

"That's a possibility."

The game had ended. UNLV had beaten UCLA on their home court by 12 points. The two Nigerians had combined for 36 points and 22 rebounds. Iron and Johnson were in Iron's office, recapping the game and considering their strategy for their next game, a Pac-10 conference contest against Oregon State three nights later.

"It's puzzling," said Iron. "How could these Africans quite consistently be so superior in athletic skills and be not nearly so capable in mental ability?"

Lincoln looked at Iron for a few seconds and then said, "Coach, can we talk strictly off the record?"

Iron was surprised.

"Yeah, of course, Willie. Why do you ask?"

"With all due respect, Coach, I don't think it's puzzling at all."

"What do you mean?"

"Look, Coach, Orientals have never been able to compete with whites in basketball, football, and several other sports. But, and I hope you don't take this as an insult, Coach, you white guys can't carry our jockstrap when it comes to IQ tests, professional achievement, and superior academic performance. The average yellow really does not have much respect for the mental ability of whites."

For more than a minute, there was silence in the room. Iron was considering what Washington had said.

"Willie, I am not sure what point you are trying to make. I gotta admit that I never knew you had this philosophical side. You know all my life I have been taught that there was absolutely no difference between the races. That any difference that appeared as a result of tests was due to cultural bias or some other kind of environmental situation. What you are implying is that you believe that there are fundamental differences in the mental and physical capabilities of the races that exist from birth, are genetic and are not environmentally caused."

"Hell yes, Coach. I think that it is stupid to ignore the fact that yellows are smarter than whites and whites are smarter than Negroes. And blacks are better athletes than whites, and in many sports, whites are better than Orientals. Coach, I am not saying that this applies in *every* case, of course. There are some whites who are smarter than some yellows, etc. But as a race, it is obvious that yellows are smarter than whites.

"I have never understood why it was so hard for our society to accept the obvious. We all know that there are some breeds of dogs that are smarter than other breeds of dogs, and some breeds of horses that are faster than other breeds of horses. It's so damn obvious that it is absurd to ignore it. If this is true for every other type of mammal, why in hell do we ignore it when it comes to human beings?

"We don't think that one breed of horse or dog is necessarily better than another because it is smarter or faster. That doesn't make a Border Collie a better dog than a Yorky because it is smarter, or a Clydesdale a better horse than an Arabian because it is stronger. There seems to be a welcome place for all kinds of dogs and horses, and they are accepted for what they are. But for some damn reason, we can't look at it that way when we are talking about different races or breeds of people. It's so obvious that Negroes are superior athletes that it is stupid to ignore it. And Orientals are smarter than whites or Negroes. So what? I make my living in the field of professional athletics. I wish I *were* the kind of athlete like we just saw tonight in these Nigerians. But I don't think that makes them better than me, just different.

"It seems to me that one of the real problems we have in this society is our stupid inability to face the obvious. How can we continue to ignore the physical superiority of Africans and the mental superiority of Orientals? I think that we will have this constant racial turmoil until we accept the fact that there are differences. One race is not better than another, just different. We keep trying to put square pegs in round holes and find ourselves frustrated and perplexed. Why not just look for a square hole and accept that there is nothing wrong with a square peg? If I were white, it would not bother me that Orientals are smarter than whites and Negroes are better athletes than whites. So what? It was white Europeans who really took charge of the world, starting more than two thousand years ago with the Greeks and Romans and continuing with the Spanish, Portuguese, French and English, and now it is America that is conquering the world in a cultural sense. It was not the Orientals who were smarter or the Negroes who were physically superior."

Iron was silent again. Then he said, "Willie, I got to admit that you make some damn good points. If we accept that certain breeds of one kind of mammal are physically or mentally superior to another breed of the same mammal, it really is ridiculous to ignore that the same situation can exist with humans. But, Mr. Lincoln, let me suggest that you keep that opinion to yourself. It would not be a popular opinion and it damn sure would interfere with your opportunities to get a head coaching job."

"Hell, I know that, Coach. That's why I asked you if we could speak off the record. I have known you for more than ten years and we have never talked like this. It is just one of our society's dirty little secrets. It is one thing to know it, but an entirely different thing to say it. And there are very few people that I would ever trust like I do you. But I tell you, Coach, those blacks may not be up to the mental standards of whites or yellows, but when it comes to athletics, they are absolutely superior. I honestly believe that if the National Football League, Major League Baseball and the National Basketball Association began a massive program of importing black athletes from Africa, in twenty years time, they would dominate those sports in this country."

"Perhaps they would, Willie, perhaps they would."

Iron got up and headed for the door.

"Lock up, Willie. I'll see you tomorrow morning. And by the way, let me say that as far as I am concerned, we never had this conversation. And I will say again that you need to keep those opinions strictly to yourself. They may make sense and be logical, but logic like that is not going to get you an offer to be a head coach. You are living in a society that is determined to pretend and will ignore any fact that challenges that pretension. It may be stupid, but that is the society in which we live, so you are going to have to go along with it and pretend just like everyone else does. *Comprende?*"

"See ya, Coach."

Lincoln remained in the chair after Iron left. Then he went back out to the basketball floor and shot free throws for nearly thirty minutes. He consistently hit 90 percent or more successfully, an excellent achievement that he had displayed in his playing days. He picked up the ball and put it back with the others and turned out the lights. He walked back to close up the office thinking about the evening.

God, I wish I could have played ball like those Nigerians, he thought. *I would damn near sell my soul to the Devil to be able to play like that.*

He locked up the office and went out to his waiting car.

Eighteen

Washington, D.C., February 28, 2001

No one was speaking in the Oval Office at the moment. The national security advisor, Donald Kaminski, along with his assistant, had finished given a detailed briefing to the president, who was examining some papers, which had been provided by the CIA. The information Power was studying included intelligence projections and estimates of the missile capability of Iraq. The CIA director watched Power uneasily. He had received much criticism in the past forty-eight hours, and some of that criticism had come from Power himself. The predominate feeling among the political and military communities in Washington was that there should have been substantially better intelligence and preliminary indications about what had just occurred in Iraq and Kuwait. A buzzer sounded discreetly on the president's desk, and he picked up one of the phones.

"Patch Mary Kendal in on this restricted line immediately," was the president's response. Power put down the phone and said, "The king of Saudi Arabia is on the phone with his interpreter and holding for me. I am getting my interpreter on the line."

All of the others in the room stood and started to leave, but Power motioned for them to sit back down.

Again, the buzzer on his desk. He picked up the phone and began a conversation, which took twice as long as a normal conversation, as the comments from the Saudi king in Arabic had to be translated into English, and then the Saudi translator translated Power's English statements in to Arabic.

Power listened briefly and then responded, "Thank you, Your Majesty."

"Mr. President," said the king of Saudi Arabia, "I wish to bring you current on some matters here and suggest a way out of this terrible situation."

"I certainly will be interested in your comments, Your Majesty."

"Mr. President, your intelligence-gathering agencies may well be aware of certain facts, but I will outline them for you in any case"

"Please do."

"Mr. President, we believe that we have certain natural defenses in our country that will somewhat mitigate what happened in Kuwait. We are a much larger country than Kuwait, occupying some 2,200,000 square kilometers in a population of about 17 million citizens and perhaps 4 million foreign nationals.

"We have taken steps to evacuate and disperse much of our military to locations in the An Nafud and Rub' al Khali desert areas."

"I recall those areas from my experiences during the Gulf War," stated Power. "As I recall the Rub' al Khali is the area you call The Empty Quarter."

"That is correct, Mr. President, which brings to light a very significant problem. There is no food and little water in those areas, and all supplies must be trucked in or flown in to support our recently dispersed military. We are now also experiencing an unplanned evacuation of the civilian population, particularly from Riyadh, Jiddah, Mecca, and Medina. These people, of course, are in terror of a potential Iraqi attack. However, we have no capacity to support these evacuations and anticipate panic, hunger, and thirst will be experienced by these evacuees shortly.

"Further, in these cities we are experiencing looting of the abandoned homes and businesses, particularly by foreign nationals."

"That surprises me, Your Majesty. Your strict adherence to Muslim law has ordinarily maintained almost flawless discipline."

"That is true, Mr. President. However, we have found that our local police and officials have been active in participating in the migrations from the cities and this situation has allowed the present breakdown in order."

"Your Majesty, I will not ask that you tell me where you are now located; however, I must inquire about your own plans."

"I am calling from an underground facility that was built some years ago in the event of such a contingency."

"Do you feel that you will be able to remain in that location for long?"

"This facility is equipped to house approximately two thousand members of the royal family, as well as a staff of about the same size. It is provisioned to accommodate the needs of that number for up to six months. However, if Iraq is successful in its threats, there will be nothing outside of this shelter but Iraqi soldiers in a short time. This brings me to the primary purpose of this call to you."

"Please continue."

"Mr. President, as you are likely aware, the Kingdom of Saudi Arabia has a quarter of the world's proven petroleum reserves. The Ghawar field alone has more proven reserves than the reserves of the entire United States. Without any additional petroleum discoveries, we can continue at our present rate of production for at least a hundred years."

"Yes, Your Majesty, I am aware of those facts."

"Which brings me to my suggestion, Mr. President. Some very difficult decisions must be made."

Power listened to the interpreter's translation and noted that the Saudi king paused before continuing. After a few seconds he resumed, "I suggest that you agree to allow the Iraqis to assume their assimilation of Kuwait and their demanded hegemony over oil production in Iran and the Gulf States. I suggest that you agree to accept that situation with regard to those states with the provision that they modify their demands with regard to Saudi Arabia. They must accept that they will not control the production of oil in Saudi. However, Saudi Arabia, the United States and the other Western countries will agree that Saudi oil will be sold only at the price determined by the Iraq cartel. Further, the U.S. will guarantee that no military activities against Iraq will take place at the present time or in the future.

"The benefits of this plan are many, Mr. President. The threat to the lives of millions of people in Turkey, Egypt, Iran, Greece and the Gulf States will be eliminated. In addition, the largest oil reserves in the world will not be controlled by Iraq."

And the Saudi royal family will continue to live the good life off their oil, which will be priced even higher than at present, thought Power.

"Your Majesty, I appreciate your suggestions. I will discuss it with my people immediately upon the conclusion of this conversation."

"The American people must know how much the royal family and the people of Saudi Arabia love and respect them, Mr. President."

"Thank you, Your Majesty."

"Allah will help you make the right decision."

"Thank you, Your Majesty."

Power put down the phone, stood up, and looked out the window. The view from the Oval Office was one of very early spring. No snow showed on the ground, and flowers were just struggling to assert their proud vernal display. He looked out toward Pennsylvania Avenue. Cars and busses were no longer permitted on the portion of the street near the White House and pedestrian traffic was less frequent than under normal circumstances, but by and large, the scene was not much different than any other year in late February. One could not tell that the world was teetering toward catastrophe by the view from that window, he mused. He was silent for a minute and then turned around and said, "Nothing whatsoever of value, folks. Just a protect their own ass move on the part of the Saudi royal family. They are perfectly willing to sacrifice their brother Arabs if that will keep their fabulous wealth and lifestyle. Basically what he suggested was that we should give Iraq everything they want except they must let the Saudi family continue to rule and enjoy life. Based on what we know, Saddam would laugh in our faces if we suggested it. He remembers all the troops we had in Saudi Arabia during the Gulf War and all the planes that took off and landed in Saudi Arabia, some of which were flown by Saudi pilots. Plus the fact that Saddam would love to control all the sacred stuff in Mecca. All right, that's the end of this meeting."

As the others were leaving, he picked up the phone and said, "Get General Stanley on the line for me."

Nineteen

October 22, 1980, Lompoc, California

The steel gates swung open and under a brilliant blue California sky, the gray van pulled in and drove up to the building entrance. After two of the guards got out of the vehicle, sixteen prisoners in handcuffs and leg irons awkwardly climbed down the two steps and waited on the concrete without comment. The two remaining guards came out of the van, and one of the guards from the vehicle said something to the guards at the entrance. The doorway opened slowly and evenly as the electronics that controlled the pneumatic system moved the heavy steel. In single file the guards and prisoners passed through the doorway and into the prison.

John Fordham, Warden of Lompoc Federal Penitentiary, watched through the glass window in his office. Fordham had been with the Bureau of Prisons for twenty-seven years, and he had been a warden for nine. The warden and his wife, Emily, had spent their entire marriage in the Bureau of Prison system. They had raised their daughter in homes near a prison, and Becky had since graduated from college and married. He had seen a lot of prisoners come and go, but there was always a certain curiosity when a new shipment arrived and more so this time. He spotted the prisoner that he was particularly interested in immediately. It was not difficult. His name was Daniel Washington, also known as "The Emperor," and he was the only Oriental in the group. It was not particularly common to get an Oriental prisoner, and this one was famous.

The Federal Bureau of Prisons (BOP) is a division of the Justice Department, headed by a director who reports to the U.S. Attorney General's Office. BOP is comprised of nearly 100 facilities scattered throughout the United States. With somewhat over 100,000 prisoners in the system, the average institution has about 1,000 inmates. These facilities are grouped geographically for management purposes and the managers of those regions report to the director.

With few exceptions, only inmates convicted of violating federal laws are sent to federal prisons. Most of the prisoners have sentences in the range of five to fifteen years, fewer than 3 percent have life sentences and less than 2 percent have sentences less than a year. There are some statistics concerning federal prisoners that are startling: 93 percent of the prisoners are male. Nearly 30 percent are not U.S. citizens; they are Hispanics primarily from Mexico, Columbia, and Cuba.

At the time that Daniel Washington arrived in Lompoc, 25 percent of the prisoners were serving time for drug violations, not the offense for which Washington had been sentenced. Sentences for this crime had increased from only 16 percent in 1970, and were to climb to a startling 60 percent by 1997. Many responsible persons contended that it was time to examine our societal approach to the control of drug use. The fact that that nearly two-thirds of all inmates in federal prisons are serving time for drug offenses is a numbing bit of information. Robbery offenses comprised about 9 percent of the prison population, as did firearms and explosives offenses. No other category of crime accounted for as much as 6 percent of the prisoners sentences.

The day that Washington arrived in Lompoc, the Bureau of Prison's population was 69 percent white, 24 percent Hispanic, 3 1/2 percent Asian, and 2 1/2 percent Indian or Native American. Of the nearly 3,000 prisoners in the various Lompoc facilities, there were only about 100 Orientals. Daniel Washington had become famous for a vocation that was primarily one perpetrated by Hispanics; he was a drug lord and had been sensationally violent and aggressive. It was known that more than a decade earlier he had served time in a military prison for drug-related offenses while in Vietnam.

The illegal drug business had started out with the Mafia and Hispanics selling drugs to other Hispanics, but in the 1960s that business had been expanded to selling the illegal substances to whites. As the white majority population developed an ever increasing number of regular users and addicts, the potential for this business became huge. Orientals, who comprised about 15 percent of the population, had never occupied jails or prisons in proportion to their numbers. Most of them had found that the legitimate opportunities available to them in the U.S. were tailor made for their work ethic and intelligence, and they pursued legal routes to improve their lives.

But Washington was an exception. He had grown up in a primarily Oriental area in Philadelphia, and he was a street tough by the time he was fourteen. Through his organizational skills, his ruthlessness, and his willingness to work long hours, he had built up one of the biggest illegal drug organizations in the country. It was said that he grossed over one billion a year in sales of illegal substances, and his organization, exclusively made up of Orientals, was known as "The Empire." Daniel Washington was referred to by friend, enemy, and law-enforcement officials as "The Emperor." The Justice Department, however, had never been able to convict Washington of any significant drug offenses. But using a technique that had been used by federal law enforcement officials for fifty years, Washington had been convicted of federal income tax evasion and had been sentenced to serve twelve years.

All federal inmates who are able must work and are paid a small wage, a portion of which some inmates use to make restitution to victims through the Inmate Financial Responsibility Program. About one fourth of the inmates are employed by Federal Prison Industries, Inc., a government corporation that produces a range of goods and services from office furniture to electronic cable assemblies for sale to federal government clients. Research has shown that inmates who work or receive vocational training adjust better to prison, are more likely to hold a job after release, and are less likely to commit new crimes.

Warden Fordham had been pondering about the work assignment for Washington. On one hand his exceptional skills as an organizer could be a problem. On the other hand, he had previously functioned exclusively with other Orientals as his cohorts, and as few of those were incarcerated in the prison, scattered throughout the various job assignments, it would be very difficult for Washington to generate any problems through them. Fordham intended to treat Washington with his usual "no nonsense will be tolerated, but I am fair" approach, but he was cognizant of Washington's reputation and contacts outside of the prison.

After all the years that John Fordham had been involved in the federal penal system, he was aware that there was a certain threat to his welfare and especially that of his family, which might be caused by former convicts or the associates of convicts. If his family was to be able to lead any kind of a normal life, they had to be able to go on about their normal routines of schooling, shopping, entertainment, and other activities. But an individual determined to "get back" at the warden would find that his family was relatively easy prey. Daniel Washington had a small army of associates outside of the prison who would follow his orders, including orders to do harm to Fordham and/or his family.

Fordham had received threats before and thus far nothing serious had occurred. The strangest and most memorable was an event that had occurred some years back. He and his wife had purchased a new car and soon after that his wife was contacted by a woman who stated that she represented the automobile manufacturer, and that she was following up with a customer-satisfaction procedure. The woman and his wife had several phone conversations and became quite friendly. Eventually they agreed to meet for lunch. The friendship continued and they met a couple of times for drinks. One night the woman showed up for such a meeting with a couple of men. One of the men, who was a relatively attractive and ingratiating individual, made a very determined approach to Fordham's wife. He suggested that they get to know each other much better and perhaps take a discrete trip some place. Emily Fordham was flattered, but not interested.

She told Fordham what had happened, and that was the end of her meetings with the woman who claimed she was representing the automobile manufacturer. Some time later, Fordham and his wife learned that the woman was actually a private detective who had been hired by an ex-con. The remarkable thing to Fordham was that the man would go to such trouble and expense in an attempt to hurt Fordham from an emotional standpoint. It would serve no benefit whatsoever to the ex-convict, it was simply the activity of a disturbed mind attempting to hurt Fordham for the sheer sake of inflicting hurt. But the warden had long since quit trying to make any sense out of the actions of the majority of his charges. He just did his job.

As was his custom, Fordham left his office and headed for

the area where the prisoners were being issued clothing, bedding, and assigned to a cell. Washington would be placed in a cell by himself. That ten-by-seven-foot cell would be a big difference from the life that Daniel Washington had been accustomed to. The warden would give the new prisoners what his staff called his "no-shit talk." He would tell them that they would be treated fairly and honestly, but he would also tell them that he expected 100 percent adherence to the rules and the routine. It would be pointed out that their goal should be the earliest possible parole, which would be enhanced by model behavior in Lompoc. Fordham entered the area where the prisoners were being held, grouped in line in front of the warden.

Fordham began delivering his customary initial comments and soon was aware that he was being studied. Washington stared intensely at Fordham, almost without any movement, he scarcely blinked. His eyes bore in on the warden's as if he were boring into him and through him. The warden felt as if Washington was penetrating his very being to find a weakness. Fordham looked directly into The Emperor's eyes at one point, but found that he could not continue to look and must turn away. It was very disturbing to Fordham, and he did not deliver his remarks with the same effectiveness that was normally the case, concluding in a somewhat stumbling manner. The guards took the prisoners on to the next stop.

The warden left his office and went out to his Oldsmobile. He drove out to the coast about ten miles west of the prison and got out of his car. For nearly an hour, he watched the waves and the sea birds. Then he said to himself, "Goddamn it, I'm the warden and he's the prisoner." He drove back to the penitentiary, unsure if he had convinced himself. He had never been affected by a prisoner like this before, and he did not like it.

Twenty

Washington, D.C., February 28, 2001

It was a few minutes after 1:00 A.M. The president sat alone at his desk in the Oval Office studying the recommendations that he had received from the cabinet members and others the previous afternoon. He sat for a few moments, staring ahead while he was thinking, then got out of his chair and opened a door. Entering a room off the Oval office, he was now in the area, which had existed for decades, but was largely unknown to the public until it was revealed that Bill Clinton used this as one of his venues for extra-marital sexual activities. Power poured a cup of coffee and thought to himself that he must have consumed at least five cups already, and there was no way he would be able to get to sleep. Then he rationalized that he would not be able to sleep tonight even if he had no coffee. There was far too much on his mind. A steward on duty in the adjoining kitchen heard the activity and came into the room.

"Mr. President, please. I didn't know you wanted anything. Let me get the coffee for you."

"Larry, that's quite all right. I've been sitting for a long time and it feels good to move around a little. I'll just get the coffee myself."

"What can I get you to eat, Mr. President? How about some eggs?"

"Nothing, thank you, Larry."

"You sure?"

"On second thought, I will have an English muffin with some of that wonderful French jam that you have."

"Yes sir, coming right up."

The president went back to his desk, carrying his coffee cup, and began to reread the recommendations. The steward came in a few minutes later carrying a tray and placed the contents of the tray on his desk. Power looked at the delivered items and thought to himself that there was monumental overkill. On the desk was a linen napkin, a small vase with a rose bud, and a dinner plate. On top of the plate was another linen napkin and on top of that was a smaller plate. On that plate was the English muffin and a garnish of parsley, orange slice and kiwi fruit. In a separate bowl, also seated on a napkin, were the raspberry preserves that Power had requested.

All that for a damn English muffin, thought Power. *I hope the taxpayers don't learn about this.*

He returned to the recommendations. Not too many surprises, he thought. The Secretary of Defense, National Security Advisor, Director of Disease Control, Chief of Staff, Ambassador to the UN, and CIA Director all had variations of the same plan. Basically, they suggested that the president do nothing at the present time. In varying manners they all suggested that the president wait and see what happened on March 3rd. If Iraq was able to follow up on its threat, the U.S. still should continue to do nothing overt, but appear to go along with the Iraqi demands while planning future activities to solve the problem.

The Vice President and UN Ambassador felt that the U.S. should negotiate immediately, and that with effective dialogue, Iraq could be convinced to mitigate some of their demands. The UN Ambassador particularly felt that she had a very good relationship with the Iraqi representative to the UN and that she could get some concessions. The CIA Director suggested that we initiate a massive plan of infiltration of agents in Iraq and reach our long-range solution through clandestine activity. Dr. Tripp, Director of the Disease Control Center, suggested an all out effort to develop an antidote for the Botulinal Toxins, specifically one that could be airborne. She proposed that a massive saturation of all threatened countries with such an antidote, followed by military action against Iraq, would be the most humanitarian and successful course. *She is a bright lady*, thought the president. *I know she is extremely upset that she could not offer more.*

The recommendations from General Stanley did not surprise Power. Stanley was a straight arrow with basically tunnel vision. The general stated plainly that all of the key figures involved in this emergency had a duty to the Constitution and the American people. Period. It was most unfortunate if that duty resulted in the deaths of millions of Turks, Egyptians, etc., but their clear duty was to serve the United States. He suggested an immediate and comprehensive attack on Iraq, possibly including nuclear bombing. This would be followed by a military occupation of Iraq, the establishment of a democratic government, and U.S. control of their oil fields for whatever time was necessary. Stanley had made it clear in his proposed course of action that he was a soldier, that he had seen much suffering as a result of war, and that he deeply regretted that his plan would entail the likelihood of much more suffering and deaths.

Stanley went on to point out that the officials who were responsible for running other countries had a similar duty to their nations, and that such a duty might mean that they inflict great harm on the U.S. As a soldier, he would do everything possible to prevent such harm to his country, but he would understand the duty that compelled others. The duty of a soldier was to serve his country, and to him it was clear that his proposed course of action, though awful in its consequences, clearly served his country best. He concluded by saying that when he was seventeen years old and a plebe at West Point, he had been first presented with the motto of the Military Academy: "Duty, Honor Country." He said that he felt that there was no finer expression of his recommendation to the president than those three words. Those words told them all they needed to know about what their course of action should be. Duty, Honor, Country.

By far the biggest surprise to Power was the proposal of the secretary of state. This complex man had written that his first reaction was to do nothing at present but plan for future action. But he said that the comments he had heard from General Stanley had moved him. He wrote that he realized that an attack on Iraq would possibly cause catastrophic harm to many people, but his responsibility was not to humanity, but to the state of which he was secretary and concluded by stating that with great regret he found that their overriding obligation was to the United States and that military action was the best course to further the interests of the U.S.

Power picked up his phone, pushed a button and said, "Larry, bring me another one of those muffins with jam and another cup of coffee."

He was tempted to tell the steward not to worry about all the plates, napkins, and garnish, but then decided that the man might take that as criticism of his service. Putting his hands behind his head, he leaned back in his chair, put his feet on his desk, stared into space and thought. Then he went over to a wall on which there were shelves and he studied some photographs. There were pictures of Marcie and the children, and one of him taken during the Gulf War with President Bush. There was a photo taken on a book tour

showing a huge queue of people lined up to have him autograph his memoirs, and several other items of photographic
memorabilia. He went back to his desk and once again read
through the recommendations and some notes he had made
on the pages. Then he again leaned back in his chair and
muttered, "Harry Truman had it right. The buck sure as hell
stops here."

Twenty-one

August 27, 1984, Chicago, Illinois

"White people discovered this country, white people settled this country, white people cleared the land and farmed. white people fought the British, the Indians, the Mexicans, the Spanish, the Germans, the Japs, the Italians and God knows who else to keep this country and build what we have. White people made this country what it is!"

The audience was in a near frenzy by now. It was hot in the auditorium and the sweat was pouring down the face of the speaker, who had come out from behind the podium and was pacing back and forth on the stage as he talked. The cheers and screams were so loud that one could not have heard what he was saying without the amplifier being up, almost to the point of pain.

"So what does the white man get for his blood, his sweat, his effort and his pain? I'll tell you what he gets. He gets the shaft!"

Still louder screams of approval from the audience.

"We got the Mexicans, many of whom are wetbacks, who are taking the laboring jobs from the white man. We got the Orientals who are taking over the schools, the universities, the law, medicine, the sciences, and thousands and thousands of high-paying jobs. Now on top of everything else, we got the Koreans and the Vietnamese coming in and taking over the white man's small businesses. What about the white man who founded this country? What is he supposed to do? Is he supposed to starve?"

"No, no, no, no," screamed the audience.

"We got a government that is letting the white man go down the tubes," continued the speaker. He took off his jacket. His shirt was soaking in the front and in the armpits.

"We got to send a message to Washington. No more of this. We have to have protection for the white man. Quotas to protect white people's jobs. Stricter quotas to see that white kids can get in the good schools. Subsidies for white people who are out of work. This is a white people country and we need a government to see to it that the white man is protected."

The audience screamed its approval.

"I am not a racist. I have nothing against yellows or Latinos, but the white man needs a level playing field, and the place to see that that happens is in Washington D.C., and that is why I agreed to run for president on the American Party ticket. And when I say run, I mean run, not walk, not trot, not jog, I am running, running, running!"

"Run, Jesse, run; run, Jesse, run; run, Jesse, run!" The audience was wild.

The speaker picked up his jacket and threw it over his shoulder. He raised both of his hands in the air and walked back and forth across the stage.

"Jesse, Jesse, Jesse, Jesse, Jesse." Near pandemonium.

Finally he walked off the stage waving his hand as he left. An assistant handed him a glass of water and began wiping the perspiration off his face and neck. The speaker pushed the man away and together they walked back to the dressing room. As they walked the speaker was beaming and excited.

"Damn, I got to 'em tonight."

"You sure as hell did, Jesse. I thought they were going to tear down the building, they are so high."

"I don't think I ever saw a Yankee crowd as worked up as this one. I am feeling better and better about this campaign."

"Jesse, we have never kidded each other about the facts. A third-party candidate can't win. But I think we got a damn good shot at keeping both the Democrats and Republicans from getting a majority of electoral votes. By God, if we do that, we are in the catbird seat. They can come to us on their goddamn knees. We will decide who is going to be the next president. Who wants to be president will need our votes and to get our votes, we get one hell of a lot of concessions. This country is going to go back to the white man."

"Okay, Freddie. It's been a great night, but I am beat. I want to go back to the hotel. Tell room service to bring me a steak, a baked potato, and a double scotch. We got Milwaukee tomorrow, so I can get a decent sleep. It's only a couple of hours drive."

Freddie picked up a phone and dialed a number. He gave instructions.

"Pick up Mr. Jacksen right away. Order his usual dinner for his room one hour from now. Call his wife and tell her that he will talk to her later tonight."

"Shit, I'm soaking wet. You should have brought a change of clothes."

"You'll be in the shower in fifteen minutes, boss. You'll be okay." They both left the room.

Jesse Louis Jacksen was still a young man. Born in South Carolina in 1941, he still had the soft accent typical of that region. His father, of Scandinavian heritage, was a drifter and never participated much in Jesse's youth. The young man had first arrived in the Midwest in the early 1960s to attend the University of Illinois, but returned to the south where he earned a degree from a school in the Carolinas. After graduation, he returned to Illinois in 1964, and shortly after that became active in the Whites Rights movement. As a neophyte he played a minor role in the Selma, California, Whites Rights demonstration, and he rapidly learned the power of using the media successfully to advance his goals and reputation.

Jacksen gained international attention as a gadfly, traveling anywhere and everywhere to attempt to mediate disputes and thrust himself onto the stage, such as visiting South Africa, speaking on behalf of apartheid, and Israel, opposing a Palestinian state. It had been said, not entirely in jest, that the most dangerous place in the country was the space between Jesse Jacksen and a TV camera. A member of his staff had recounted that at one time she and Jacksen were leaving a debate in Atlanta, when Jacksen slugged her in the back and pushed her aside, snarling an obscenity as he raced toward a TV camera that had suddenly appeared.

Another time an aide told of Jacksen delivering a public chastisement because this unfortunate staff member had shared the spotlight during a campaign stop. Jacksen's efforts on behalf of Whites Rights were twofold. He sincerely believed that the white man was being put in a subservient position in American society, and he thought that such was morally wrong. But he also reveled in attention and being in a position of a statesman and representative of a movement. In a sense he was drunk on power and notoriety. Success was not measured by results but by the amount of media coverage. It was far more important to him to have the TV and newspapers give broad coverage to what he said rather than concern with any actual effect it might have. Actually, if he had been highly effective in producing change and results, it would have proven an agonizing frustration for him. If his demands were fulfilled, how would he get media coverage? With a goal of becoming such a presence that he could not be ignored, he would use that presence to get power. His dream was to garner sufficient electoral votes so that either the Republicans or Democrats would have to pay his price to get his votes. And his price was as high as it could get. He would demand to be appointed Secretary of State. With that august position as a platform, he would have constant media coverage all over the world. His face would be on TV daily!

Many people, including many white people, felt that he was a bore, bigot, publicity hound, and monumental pain in the ass. Jacksen was known by intimates to be a petulant, thin-skinned bully, incapable of sharing the limelight or delegating responsibility, and a man who treated the women on his staff as second-class citizens, looking on them basically as sexual objects. Although his original constituency had been working-class Southern whites, in recent years as yellows became more successful, that constituency had grown to include citizens of Northern states, again primarily working class. Those individuals had been particularly resentful of the rise of the Oriental in society, and Jesse Jacksen was a man with a mission. Whites Rights.

Jacksen had returned to his hotel, showered, dined and relaxed. He called his wife and they talked for about fifteen minutes. Many people felt that he was harmful to the country, promoted extreme divisiveness among the races, and fostered a course of social action that was very wrong. But no one could question his dedication. You could despise him, but you could not ignore him.

Twenty-two

Washington, D.C., March 1, 2001, 6:17 A.M. EST

Gerald Gordon Sauer had been assigned to the White House for most of his fifteen years with the Secret Service. Four years in the Marine Corps had preceded his Secret Service gig, and Jerry Sauer had the professional, military bearing and presence that did both of those organizations proud. Over the years Sauer had realized that some of his colleagues in the service got much closer to the presidents that they served than he did. That did not bother Sauer at all. He considered himself a professional and personalities were irrelevant in his mind. The professional distance that he maintained had some advantages. When Bill Clinton's extracurricular sexual activities were being investigated three years earlier, several of his fellow agents had been subpoenaed and questioned and found that the things that they knew about Clinton were embarrassing and awkward. But Jerry Sauer had never been one of Clinton's favorites. Sauer just could not be one of the boys. It was not in his makeup. But he got along with President Power very well. In Sauer's mind, Power was a professional, and he could tell that Power felt the same way about him. So Agent Sauer was one of those chosen to serve not only as field protection for the president, but also to function directly with the president in the White House in a closer, somewhat social situation.

The secretary of state had called on the president's line, and the man assigned to answer this line had asked to talk to Sauer. Sauer got on the phone with the secretary of state and was informed that the president of Egypt was insisting that he talk to Power immediately.

"Mr. Secretary," Sauer offered, "the president was up late last night and asked to be awakened at 7:00."

"I will take the responsibility, Jerry. Please tell him that I feel that he should talk to President Mubarak as soon as possible."

"Yes, sir."

Sauer considered waking the president with a telephone call, but decided instead to get a cup of coffee from the kitchen. He carried the coffee on a tray and went to the anteroom, which led to the president's bedroom, opened the door, and knocked gently on the bedroom door.

"What is it?"

"Mr. President, it's Jerry. I just talked to Secretary Winslow, who asked me to wake you. I have a cup of coffee for you if you like."

Silence for a moment. Sauer could hear the president getting out of bed. After a moment, he said, "Come in, Jerry."

Sauer opened the door. Power had put on a bathrobe and was rubbing his eyes, which were red. The president had not gone to bed until nearly 3:00 and was having a hard time getting awake. Sauer put the tray with the coffee on a table and left. Power sipped some coffee and picked up the phone, asking to be connected to the secretary of state. Shortly he was speaking to Ronald Winslow, a former U.S. Senator from Virginia and a member of a wealthy, well-connected, politically active, old and powerful family. Winslow was one of the most honorable men that Power knew.

"Mr. President, I apologize for waking you, but President

Mubarak is extremely concerned. Knowing him as I do, I take this very seriously. He is not the kind of man to go off half-cocked. In my judgment if Hosni says he needs to talk to you immediately, you should strongly consider that request, and he all but demands to talk to you."

"Do you know specifically what he wants?"

"I get the impression that Egypt is in complete chaos."

"Hell, Ron, most of the world is in chaos."

"Once again, Mr. President, I know Hosni well. He has been a tower of strength in the Middle East. He is a cool customer who has spent his entire adult life in the eye of the storm. If he is as upset as he is, it would be my judgment that extraordinary circumstances exist. I urge you to talk to him."

"All right, I'll take a fast shower to wake up and call him."

"Mr. President, if I may presume. I request that you call him immediately."

There was silence on the phone for several seconds. Then Power said, "All right, Ron." Power flashed the operator and gave instructions. He would not need a translator. Mubarak spoke fluent English.

Hosni Mubarak had been the president of Egypt since the assassination of Anwar Sadat. In some respects Mubarak was the glue that kept the Middle East from coming completely apart. He was a voice of reason and negotiation in an Arab world that was punctuated by radicals, militants, terrorists, fanatics, unbelievable wealth, and crushing poverty. He had hosted numerous meetings and discussions to bridge the immense gaps that stood between Arabs and Israel, Arabs and Western countries, and Arabs and Arabs. Power had a great deal of respect for Mubarak, who had a near impossible challenge in running Egypt itself.

Egypt is by far the largest Arab nation in terms of population, but by the fortunes of fate, it has virtually no oil. This

140

stands out in preposterous relief when compared to countries, such as Saudi Arabia, Kuwait, and the Emirates, which have almost no people and immense reserves of petroleum. As a result, those countries with oil were able to provide magnificently for their citizens. The citizens in the wealthy Arab countries were so pampered that they refused to do any of the mundane, dirty work necessary to maintain a society. In some of these countries, a third or more of the entire population consisted of expatriates imported from Pakistan, Turkey, and India to collect the garbage, scrub the floors, wash the clothes, and do the manual labor, while the native citizens spend their time in shopping and socializing. Perhaps one percent of their neighbors in Egypt lived in similar luxury, but the majority of the nearly sixty million Egyptians lived in abysmal poverty, and the overcrowding and squalor of Cairo was wretched.

Militant Arabs, both native Egyptians and many from other countries, had done everything they could to destabilize Egypt and throw the country into turmoil, hoping to bring about a coup and an Islamic state. Tourism had long been a source of income and employment in Egypt. Millions of people throughout North America, Japan, and Europe were potential tourists. The mystique of the Pyramids, the Nile, and the Sphinx were legendary, and the potential tourist income for Egypt was considerable. So the militants, in an effort to further destabilize the country, attempted to destroy tourism by terrorist assassinations and attacks on visiting tourists, thus discouraging others from coming to Egypt. Somehow, Mubarak had managed to hold the nation together and his presence and reputation in the Middle East was unmatched.

Power was notified that Mubarak was on the line and picked up the phone.

"Good morning, Mr. President. It is good to hear from you."

"Mr. President, I am deeply sorry to disturb you in this manner, and I realize that it is early in the morning in Washington. I would not have done this unless I felt that it was absolutely necessary."

"That's all right, Hosni. Tell me why you called."

"I call you with the most urgent possible request to do what is necessary to prevent a calamity in Egypt."

"Go on, Hosni."

"Mr. President, if you will refer to your knowledge of history, you will have a comprehension of the situation today in Egypt. The circumstances in Cairo today are frighteningly similar to those in Russia in 1917. You are aware of the problems and challenges that we have faced with Islamic fundamentalists in recent years. The situation regarding Iraq has brought this threat to a point of peril. Egypt is in a state of panic. The fear that Iraq will do to Egypt what it did to Kuwait has caused pandemonium. Stores have been looted, homes have been abandoned, and hundreds of thousands of people are in the streets and highways leaving the cities, particularly Cairo, heading out into the desert. There is little or no food or water for these people, and there is continual violence as the strong steal from the weaker ones in an attempt to survive. The police are basically as insecure as the rest of the population and the cities are largely without police control or protection.

"Just as the Bolsheviks did in 1917, the Islamic militants have issued an order to the Army to obey no orders other than the orders issued by these militants, and much of the Army seems on the verge of following that instruction. If that happens, and I believe that the next 24 hours will determine that situation, regardless of the outcome of the Iraqi threat, what remains in Egypt will be an Islamic fundamentalist state similar to Iran. As you are aware, Mr. President, these groups consider the United States to be 'The Great Satan.'"

"Hosni, you said that you had an urgent request. What is it?"

"Mr. President, you must immediately make a formal statement that the United States will not attack Iraq, that the United States accepts the Iraqi demands, and that there is no need for any further attacks by Iraq on any country. I feel that over a reasonable period of time your great nation will find a way to solve the Iraqi puzzle and return the world to stabilization. In the meantime you will prevent the certain deaths of millions of people and the certain complete destabilization of the Middle East due to the fall of Egypt to the Islamic militants."

The line was silent for a few moments. Then Power said, "Mr. President, I can give you no immediate answer. I do understand the urgency of the matter and will give it the consideration it deserves."

"Mr. President," Mubarak pleaded, "millions of lives are at stake."

"I know that, Hosni. I need to conclude our conversation,"

"Thank you, Mr. President."

Power put down the phone, sat for a minute, sipped some coffee, which was now only warm, picked up the phone again and asked to be connected to the secretary of state. He talked to Secretary Winslow briefly, repeating for him what Mubarak had said.

The Secretary responded, "Mr. President, based on what I know of the situation, I believe that Hosni is not exaggerating. This mess has provided just the crisis the Islamic militants need. Mr. President, at your request I gave you my thoughts in writing on the action that we should take two days ago. I urge you to take that action immediately."

"Ron, I hear what you are saying."

"Have a good day, Mr. President."

"And the same for you, Ron."

Twenty-three

Bandar Seri Begawan, State of Brunei, March 1, 2001, 11:46 P.M.

The girl in the red dress was beginning to perspire slightly. She had her eyes closed and was moving to the blaring disco music. She was dancing with a girl who also had her eyes closed, and they could have just as well have been dancing alone as each one of them was responding to the pounding beat of the music and each was "doing her own thing." Her long blonde hair swished back and forth across her bare shoulders as she moved. The red dress, styled in mini skirt length several inches above the knees, exposed nearly perfect tan legs, and the low neckline revealed much of her very full breasts.

Those breasts had not always looked like they did now. They had been improved by a very creative cosmetic surgeon in Newport Beach, California, who had developed an implant technique that was nearly free of scarring and virtually undetectable. While under anesthetic, the surgeon had also altered her nose slightly and placed a small implant under her chin to improve her profile. The nearly fifteen-thousand-dollar cost of this cosmetic improvement had been paid for by a Southern California land developer, who had also gifted the girl with considerable in jewelry, clothing, and a Porsche convertible. His wife's lawyer had later used information concerning these gifts very successfully in securing an extremely satisfactory divorce settlement for his client.

There were about a dozen girls dancing and two men sitting and watching. There was no one else in the room other than three attendants. This was a private disco and no liquor was served. However, the flashing of the colored strobe lights in the ceiling, the changing of color in the tiles in the floor and the beveled mirrors on opposite walls produced a surreal, almost psychedelic effect. The two men were talking, particularly about the girl in red. She was twenty-seven, which was somewhat older than most of the girls, who were from the United States and a number of European countries. There were highly paid agents in several countries, who contacted beauty contest winners and models with regard to the opportunities to earn a great deal of money in a short period of time in Brunei. The younger of the two men was describing his experience with the girl in red two evenings earlier. After a few minutes, the older man motioned to one of the servants, who immediately came forward and bowed. The man gave some instructions to the servant and then Haji Hassanal Bolkiahm, the Sultan of Brunei, got up from his chair and left the room. His younger brother stood and the servants bowed as he exited.

The State of Brunei occupies an enclave on the northwest coast of the island of Borneo, facing the South China Sea. It is surrounded by and divided by the portion of Borneo that is part of the Malaysian Republic. It is a tiny country with less than two percent of its land being arable and a population of less than three hundred thousand and would be completely insignificant to the rest of the world if it were not one for one thing. Oil. About two-thirds of the population is Malay and most of the rest is Chinese. Two-thirds are Muslims.

Malay is the official language, but English is widely understood. Eighty percent of its food requirements are imported. It is a welfare state with one of the highest standards of living in the world. Education, medical care, and many other benefits are free. There is no income tax. Brunei had been part of the British Empire and achieved full sovereignty in 1984. It is a Sultanate; the Sultan passes on his title to his oldest son. Japan, the industrial giant of the Orient, has virtually no petroleum. It has been said that one could walk from Malaysia to Japan on the oil tankers that are constantly bringing petroleum to fuel the Japanese engine; however, South Korea, Thailand, and Singapore also depended on oil from Malaysia.

The Sultan preferred Caucasian women. So he and his brother enjoyed the company of attractive young women from America and Europe on a regular basis. Their agents were on the lookout for young women who would be interested in spending three to six months in Brunei. For this contract they were paid as much as a hundred thousand dollars, and they were expected to be in the private disco, appropriately dressed every night and available to talk to and dance with the Sultan, his brother and their guests. They were not required to sleep with any of the men if they were not so inclined. Those that did, however, found that it was financially very rewarding. These women also had opportunities from time to time to be the companions of certain of the Sultan's guests. Although they were expected to be courteous and friendly to the guests, nothing more was demanded. The girls could dance with the guests, talk to the guests or, if they chose, spend the evening with the guests.

It depended on the individual girl's appraisal of the guests and their own ambition to be rewarded by these men. Certain of the girls were quite willing to entertain anyone as long as they could bathe them prior to any close embracing. Other of the women confined their activities with all the men, including the Sultan, to dance and conversation. The following morning

147

the girl in the red dress, who had impressed the Sultan's brother earlier with her creativity in the bedroom, was gifted by the Sultan with a piece of jewelry easily worth $20,000. What she had done for the Sultan, she had not learned in California; she had listened attentively as two of her colleagues described some boudoir techniques that resulted in a generous spirit of gratitude.

But it was not the girls or bedroom favors that were primary on the Sultan's mind these days. It was Iraq. It was obvious that his already valuable oil was going to be worth many times its previous value. The industrial world was in upheaval over the petroleum situation, and the Sultan had already cut off the flow of his petroleum, waiting to see what it was going to be worth. Petroleum purchasers were screaming about the contracts they had with Brunei, but the Sultan paid no attention to them. A few years earlier, he had been considered to be the richest man the world. Then he was overtaken for that distinction by a Japanese industrialist and an American software developer. The Sultan smiled when he thought about the future. Oil at perhaps $50.00 per barrel! He would soon be again looked on as the richest man in the world. Iraq was a gift from Allah!

Tonight, perhaps he would invite both the girls from Sweden to his bedroom suite. The girl in the red dress had satisfied all his immediate physical needs last night, but he somehow found that watching the two Swedish girls in bed, vigorously laboring on each other, was almost more erotic than personally being in bed with one of them. His brother knew that he frequently invited two girls in at a time, but the Sultan had not told the heir apparent that he was watching, not participating. But even more exciting than the Swedish girls were the actions of Iraq. Truly, a gift from Allah!

Twenty-four

Alexandria, Virginia, March 1, 2001

Ronald Franklin Winslow was fifty years old and had been the secretary of state for a month and a half. A person who had known him for only the past twenty-five years would say that such responsibility and position was inevitable for a man with the character, intelligence, and talent of Ronald Winslow. A person who had known him for only his first twenty-five years would say that, considering his personal habits, it was remarkable that he was alive.

Winslow had been, as they say, born into privilege. The family's money was first acquired three generations earlier, and through capable management and skillful investment, it had grown to be one of the nation's great family fortunes. His father had entered politics early in his life and had served as a United States Senator from the State of Virginia for thirty years, at one time prominently mentioned as a possible presidential candidate.

Ron Winslow was raised by nurses and nannies, and by the time he was four years old, he was manipulating them to his own satisfaction. In 1964, at the age of twelve, he was expelled from the Hill School for drinking alcoholic beverages in his dormitory room. This was a situation of anguish and awkwardness for all concerned. Ron was the third generation of Winslows to attend the Hill School, and his father, who at that time was in his second term in the Senate, was not only a high-profile alum, but also a significant financial benefactor of the Pennsylvania school. But the headmaster and the school trustees simply could not overlook young Winslow's actions. His quiescent interest in academics, was not really a problem; there were plenty of other boys with that propensity.

When, at the age of eleven, he had been discovered drinking wine in his room with a seventeen-year-old local girl, the school administration justified the transgression as the fault of a much older woman. In fact, Winslow was manipulating this young lady much as he had done with the household servants. This was not the first time she had been in his room, just the first time they were caught. On an earlier liaison, he had persuaded her to take off her bra and let him play with her modest young breasts. On the occasion when they were caught, his goal had been to get her to remove her panties.

A few months later, Winslow had been in his room with three of his classmates drinking scotch and mixing it with Pepsi. They were discovered when one of the boys, drunk and sick beyond control, was screaming and vomiting in the lobby of the dorm. After this episode the senator personally visited with the headmaster and Ronald. The headmaster desperately wanted the problem to go away, and Ronald assured them that he would walk the straight and narrow.

Things became testy that summer when one of Winslow's school mates explained to his mother and their family physician that he had likely acquired his gonorrhea affliction in Winslow's room, after Ronald had persuaded a far over the hill local hooker that there was money to be made in his dormitory room. And indeed the lady had generated significant revenue from Winslow and his buddies that evening. The boy's family raised all kinds of hell and pulled their son out of the school. At this point Ronald was affecting the school from a standpoint of both reputation, gifts, and tuition income. Senator Winslow had managed to keep his son in the school by persuasive words and a substantial donation to the school building fund. However, the headmaster, the rest of the administration, and the trustees by now were anxious to get rid of this kid. The senator and the boy were told that any more trouble at all and he was history.

That history was not long in arriving when Ronald was discovered drinking a bottle of Cabernet in his room. Young Winslow tried to mitigate the offense by pointing out that this was not some banal jug wine, but a fine bottle of Heitz Martha's Vineyard, and his good taste in selection certainly brought credit and prestige to the Hill School. But the administration was relieved to have a final episode and anxious to get rid of him. Which they did. The remainder of his pre-college schooling was distributed fairly evenly over three other schools, finally settling on an institution that was in need of funds and willing to put up with anything to get them.

After attending the Hill School, it was family tradition for the young men to attend Princeton. It took much of the Senator's influence to get Ronald accepted by Princeton. It never would have been accomplished without the assistance of both of the U.S. Senators from New Jersey, who wrote glowing letters praising this young man, whom they had never met. By this time Ronald had discovered that his recreational substance of choice was not alcohol but marijuana. He would have flunked out of Princeton at the end of his first year, but he never got that far. One of his associates proposed that they try LSD one Friday night. Winslow had used acid a couple of times earlier with no bad side effects, but this time a memorably "bad trip" resulted in Winslow being incarcerated in the city jail charged with defacing both campus and private property.

His father, at this point completely disgusted, told him that he was now on his own, which was no great problem for

Ronald Winslow, who was shortly earning big money dealing in marijuana and occasional mushrooms. He maintained this lifestyle for several months. But he was getting bored and looking for a new excitement. One day he enlisted in the Army. His family was appalled. People were getting killed every day in Vietnam. Boys from his background did not need to go to Vietnam, certainly not as enlisted men. His father considered using his connections to get the enlistment voided, but he realized that from a political standpoint, if he did put pressure on the Pentagon and it was learned by the press, it would be political suicide.

So in 1971 nineteen-year-old Ronald Franklin Winslow found himself near the Cambodian border serving as a combat infantryman. By 1971 the war in Vietnam was a disaster. The Tet Offensive in 1968 had ended all pretensions that the U.S. was going to defeat the North Vietnamese. The American public, slowly at first, but by now at an ever-hastening pace, was tired of the war and just wanted it over. Lyndon Johnson's political career was ended because of the war and Richard Nixon was under huge pressure to get the country out of Vietnam before it ruined his. The word of the day was "Vietnamization," which was represented as turning the war over to the South Vietnam troops, but was basically an excuse to get the hell out with some modest honor left.

For young Winslow it was quite an experience. He was never wounded, but he saw several soldiers in his company wounded and killed, which circumstances he confronted in Southeast Asia just as he had in the States, staying stoned most of the time. This habit did not offend most of his comrades, who were as stoned as he was. Returning from Vietnam, he brought with him several military decorations, corporal stripes, an honorable discharge, genital herpes from a Vietnam whore and a stash of the most potent marijuana that he had ever encountered. Instead of going back to Virginia, he decided to stay in California after he was processed out of the Army.

The young military veteran spent about a year in the Sunset Strip, Hollywood area, selling and smoking dope and hanging out with wannabe musicians and actors. He worked as an extra in a couple of movies and learned to surf in Huntington Beach, had a series of girl friends and live-ins, but never any that lasted longer than a few months. One of the girls got pregnant and had an abortion. That bothered Winslow for some reason, and he stayed stoned for several days after that. Journeying up to San Francisco, he checked out the flower children, but decided he preferred LA, smog and all. By 1976 he was twenty-four years and had no direction, no plan, and his only goal was to get stoned again. On a lark he decided to join a friend who had enrolled in a course in political science in a community college.

For the rest of his life, he had tried to understand how and why he had changed so. There was no traumatic event, he was not impressed by some inspirational speech, and nothing dramatic occurred. But for some reason, he studied the other students, nearly all younger than he was. Most of them were working and going to school at the same time. They seemed to be trying hard to make something of their lives. Some had families to support. At the end of the first week of classes, he decided that he would not go to class stoned. He paid some attention to the instructor, he read the assignments, and he participated in the class discussions. He was astonished to find that he not only rather enjoyed it, but he felt good about doing something that had at least some intellectual value. After a couple of weeks, he was not getting stoned even when he was not in class. He never made a profound decision, but one day he realized that he had not used any substance for more than a month. At the start of the next semester, he registered as a full-time student. Miraculously, he had become an excellent student. He earned one "B" and four "A"s.

Winslow called his father in Washington, D.C. He said he would like to talk to him and asked for a plane ticket. He and his father had not been face to face in three years. They talked for a couple of hours and agreed to meet again for dinner that evening. After that dinner the senator went back to his study in his Virginia home and sobbed for nearly an hour. Ronald had told him that he realized that he had been a disappointment and had wasted a lot of his life. He said that he did not know why, but he had changed and showed his dad his most recent and excellent report card, and said that he would like to transfer to a regular four-year college. Ronald admitted that he realized that at his age he should be on his own financially, but he asked for help to pay for school. Senator Winslow maintained his poise during their meetings, but he could not control his emotions when he was alone.

With some help from his father's friends, he was accepted at the University of Virginia. He decided that he had really enjoyed Political Science and elected that discipline as his major. Now studying long hours, he was completely drug free and rarely consumed anything alcoholic. Winslow appeared to be trying to make up for years of wasted time, but he didn't really think about it that way. After graduating with honors, his father offered him a job in his senatorial office, and soon Ron was his dad's legislative assistant. He decided to run for Congress in 1982, and with enormous help from his father and his family connections, was elected to the House of Representatives, representing a Virginia Congressional district.

Winslow's first congressional assignment was as a member of the Foreign Relations Committee and soon he had a reputation as a hard-working and quick-learning young man with a great deal of promise. In 1986 his father decided to retire after thirty years in the Senate, and Ronald Winslow ran as a candidate to replace him. His election victory established him as the youngest member of that exclusive club of one hundred. The young Senator Winslow worked hard on his specialty in the field of international relations, and during the next fourteen years, he traveled extensively all over the world and became well acquainted with most of the world's leaders. His reputation was as a man of unquestionable character, dedicated, hard working, and extremely intelligent. After Colin Power's election in November of 2000, the president-elect announced that Ronald Franklin Winslow was his choice to be the incoming secretary of state. His Senate colleagues approved the appointment by acclamation.

On March 1, 2001 at 9:15 P.M., the secretary of state was in the office in his home in Alexandria, Virginia. The room was deliberately not furnished in the dark-paneled, somber manner favored by most of his colleagues. It was quite contemporary with lightly hued woods, chrome, and Lucite. There were few photographs and almost no memorabilia. On the desk were a computer monitor and keyboard, a telephone and a few papers he had been reading, primarily concerning the Iraq crisis. He was somewhat startled when his phone rang. This was a number known only to his political intimates, and Winslow answered it promptly. General Robert Stanley was on the other end.

"Ron, I apologize for calling you at this hour."

"No problem, Bob. I was just doing some reading."

"Ron, if it's not too inconvenient, I would like to come over and see you."

"When?"

"Now. I can be there in fifteen minutes. It's damn important."

"Come on over. Is there anything I should do or get to prepare for your visit."

"No."

"See you shortly." Winslow hung up the phone, apprehensive about what was on the general's mind. Why would the Chairman of the Joint Chiefs want to see him at night and in his home? They had a cordial professional relationship, but they were certainly not close friends. *I can't see anything positive about this*, thought Winslow. He went to the wall and switched on an exhaust fan to help clear the room of the smoke from his cigar, considered pouring a glass of brandy and decided against it. *I just can't see anything positive about General Stanley coming over here tonight*, he repeated to himself.

Twenty-five

Georgetown, March 1, 2001

The general put down the phone and walked toward his garage where his Cadillac STS was parked. Ordinarily, he traveled in a chauffeured military vehicle accompanied by an aide, but tonight he would drive to Secretary Winslow's house by himself. Ordinarily, he was dressed in full military uniform, but tonight he was in mufti, as he wanted to attract no attention this evening. He drove away from his Georgetown home and headed for the Key Bridge.

Robert Talmadge Poindexter Stanley came from perhaps the finest example of Southern military tradition. He was the sixth-generation Stanley to graduate from West Point, a chain started when his great-great-great-grandfather had graduated in 1831. That Stanley had joined the Confederacy in 1860 and had been killed at Vicksburg when his horse was shot and his neck was broken from the animal's fall. But he had sired a son before his death, and that son had graduated from the United States Military Academy one year prior to the start of the War between the States. Although wounded twice in the war, he had survived and produced General Stanley's great-grandfather, among others, and that young man had graduated from The Point in time to see action at San Juan Hill.

After returning from Cuba, he fathered a son who, following family tradition, graduated from the United States Military Academy just two years before American troops headed for

France to take on the Turks and the Kaiser. His son, the general's father, had continued the remarkable procession when he was commissioned early with his class in 1943. Stanley's father had married in haste, as did many others that year, and the general, who was conceived during a brief, hurried honeymoon, never saw his father, who was killed by a German hand grenade in Maarland, Holland, in 1944.

Robert Stanley graduated from The Point as an outstanding military student in 1962. By 1972 he had served three tours in Vietnam and was the youngest full colonel in the U.S. Army. He was considered to be a brilliant officer, fearless to the point of recklessness, adored by his troops and a soldier's soldier. His only apparent failing was that his now ended marriage had resulted in only one child, a daughter, who had no interest at all in a military career, and the sequence of Stanleys in the United States military would come to an end when he retired. He had been appointed, as Chairman of the Joint Chiefs in 1998 and President Power had not indicated whether or not he would be reappointing Stanley to that position when his tour was completed.

The general arrived at the gate of Secretary Winslow's estate and pressed the speaker button. Winslow himself answered and activated the electric motor, which opened the gate. Stanley drove through the tree-lined drive and parked his car in the portico in front of the house. When he got out, he saw that Secretary Winslow was waiting for him on the front stoop. It was still cold in March and they both hurried inside to escape the chilling breeze. The two men had been acquainted for about ten years, but had never been on a first name basis until Stanley had become Chairman of the Joint Chiefs. Since that time they had developed a relationship based on mutual admiration and respect.

"Can I get you a drink, Bob?"

"No, thanks, but I'll take a cup of coffee if you have it."

"I'll have a fresh pot made. Too late for me to drink coffee, though. I'll just have a Diet Coke."

The men engaged in brief small talk, while Winslow's houseman served their beverages. When he left the room, Winslow said: "All right, Bob, what's on your mind?"

"Mr. Secretary, two days ago the president instructed several of us to provide our handwritten recommendations indicating how we felt we should handle this Iraqi mess."

Winslow was somewhat startled that Stanley had addressed him by his title. They were accustomed to speaking to each other on an informal basis.

"Yes, General," he replied.

"I think that everyone in that room knows what my position is. I feel compassion for the people of Iraq and all others who may suffer, but my oath is to this country and this country alone. In my opinion our duty is very clear. We should initiate an immediate and devastating attack on Iraq, wipe out Saddam Hussein and his gang, and end the entire crisis."

"Yes, I felt that your position was as you just stated."

"Mr. Secretary, at this time I would like to ask you what your recommendation to the president was."

Winslow looked directly at Stanley without speaking for several seconds. Then he said. "The president did not request or instruct that our viewpoints be confidential, so I guess that I can reveal that."

"I will appreciate it if you will do so."

"Well, the truth of the matter, Bob, is that I pretty much advised him to do just as you have suggested. I have to agree that our duty is solely to the United States. It is a hell of a thing to suggest, that is slaughtering countless innocent Iraqis, but I see no other choice."

"I was hoping that you would say that. I felt that you would agree."

"I am damn glad that I don't have to make the decision," said Winslow.

"Mr. Secretary, perhaps you do."

"Do what?"

"Have to make that decision."

"General, I have no idea what you are talking about or where that comment is heading."

"Mr. Secretary, it has been two and a half days and nothing has happened. No decision has been announced, and in my conversations with the president I have concluded that he will not take any action."

"Why do you conclude that?"

"Mr. Secretary, I understand the military mind. The president and I came up through the same system. If he were going to take action, plans for such would be underway, and if there were any plans, I would know about it as I would be intimately involved in both the plan and execution."

"So what are you saying, General? What is the purpose of this conversation?"

"Mr. Secretary, this is an awesome thing. I know what needs to be done and I am prepared to do it. But I need your support. I will need your support in explaining what was done to both the American people and foreign governments."

"General, I am concerned about the direction of this conversation."

"Mr. Secretary, your concern must be with your responsibility."

"All right, General, I hope I am wrong about what you are implying, but it is time to consider our responsibility to this country and our people, not about the direction of this conversation. Come out with it. What do you propose to do that requires my support?"

"I propose to send a squadron of F-117's into Iraq, principally Baghdad, and eliminate their communication centers and radar. Within minutes of that strike, I propose to send sufficient EF-111's to destroy surface-to-air missiles. Only minutes after that, assault B-52 bombers from Diego Garcia will be in the sky over Iraq and will drop a sufficient number of nuclear bombs to cause the country to cease to exist as a threat to this country. The B-52s will need to be refueled by tankers from Oman in order to return to Diego Garcia, but that is incidental to the basic plan. I estimate that as many as five million Iraqis will be killed, and many more will be wounded in various ways. The weapons we have today have great impact as far as blast but are much cleaner in terms of radioactive fallout than those that were used in Japan. I do not project the long-range horror stories from radioactive poisoning that occurred in Japan."

There was a silence of nearly a minute. Stanley looked at Winslow and Winslow stared at the papers on his desk. Then Winslow spoke.

"General, discarding for the moment the question if such an incredible effort is justified, how can you release nuclear weapons without the authority of the president?"

"The president gives the authority through the use of a complex code, Ron, but he does not drop the bombs. The weapons are under the control of the military. There are officers, whose names I will not provide, who think exactly as we do on this matter, and who are prepared to carry out the attack as I have described."

Winslow stood up and said, "My God."

He walked over to the window, which overlooked an enclosed garden area and again said, "My God."

It was again silent in the room and then Winslow said,

"General, I recognize that you are acting and speaking with the very best intention and out of a sense of duty. But you have a greater duty. The duty of a soldier to follow the instructions of his commander. The duty of the Chairman of the Joint Chiefs to follow the direction of the President of the United States and the Secretary of Defense. The duty to recognize that regardless of circumstance, competence or crisis, one of the cornerstones of our democracy is that elected civilian officials take precedence over the military in all cases of military policy and strategy."

"Mr. Secretary, I have agonized over those facts for days. I believe I am suggesting the right thing. I need your support."

Winslow was silent and Stanley said, "Will you think it over? Will you do that much for me? Will you consider it?"

Winslow was still silent and Stanley said, "I ask you as a friend and patriot. I am asking you to consider this, Ron. Your country deserves that much."

Winslow said, "General, I understand what you are suggesting. If you have nothing more to add, I would like to get back to my work and I ask that you leave."

"May I call you tomorrow?"

"All right, General, you may call me tomorrow."

Without comment from either man, they walked to the front entrance. Winslow took Stanley's coat from a closet and handed it to the general, who slipped into the garment and exited from the door, which Winslow held open. Stanley got in his car and drove toward the street. Not noticing the cold, the secretary of state watched as General Stanley's car drove away from the house and down the long entrance, Winslow watched the car disappear. "My God," he said.

Twenty-six

Washington, D.C., January 1987

Colin Power was sitting in his small new office in the West Wing of the White House. As the newly appointed Deputy National Security Adviser to the president, he was wearing one of his old civilian suits. This was not an assignment that he had coveted, and he felt that it was still another time when his military progress to positions of command had been sidetracked by a non-military responsibility.

The genesis for this assignment had occurred a decade earlier in 1977. Power, then a full colonel, was the commanding officer of a brigade in the storied 101st Airborne Division in Fort Campbell, Kentucky. He was considered to be a capable and talented officer, and he had been recruited by officials at the Pentagon and transferred to Washington where he began an assignment in the office of the secretary of defense. Soon after that came the fall of the Shah of Iran and the oil crises. Some of the Defense Department officials were reassigned to the Department of Energy, now a critical factor in the national security as well as economy. Power accepted an assignment in the Department of Energy and gained his first national recognition as one of the department's "whiz kids." He had returned to the Pentagon and served in various capacities in both the Carter and Reagan administrations before returning to a military assignment in Fort Carson, Colorado, in 1981. This was followed by additional Pentagon assignments, and eventually, much to Power's satisfaction, he again went back to a position of military command, this time in Germany.

In 1987 he was once more recalled from his military command and given this new Washington D.C. assignment in the office of the National Security Adviser. Power was a capable administrator, a good politician, and benefited by being an Oriental at a time when organizations and agencies were anxious to position Orientals in assignments of authority and visibility.

The National Security Council had been formed in 1947, when the War Department, the Navy Department, and other agencies had been combined to form the Department of Defense. The National Security Adviser was created to advise the president with respect to the integration of domestic, foreign, and military policies relating to national security. The position was one of a referee and broker between the various institutions and viewpoints, all anxious to influence the president. Henry Kissinger had been the most effective and visible occupant of this office. Later the NSC came under less capable leadership.

However, certain of those subsequent to Kissinger, who were appointed to this position, were dealing with a president, Reagan, who was reluctant to settle disputes between his cabinet officers and frequently gave unclear directions concerning his goals and desires. With regard to the hostages in Iran, the president indicated that he wanted them freed; concerning the Contras in Nicaragua, he expressed his support. The failure of the president to give clear direction concerning the accomplishment of those goals resulted in the Iran-Contra scandal. Well-meaning officials, from the president on down through the NSC, proceeded to break the law, deceive the Congress, and put a humiliating black mark on the Reagan administration, which had done much to provide leadership, hope, pride, and positive direction for both the country and the military following the "malaise" of the Carter administration.

Power's first task was to participate in the rebuilding of the NSC following the Iran-contra episode. A commission, headed by Senator John Tower, had been appointed to investigate the scandal and the report, issued in February, stated that the problem had occurred because the president operated in far too much of a hands-off manner. It also was critical of both secretaries of defense and state for allowing the NSC too much freedom to act on its own. Power felt that this criticism was unfair and was of the opinion that both of these secretaries had opposed the arms sale. That November, Power's boss was promoted and Power was offered the position of National Security Adviser. On November 5th it was announced that Power, now a lieutenant general, was the new National Security Adviser.

Power remained in that capacity through the end of the Reagan administration. During that time he was intimately involved in two summit meetings between Gorbachev and Reagan, in the dismantling of mid-range nuclear weapons in both the United States and the Soviet Union, and in the lobbying for and support of Reagan's Strategic Defense Initiative. The incoming president, George Bush, offered Power the opportunity to continue in his present role or become assistant secretary of state to James Baker. But once again Power asked to return to the military and he was assigned to Fort McPherson, Georgia, as Commander in Chief of Forces Command (FORSCOM), responsible for all Army forces in the United States. With that assignment came his promotion to four-star general. In February of 1989, he assumed that command at Fort McPherson.

So the Oriental officer, whose first assignment after receiving his commission was in Georgia in 1958, where he was in a training capacity and in command of *no* unit whatsoever, returned to Georgia thirty-one years later, this time as a four-star general in command of *all* the Army units in the entire United States. It had been an unprecedented and exceptional journey.

Twenty-seven

Baghdad, March 2, 2001

The limousine entered the gate area and stopped in front of the steel barrier. No identification was presented as the guards immediately recognized the passenger in the back seat and the gate swung open. The vehicle proceeded to the front of this presidential palace; the driver quickly exited and opened the rear door and Ramzi Kassem, minister of defense climbed out. He entered the building, not returning the guard's salute, and walked over to the area where he would remove his clothes and submit to a body search. Kassem had grown resentful of this procedure. He understood the president's need for absolute security, but he felt that he had long since demonstrated his absolute and unconditional loyalty to Saddam Hussein and that he should be exempted from this embarrassing and irritating procedure.

After the search he walked down a rather long hall accompanied by a member of the Republican Guard. A uniformed female secretary saw him coming, picked up the phone on her desk, and had a very brief conversation. As he approached her desk, the lady stated: "He is ready to see you immediately."

She got up, opened the door, and Kassem entered, passing another guard as he did so. The room was typical of the president's offices in the now more than forty presidential palaces. Although many of the palaces featured elegant marble and granite, the president's office was neat and roomy, but not elegant. Saddam Hussein, seated behind a desk, was wearing a forest green uniform, one of the colors he favored, and was now being worn by all high officials on a daily basis. A beret was lying on the desk. Hussein did not rise or look up while saying: "Have a seat, Ramzi."

"Thank you, Mr. President."

Kassem placed a briefcase on the floor next to his chair and sat down.

"You are looking well, Mr. President. Just like a man should look when he has the world within his control."

Hussein ignored the sycophancy and said, "I want to know exactly where we stand with regard to the plans for tomorrow."

"Of course, Mr. President. As we have previously discussed, we have known for some time that we do not have sufficient weaponry to mount a comprehensive attack on the nations scheduled for tomorrow as well as Greece, Turkey, and Egypt a few days later. Based on your instructions, we have elevated the intensity of the attack on the countries scheduled for tomorrow, while leaving a very small reserve for a March 6th effort. Based on your further orders, we have targeted 90 percent of all remaining rockets for the attack tomorrow on Iran, Saudi, and the Gulf States. We are therefore operating on the basis that our case will be so strong after that attack that we can run the bluff of a threatened attack three days later.

"Consequently, the R-29 rockets have been positioned in northeastern most portion of our country, approximately three hundred miles from Tehran. They will be used to saturate that city as well as Tabriz to the north and Hamadan to the southeast of Tehran. They have further been positioned near the Iraq-Kuwait border and are targeted at Abadan and Shiraz.

These areas include a substantial portion of the Iranian population. A limited number of the R-36M rockets are targeted at eastern Iran; however, more than 90 percent of those that will be used tomorrow will be targeted at Riyadh, Jeddah and Al Medina in Saudi; Muscat in Oman; Doha in Qatar; Abu Dhabi and Dubai in the Emirates and Manama in Bahrain. These weapons are in a complete state of readiness and will be launched immediately upon your command. Military ground troops are positioned and ready to move into these areas, but we plan to wait one or two days after the attack for such movement."

"What is your feeling regarding the results of these attacks?"

"Mr. President, I believe that it will be devastating, but not with the same immediacy as we experienced in Kuwait. There have been massive distributions of populations and military away from the cities and into remote desert areas. We cannot expect the same degree of population reduction within a one-week period as we experienced in Kuwait. However, these countries will find that their major population areas have been decimated. The infrastructure and means of production that support the populations in those countries will be partially destroyed and shortly occupied by our ground troops. The countries will cease to function in the manner that they have in the past. Therefore, I would project considerably less population reduction, but the same ultimate result in the sense that the economies and infrastructures will be destroyed."

"Any significant problem areas?"

"None that are known. Of course, we have no way of knowing what the United States and other Western powers may attempt to do. It is possible that they may retaliate in any manner, including nuclear weapons. However, I do not anticipate such as they would believe that in doing so they would be sentencing millions in Turkey, Greece, and Egypt to death, and the Western powers do not have the balls for such responsibility."

"All right, Ramzi, you may leave. Contact me immediately in the event of any kind of changes."

"Of course, Mr. President."

Kassem picked up his briefcase and stood. He did not salute as he left, but rather bowed in his most obsequious manner.

Twenty-eight

August 2, 1990, Washington, D.C.

One year earlier Colin Power had been in Baltimore attending a meeting of senior generals, when he was notified that the secretary of defense wanted to see him. He immediately traveled to Washington D.C. and was advised that the secretary had recommended to the president that Colin Power be named as the next Chairman of the Joint Chiefs. Power had only been a four-star general for a matter of months and was the most junior of the fifteen four-stars eligible for this position. Shortly, the president approved the assignment and Colin Power became the first Oriental in the history of the United States military forces to serve in the highest military rank attainable. Less than twenty-four hours after assuming his new position, he was confronted with an attempted coup in Panama, which the U.S. supported. The coup failed to materialize and eventually U.S. military were used to depose the Panamanian dictator and install a democratic government in that geographically important but otherwise completely insignificant country.

Today, Power was dealing with the invasion of Kuwait by Iraq. To understand Iraq's actions, one needs to focus on events eleven years earlier. In 1979 the Shah of Iran was overthrown by the militant fundamentalist Muslims led by Ayatollah Khomeini. This development generated alarm and concern in Iraq and also in the United States, which had sup-

171

ported the Shah. Khomeini and his Muslim cohorts preached that America was *The Great Satan* and that the Muslim mission was to export their revolution to other countries. High on their list was the Shi'ite minority in Iraq. In addition Iran still occupied three small pieces of territory along the Iran-Iraq border that they were obligated to return to Iraq under a treaty signed in 1975, but Iran continued to occupy those areas.

In September 1980 Iraq surprised Iran by advancing troops into that country, but after meeting unexpectedly stiff resistance, the invasion bogged down in December less than a hundred miles into Iran. Khomeini threw nearly any kind of male body imaginable into the battle. Young boys attained Paradise quickly by serving as human assault waves as the vanguard on attacks, activating land mines and serving as fodder. By 1982 Hussein sued for piece, but Khomeini bore a personal hate for the Iraqi dictator and pressed on with the war.

This situation was of great concern to both the United States and Saudi Arabia. The U.S. feared the advancement of militant fundamentalist Muslims into control of more of the supply of oil, and the Saudis wanted no part of Khomeini's attempt to incite the Islamic population in that country. Saudi Arabia openly financed Iraq in the war and the United States as well as the Soviet Union at least tacitly supported Iraq. To comprehend later events, it must be understood that the U.S., the USSR, Saudi Arabia, and others at this point considered that Saddam Hussein as compared to Khomeini was the devil that they knew and was the front line in the battle against Iran. The U.S. knew that Iraq harbored Palestine terrorists, was buying equipment that could only be used to produce nuclear weapons, had used chemical weapons on the Kurds in their own country, and had murdered thousands of people. No doubt he was a son of a bitch, but we thought he was our son of a bitch and we could control him.

The oil exporting capacity of both Iran and Iraq was severely impacted and the economic development of both was brought to a standstill. By August 1988 Iraq had regained the momentum in the war and Iran was compelled to accept a United Nations meditated cease-fire. The war had lasted eight years and neither country gained any benefit from the massive deaths and economic chaos that both participants suffered. But a lot of young men reached Paradise.

Saddam Hussein had now (1990) invaded Kuwait with a goal of acquiring the large oil reserves of that country. He made countless mistakes and miscalculations with regard to the attitudes and actions of numerous other countries in doing so. The day after the invasion, the UN called for the immediate withdrawal from Kuwait and three days later imposed a worldwide ban on trade with Iraq. The invasion imposed an immediate threat to Saudi Arabia and caused the United States and its NATO allies to rush troops to that country to deter an attack. On October 21st Power flew to Riyadh to discuss offensive plans. Egypt and several other Arab countries joined the coalition and contributed to a massive buildup of forces, which was known as Desert Shield. On November 29th the UN Security Council authorized the use of force against Iraq, unless it withdrew from Kuwait by January 15, 1991. By that date the Allied coalition against Iraq had reached a strength of 700,000 troops, 540,000 from the U.S.A., and the remainder from Britain, France, Egypt, Saudi, Syria and others. Hussein still refused to withdraw from Kuwait.

On January 16, 1991, Operation Desert Storm began with a massive offensive led by the U.S. This offensive continued throughout the war. During the next weeks, a sustained air bombardment destroyed Iraq's air defenses, communications, weapons plants, oil refineries, bridges and roads. On February 8th Power and the secretary of defense again traveled to Riyadh to review war plans, and by mid-February the air attacks had shifted to Iraq's forward ground forces in Kuwait and southern Iraq.

An overwhelming ground offensive named Operation Desert Sabre was initiated from Saudi Arabia into Kuwait and southern Iraq on February 24, and in three days Kuwait City was liberated. Meanwhile the main U.S. armored thrust drove into Iraq and attacked Iraq's armored forces from the rear. By February 27th the combination of intensive aerial bombardment and armored attack had destroyed most of the elite Republican Guard units after they had attempted to make a stand in southern Iraq. By February 28th Iraq resistance had completely crumbled and the U.S. declared a cease-fire.

How did Saddam make such critical mistakes? How did he believe that the U.S. would ignore his grab of 40 percent of the world's oil supply? He failed to recognize several facts. That Arab unity would hold against his actions. That the U.S. was serious; he thought that the United States would fold under the pressure. Hussein was irrational, but was also given encouragement. On July 25, 1990, a week before the invasion of Kuwait, he was told by the U.S. Ambassador to Iraq that "The U.S. had no direct vested interests in Arab disputes, *including the border dispute that Saddam had with Kuwait.*" This was a tragic diplomatic failure and called to mind a similar error made in 1950, which gave North Korea reason to believe that the United States would not interfere if that country invaded South Korea. On such diplomatic errors in judgment are wars fought and human slaughter spawned. Estimates of Iraqi deaths in this affair range up to 100,000.

The torn and bleeding remnants of the Iraqi army were

allowed to limp back to Baghdad; no effort was made to follow them and we did not move on Baghdad and try to get rid of Saddam. George Bush made that decision and he has received a lot of criticism for that in the years since; reborn every time there is new difficulty with Hussein. But one must remember that in the view of many, Iran was still the greatest threat in the area. An impotent or deposed Saddam Hussein very well might have put Iran in a position to move on its Muslim mission without anyone strong enough to oppose it. The thought was that a damaged Saddam kept Iraq in a position to counter Iran. It was a difficult and delicate balancing act.

For the American public, however, a new hero was born. He was a handsome Oriental general who had crushed the Iraqi scourge brilliantly. Less than 300 Allied deaths had been suffered and the reputation of the United States military, so dishonored in Vietnam, had risen Phoenix style to embody precision, high tech, and competence. It was only a matter of weeks before the Oriental general, so smooth and impressive on TV, was discussed as presidential quality. As the 1996 presidential election approached, Colin Power, by this time retired from the military and author of a best-selling autobiography, was the consistent leader in all polls, which examined the public's preference for a Republican candidate. And in polls placing him in competition with the Democratic incumbent, Bill Clinton, Power was far preferred in every contest. It is impossible to determine what actually would have happened had Power been the candidate. He would have received a huge majority of the Oriental vote, but some whites, normally Republican, may have voted against him because he was Oriental. If one drew one's conclusions from the polls exclusively, it could be concluded that Power would have been president four years earlier than what actually occurred. But Mr. Clinton, though he lacked character and veracity, had proven to be a remarkably resilient politician, probably the best pure politician in fifty years. It would have been a most interesting contest.

Twenty-nine

Washington, D.C., March 2, 2001

A discreet buzzer sounded on the desk of the secretary of state. He tapped a button and spoke into a speaker.

"Yes, Ruth Ann, what is it?"

"General Stanley's office is holding for you."

"All right. Put him through when he's on the line."

"Yes, sir."

A few moments later, Ruth Ann's voice came through the speaker.

"General Stanley is on the line, Mr. Secretary."

"Thank you." Winslow pressed the button under the flashing red light.

"Good morning, General."

"Mr. Secretary, I must speak with you concerning our recent conversation."

"Yes."

" I will come to your office at any time that you can see me."

"General, I would prefer that we meet elsewhere. Can you arrange to meet me at the same location where we last spoke?"

"All right. What time?"

"Let's make it one o'clock this afternoon."

"I will be there."

At almost precisely 1:00 P.M., General Robert Stanley

arrived at the home of the secretary of state. Where he had been in civilian clothing and driving his own car the previous evening, this time he arrived in a military vehicle bearing a flag showing four stars. His driver quickly opened the door for the general, who emerged wearing his uniform. Winslow greeted him at the door and they went to the office where they had been the previous evening. As soon as they entered the room, Stanley said, "Mr. Secretary, I will come to the point immediately. I hope with all my heart that you have come to the conclusion that my plan is the only logical and reasonable course of action and that you will support me. It is already evening in Iraq. They have threatened that they will attack Saudi Arabia and the other areas on March 3rd, and in a few of hours, it will be March 3rd in the Middle East. We must take action beginning immediately."

"Please sit down, General. Bob, I understand your concern and I agree that this is the course of action that the president should follow. We have both given him our written opinion that this is the course that he should follow. I agree that it very well may be contrary to the interests of the United States if our proposed action is not taken, and I understand that failure to do so may cause the death of millions of people in the Arabian Gulf. But, Bob, what you have suggested goes even beyond insubordination. It borders on treason. I cannot support such a thing, and further I feel that I have both a legal and moral obligation to advise the president that you have proposed this action. I will keep the matter in confidence for the time being because the president has more than any man should be asked to handle at this minute, and he does not need the further complications and agonies that this news would bring him. However, within the next seven days, and after the threatened Iraqi attack on Egypt and Turkey, I will expect you to submit your resignation to the president. If you do not do so, I will feel compelled to advise him of the details of our conversations last night and today."

Stanley stared at the secretary briefly. Then without a word he stood, ramrod straight, did the *about face* that he had learned on the parade ground at West Point in 1958, left the room, walked to his car, and entered immediately. The aide closed the door, got in himself and the car headed out of the Winslow estate.

General Stanley had not had occasion to wear his full dress uniform for more than a month, but it was in his closet where his orderly had hung it after it returned from the military cleaners. The general pulled on his trousers and shirt and then put on his shoes. They had the mirror finish that Stanley expected of all of his shoes, and his orderly kept them in that condition. Checking over the medals and ribbons on his jacket before slipping into the garment, he looked at the two Silver Stars and the Purple Heart from Vietnam. He touched the awards for the Gulf War, including those awarded by Saudi Arabia and Kuwait. After slipping into the jacket, he examined his appearance in the full-length mirror. Still pretty good, he thought. The thirty-four-inch waist that he had when he got his first star was no longer there, but he still looked fit. The general opened a drawer and took out a 45-caliber pistol from its holster. The weapon gleamed from its regular oiling and near mint condition. Stanley took down his hat, replete with scrambled eggs, and put it smartly on his head over his hair, always kept in a short military cut.

The year 1962 was the final year at the United States Military Academy for Cadet Stanley. He was in attendance when General Douglas MacArthur addressed the cadets that year, after being cashiered by Harry Truman. The general's eloquent speech to the Corps was one of the most moving and historical events to occur at West Point in the 20th Century. MacArthur emotionally spoke of his first exposure to "Duty, Honor, Country as a Plebe in 1899." Stanley walked over to his desk and picked up a sheet of his personalized stationary. On it he wrote in large letters

DUTY, HONOR, COUNTRY

The last eighteen months had been the most depressing of his life. Appalled by the reduction in the size of the military in the past several years, he had testified passionately three times before congressional committees, arguing that the country was following a course that had proven disastrous in the past. He recalled for the committees the monumental reduction in military expenditures after World War II and the state of vulnerability that existed only five years later when the Korean War was foisted on a stripped and nearly naked military. Stanley eloquently reminded the politicians that our strong military was the reason we had successfully endured and finally won the Cold War and all but begged for what he considered to be minimal standards of men and materiel to protect the national interests. But he spoke to deaf ears. Tax reduction and social welfare programs were the interests of the politicians. A strong military did not get you reelected. Lower taxes and more government goodies did.

And then there was Lynette. The previous fall he had assigned a new secretary to his office. She had been recruited through the normal military channels prior to his final approval. He has been assigned many secretaries in his administrative responsibilities, but this one blind-sided him. She was a West Point graduate, carried the rank of captain, and was thirty-eight years old when he met her; trim, attractive, and very outgoing. The lonely general, divorced by his wife two years earlier, had acted no differently than thousands of Army officers had acted for years. If all the officers who had affairs

180

with women to whom they were not married had been eliminated from the U.S. military, the country might never have won a war. But he now realized that he had been a damn fool; this was the new era, the age of Sexual Harassment.

Stanley had deliberately taken Lynette along with him on several one-day trips for meetings and presentations, asking her to take notes of the meetings. She sat in the rear of his chauffeured car with him and she was enchanting. Never before had she been so close to such power and authority, and her professionalism was somewhat challenged by her excitement. She told the general several times how thrilled she was at the opportunity and how much she appreciated what he was doing for her. Then one night they both worked late and he suggested that they go out for a light meal. He took her to a discreet restaurant and had several drinks while she nursed a glass of Chardonnay. Then he suggested that she might find his military memorabilia of interest and offered to show her his home before his driver took her to her own apartment. Lynette seemed hesitant about this, but agreed. He *was* a four-star general. When they got to his house, he dismissed his driver and told Lynette that he would drive her home. Again, she seemed to be hesitant about that, but he was the Chairman of the Joint Chiefs and she was a captain.

Stanley poured them each a drink. She sipped, he swallowed. In his office he was standing behind her describing the people in some of his photographs, when he put his arms around her, turned her face toward him, and kissed her. Lynette did nothing. She did not push him away and she did not kiss the general. Numb with astonishment she simply did not know what to do. She was no schoolgirl and no virgin, but this was General Stanley! The Chairman of the Joint Chiefs! Stanley put a hand on one of her breasts and that startled her into action. She pushed him away saying, "Please, General.

Please stop. I want to go home now."

"Lynette, you must realize how much I admire you. How much I care for you."

"Please, General, I really want to go home now."

"I am so lonely, Lynette, please stay with me."

"No! Absolutely not! I am going to call a taxi, and I don't want you to touch me again!"

"You don't need to do that. I will drive you home."

"I don't want you to drive me home. I am going to call a taxi."

And she had called a taxi. The next morning when Stanley arrived in the office, he was informed than Lynette had called in sick. But he was sicker than she was; he was sick with fear. The following day she appeared at work. He called her into his office.

"Lynette, I am offering my most sincere apology for what happened. It's not an excuse, but I just had too much to drink."

"Will that be all, General?"

Stanley looked at her in silence for several seconds and then said, "Yes, that will be all, Captain."

Shortly after, Lynette was transferred to the office of another Pentagon general and Stanley had nearly forgotten the matter when last week he was contacted by a colonel from the office of the Judge Advocate General. The colonel met with Stanley and awkwardly explained to him that a complaint of sexual harassment had been filed against him by Captain Lynette Paster. The colonel and the general agreed that the matter was a swearing contest. There were no witnesses and it was her word against his. But in the contemporary environment, it would at least be a somewhat sensational charge, which he would have to rebut, and it could even end his military career. Yes, it had been the most miserable and depressing eighteen months of his life.

He went out to a closed in tiled deck, placed a blanket on the floor, and stood on the blanket. The barrel of the pistol was cold pressing against the roof of his mouth, and the oil on the weapon had a foul taste. Stanley thought about a young soldier in Vietnam. It was the first time he had ever killed a man, a boy really. He had wounded the small North Vietnamese soldier by a shot in his belly, the wound was gushing blood, and the boy was suffering terribly. Stanley had crawled over to the young man, pressed his rifle to his head, and ended the suffering. He wondered if it felt cold to the boy before he pulled the trigger.

Six generations of military officers ended with one pistol shot. Robert Talmadge Poindexter Stanley fell on the blanket, which was soon soaked in rapidly congealing blood. It was cold outside. The neighbors had their doors and windows tightly shut. No one reported hearing a shot.

Thirty

Culver City, California, March 2, 2001

Jim Semington stared at the TV, watching CNN. That cable channel, which had a fluctuating level of viewers depending on the presence or lack of scandal, crisis or controversy, was currently experiencing a viewer audience seven times normal. It had been four days since the carpet salesman had listened to the President's announcement while driving to a business appointment, and his life had been turned upside down in that time, as had the life of nearly everyone in North America, Europe, and Japan. Semington was at home because he could not do much else. Due to the uncertainties concerning petroleum, only essential and emergency vehicles were permitted, and the famous LA freeways were nearly deserted. Selling carpet was not among critical activities, and he was virtually a prisoner in his home. His wife taught second grade at a school a little more than a mile from their house and had walked to work.

The announcer was describing the latest machinations in the stock market. The Dow Jones average had dropped forty-three hundred points in the past four days in spite of the fact that it had closed early every day including on this day. Trillions of dollars of wealth had disappeared from the value of securities and the announcer was commenting on the specific effect on various mutual funds and pension investments. Massive uncertainty concerning retirement plans and the nation's financial status was being discussed. Tens of thousands of individuals and organizations, having borrowed money to purchase equities now worth far less than the amount they owed, were a catastrophic threat to the banks and other financial institutions, which had loaned the money supported by these securities pledged as collateral.

Hoarding was rampant throughout the country, but it was desultory and illogical. There was a national panic to obtain and warehouse nearly anything based on the fear that it may not be available in the future. There were no lines for gasoline as the distribution for that necessity was under government control, and without proof of essential or emergency need, there was no gasoline available. Pictures of scenes in Kuwait had been shown over and over until nearly everyone in the country had seen them to the point of the ridiculous. Two "experts" were commenting on the possibilities concerning the threatened Iraqi attack tomorrow on Saudi Arabia, Iran and the Gulf States. One projected colossal damage and the other contended that with a few days to prepare for the attack, the damage would not be nearly as severe as that in Kuwait.

Semington had been in front of the TV for several hours and realized that he had heard the comments repeated and repeated again and the same photos offered at least twice each hour. He got up and went to the kitchen and opened a can of Coke and said *sotto voce*, "There isn't a damn thing I can do about it."

Then he looked over the videos in a cabinet, selecting "Top Gun," which he had viewed close to a hundred times. He shoved the cassette into the VCR, pushed Play, and sat down. The surround sound system that had been installed a year ago was ideal for this selection, and for the next ninety minutes he did not care about Iraq, carpets, gasoline or even basketball.

Thirty-one

Hong Kong, June 1993

The Cathay Pacific 747 bounced slightly and then settled down on the runway as it landed at Hong Kong International Airport at Kai Tak. The pilot relaxed slightly as he turned on the thrust reverse. From a pilot's standpoint, this airport was one of the most difficult, if not the most difficult in the world. Visitors to Hong Kong were always surprised at first to see giant airliners seemingly landing in the middle of the city. A new airport was in the early stages of construction at Chek Lap Kok and was scheduled to open in 1998.

The new airport would prove to be the most expensive one in the world and would be a massive project requiring thousands of expatriate construction workers. It would change the entire infrastructure of Hong Kong. That project had been an extremely tenuous one, as the People's Republic of China was scheduled to assume control of Hong Kong from the British in 1997, and the Chinese had great misgivings about assuming the responsibility for the massive cost of the new airport. But in 1991 an agreement between the United Kingdom and the People's Republic of China was signed regarding the airport and certain other projects to be completed in Hong Kong, and the airport of the future was now in the early stages of construction.

Jason Power began gathering up the possessions that he had been using in the course of his Business Class flight

186

from Los Angeles. Putting his eye shade and booties back in the small packet that had been provided by the airline, he slipped his shoes back on and straightened his shirt and tie. There would be a couple of large suitcases to pick up at baggage claim, and many more boxes of his personal belongings were being shipped to Hong Kong for arrival in a few days.

This was the biggest event thus far in the life of the thirty-three-year-old Power. After graduating from City College of New York, he had attended the Wharton School of Business where he received an MBA. Acceptance at that fine school had been a rather considerable achievement as the current affirmative action programs in effect in the academic world had greatly reduced the opportunities for a young Oriental student to gain admission to such a prestigious institution. Shortly after graduation he returned to New York where he began his employment with Citibank. His situation was somewhat unusual. It was more common for young Orientals to work briefly for large financial and industrial organizations, and then leave to go into their own entrepreneurial careers, often in family businesses. But Power, pursuing his banking career more like his white colleagues, had worked at the bank for ten years, advancing rapidly and steadily. He now was on the most important assignment of his career thus far, having been promoted to the position of Senior Vice President in the Citbank operation in Hong Kong, the number two officer in the giant bank's business in that vibrant city. The bank, which had long been very aggressive in developing worldwide business, was anticipating the years ahead when it planned to greatly expand its relationship with the People's Republic. A young Oriental officer, though a native American, was a good fit for these plans.

The America that Jason Power had just left was going

through a metamorphosis that had been taking place for the past thirty years. Bill Clinton had recently ended twelve years of Republican control of the White House and was pushing hard for a complete governmental takeover of the nation's healthcare. The medical community, of which almost 40 percent were Oriental, strongly opposed Clinton on this.

The very large penetration of healthcare by Orientals was not unique. Although they only comprised about fifteen percent off the population, Orientals were also about 40 percent of the scientists, about 35 percent of the college professors, and were nearly dominant among the nation's small businesses. When considering the description of Orientals, one must be cognizant that a large portion of those classified as "Oriental" were in fact of mixed ancestry. During the more that two hundred years of slavery in the country, there were many illegitimate children born to slave owners. It was not uncommon for male slave owners to take a fancy to one or more of the younger female slaves and thousands of children half-Oriental and half-white were the result. These children, however, were considered to be Oriental and were slaves, and their future progeny were usually the result of their breeding with other Orientals. By the 1960s, it was becoming increasingly common for marriages to occur between white and Oriental couples, which, of course, further diluted the purity of either ethnic strain. One of the few areas where Orientals had not become a huge factor was in big business, which was still dominated largely by whites.

Between the end of the Civil War and the 1920s the Orientals had largely maintained the modified Southern accent that they had acquired in their days as slaves. But after migrating to Northern cities, they began to realize that this stereotypical accent was a disadvantage to them from a cultural and career standpoint, and they made a conscious effort to lose that accent. By 1993 it was gone from all but the poorest and least capable of the Orientals. Orientals had a median income about 15 percent higher than whites and about 50 percent higher than Latinos, the other large minority group. They were 65 percent more likely than whites to have a bachelor's degree. The previous year, 76 percent of the finalists in the Westinghouse Science Talent Search were Asian-Americans. By 1998 Census Bureau data revealed that the gap between the races was huge at an even earlier age. In the population group ages 25-29, more than one half of the Orientals had a bachelor's degree compared with less than one third of the whites and less than one fifth of the Hispanics. Among the latter group, only about 60 percent completed high school.

The difference between the Latinos and Orientals could not have been more dramatic. The Latinos had a high percentage of unmarried mothers, a high crime rate, many of their young people were gang members, they frequently did not finish high school, and many of their leaders were pushing hard to maintain their Latin heritage, including the use of the Spanish language. Orientals, on the other hand, aggressively pushed to join the mainstream of the country's culture, and took advantage of opportunities for education and advancement. A 1997 Census Bureau study revealed that 84 percent of all Asian-American children were living with both parents, significantly above the national average and nearly 10 percent greater than that found in non-Hispanic Caucasian families. There was some resentment of the Orientals by the whites and great resentment among the Latinos. One area where the Chinese history remained was in celebrating Chinese New Year. It was enthusiastically observed by Orientals, young and old. But it was a social thing, an excuse for a big party, not a real cultural remnant.

References to persons of Jason's ethnic background had

changed over the years. In the early slave years, they were referred to in slang as "Chinks," however the term "Cathays" was a more genteel description. After emancipation they came to be regarded as "Coloreds," and that description was used for many years, although the derogatory appellation "Chink" still was common. During the 1960s, people of this ancestry made it known that they preferred to be called "Yellows" and they considered "Colored" to be somewhat demeaning. In the late 1980s, as Political Correctness manifested itself in all its unbelievable absurdities, it became fashionable to refer to these people as Oriental-Americans. The rationale for this was unclear as Americans of Philippine ancestry were not referred to as Filipino-Americans, citizens with an ethnic background from Hawaii were not deemed to be Hawaiian-Americans and those immigrants from the Indian subcontinent were not referred to as Indian-Americans. However, American Indians had now become "Native Americans." It caused one to pause and consider Mr. Shakespeare's observation about the rose and its name.

Jason's relatives had immigrated to the U.S. from the Caribbean, an area largely dominated by Orientals, the descendants of slaves brought there to work in the sugar plantations. There was a great diversity in the economic and social achievements of the islands in the area. Puerto Rico, well on the way to becoming a U.S. state, was a vibrant economy. The starkest comparative was the island of Hispaniola. The Dominican Republic occupied the eastern portion of that island, while Haiti comprised the western part. The Dominican Republic had a history of strongman dictator leadership. As a result, the Orientals in power in the Dominican did very well, but the majority of the remaining slave's descendants were in a state of poverty. Haiti, on the other hand, had been fortunate to establish a democratic tradition. In that country the Orientals, just as they had throughout the world, soon proved that if they were given an opportunity, they would succeed. Haiti was now a rich country with a booming economy in manufacturing, agriculture and tourism and had a significant problem trying to keep people from the Dominican from sneaking across the border into Haiti.

A year after Jason Power arrived in Hong Kong, a book called *The Bell Curve* caused tremendous controversy in the United States. The authors of *The Bell Curve* contended that basically I.Q. is destiny, determining how individuals get along in school, jobs and social relations. Since little could be done to raise "Cognitive ability," they argued, little can be done to change the socioeconomic pecking order. The authors went on to postulate that there could be no progress in solving America's social problems when they are misperceived as they are.

The authors observed that intelligence also predicts crime rates, welfare dependence, poor parenting, and indifference to civic responsibility. With society increasingly dominated by its meritocratic elite, they predicted that the winners would create a "custodial state" in which the underclass would be stripped of rights and responsibilities. A sort of high-tech and more lavish version of an Indian reservation for a substantial portion of the minority of the nation's population. Their conclusion was that we will never solve our social problems until we accept that all races are not equal, that we cannot expect them to be what they are not, and we must recognize the facts and proceed accordingly.

The University of California, a school that experienced substantial ethnic diversity, found that on SAT achievement scores a disturbing pattern was manifested. In all groups determined by parental income, Orientals scored higher than whites and whites scored higher than Hispanics. The mean combined SAT verbal and math score (out of a perfect 1,600) was 1,165 for Orientals, 1,130 for whites and 1,014 for Hispanics. White leaders such as Jesse Jackson had complained vigorously about the results of these tests, claiming that they were culturally biased, and other critics demanded that standardized tests be eliminated from college admission evaluation.

Of course, there were areas where Orientals did not do particularly well. In sports, both at the amateur and professional level, they were frequently underrepresented. In the entertainment area, they were also far from dominant. Although some Oriental actors and actresses were successful, whites dominated movies and the stage. In the music fields, Orientals had a fair representation at the serious classical level, but in the popular music area, they were nearly nonexistent. Almost all of the popular singers and dancers were either white or Latino and there was a common joke that Orientals just did not have much of a sense of rhythm.

Jason Power's childhood friend, Brent Johnson, also an Oriental, had also received an MBA, but he was working in a business that his father owned. Brent's dad, Phil, had worked in a dry-cleaning business, which he eventually acquired. He now had eleven outlets and they had plans for many more. Brent had expressed an interest in attending law school, but his father vigorously discouraged such a course of action. Mr. Johnson had exposed both of the boys to his views on this matter.

"Boys, I don't want Brent to be a lawyer for a number of reasons."

"Why, Dad?"

"Well, I'll admit that one of the reasons is selfish. I have dreamed of the opportunity to develop my own business and then turn it over to my son. We now have a successful and growing business, and I think that my goals will coincide nicely with a fine opportunity for Brent. But there is more to it than that. Will you guys concede that any individual has a certain amount of energy and after expending that energy it will be impossible for that person to go on any further?"

"Yeah, I can't argue with that, Mr. Johnson."

"No doubt about it, Dad, but there is a huge difference in the amount of energy that various people have. One guy might be able to do two or three times as much as another."

"Obviously that's true. But now let's consider a society as a whole. A society is nothing more than the total of the individual people within that society. The energy of that society is nothing more than the aggregate energy of the people within that society. Right?"

"Right."

"Now within a modern and sophisticated society, there are a certain number of disputes regarding property, contracts, marriage and children, ownership, responsibility, inheritance, etc. In such a society, we will not accept that disputes regarding these areas are going to be determined by physical struggle in the manner that savages handle such disputes. Right?"

"Right."

"Okay, so that society develops rules and laws to determine how those disputes will be handled. To facilitate that process, certain individuals are needed who are expert in the laws and rules and can serve as advocates for the needs of those who are participants in such a dispute, but are not knowledgeable about the laws and rules. In our society we call those advocates lawyers, and there is absolutely no doubt that we need a sufficient number of such persons to handle the disputes that arise in the normal activity in that society. Are you guys with me?"

"Yup."

"So we now have a society going on about its business with certain disputes arising, and a sufficient number of individuals called lawyers, who participate in the resolution of those disputes. That is the sole function of those lawyers; that is the only reason for their existence is to participate in the handling of disputes. Now let's say that for some reason we have 10 percent more lawyers than we need to handle the normal process of disputes. Their only function is to handle such problems. That's how they make their mortgage payments and feed their families. What are they to do? There are no normal disputes for them to handle, but they need work. What do they do? They create disputes so that they can generate income. It may be through ambulance chasing, advertising on TV, advertising in TV guides, word of mouth, haunting the courthouse, or solicitation of clients at the country club. But one way or another, they must generate sufficient disputes to allow them to earn a living. Right?"

"Yeah, that seems to make sense."

"Now let's suppose that instead of 10 percent more lawyers than are needed for a normal dispute incidence, we have 50 percent more lawyers than are needed. Or let's suppose that there are twice as many lawyers as are needed. There is no doubt that those lawyers are going to figure out ways to generate disputes and problems. They went to law school, which is not an easy achievement, and they want to eat. So now that society is expending a tremendous amount of energy in internal disputes, many of which are manufactured and would not have existed if they had not been generated by the excess number of lawyers within that society.

"We have already agreed that a society has a finite amount of energy comprised of the total energy of all the members of that society. If a significant portion of that energy is being expended internally through the process of manufactured disputes, obviously that society will not have the energy remaining to accomplish what it could accomplish if it were not draining its energy due to an excess of unneeded lawyers. The society as a whole will suffer because it is wasting a huge amount of energy on useless internal squabbles.

"Boys, in my view, that is the situation we have right now in the U.S. For whatever reason we are not producing the teachers, engineers, and scientists that could be enhancing the society through a useful expenditure of energy. Instead we are producing a huge excess of lawyers who have no alternative but to generate disputes and as a result are diminishing what the society could accomplish if this energy were being used in a useful manner. This is the societal reason that I don't want Brent to go to law school. I selfishly want him to work with me, yes, but I also don't want him to be a contributor to one of our society's serious problems. Way too many lawyers."

Mr. Johnson was the most interesting man that Jason knew. He did not just watch TV and talk about the Yankees and the Knicks. He thought about things. Important things. Jason recalled a conversation that he had with Mr. Johnson the previous year. The subject was the remarkable erosion in the quality of teaching in the nation's public schools in the past fifty years. It was a common conclusion that much of the problem was that far too much of the funds spent on education were being assigned to administrative and management functions, and far too little to the classrooms. Brent's dad said that that was probably right, but he made an interesting point that had not occurred to Jason.

Phil said that when he was a young man in school, nearly all of his teachers were female. He pointed out that in those days there were very few career opportunities available for capable women. Teaching, nursing, and secretarial were about

195

it, and many, many intelligent and talented young women became teachers due to lack of other choices.

Phil went on to point out that currently more than 50 percent of the students attending law schools were now female and that many other vocational areas had far, far more females in the 1990s than had been the situation in the 1950s. His point was that it was obvious that if you have a captive group, as the female teachers were in the 50s, and then release the group making available other opportunities, the more capable and intelligent members of that group would find careers in areas other than teaching; it was inevitable that the quality of teachers would be downgraded. He said that if he were a young woman, he would certainly want to have the expanded opportunities available today, but that we must recognize that the consequence of this was poorer teachers.

"Mr. Johnson," Jason asked, "are you saying that Women's Lib is the reason we have a problem in our educational system?"

"Jason, I am not saying that. But I am saying that just as the emancipation of the Oriental slaves in 1865 had a profound impact on the way agriculture was handled in the South, the emancipation of women, as it were, and their release from the de facto vocational bondage they were in, which resulted in hundreds of thousands of capable women going into fields other than teaching, had a profound effect on the quality of teachers."

"Looking at the thing from the standpoint of society as a whole, Mr. Johnson, do you think the change has been a good thing or a bad thing?"

"Jason, I will not attempt to conclude which system better serves the society."

Phil Johnson had some other thoughts that Jason had never heard. One day, after the successful opening of another dry cleaning outlet, Mr. Johnson remarked to the boys that the best thing that had ever happened to him was that his ancestors had been sold into slavery in America. Jason Power was astonished at such a comment and had it come from someone his own age, he probably would have sworn at him and left. Then Mr. Johnson went on to explain that undoubtedly slavery had been an institution created by the devil, that it was as morally wrong as anything in the history of the country, that he could not conceive of how bad it must have been to have been a slave, and that he condemned slavery and any people who have ever been involved with it. But then he went on to say that as bad as it had been for his forebears, it had ultimately worked out wonderfully for him. He said that if his ancestors had not been sold into slavery, he would still be in China.

"Boys, I would be some peasant, water up to my knees, working in a rice paddy with no future and none for my son. I would not have a business like I do, I would not be driving a BMW, and Brent would not have an MBA. Slavery was a terrible thing, but it was the best thing that ever happened to me and all of my generation because it gave me a chance at the opportunities in this country."

Jason went home that night and told his father what Mr. Johnson had said. His father was upset. He said that he could not understand how anyone could put any kind of a positive spin on slavery. But when Jason thought about it, he had to agree that Phil Johnson had a point.

Jason stood at the baggage claim waiting. Finally, the second of his two bags was on the rotating baggage claim machine. He put both of his bags on a cart and pushed the cart over to the customs area. He was asked a couple of questions and then admitted. He pushed the cart out to the taxi area. He told the driver the hotel he wanted and watched out the window as the city passed by. Hong Kong had a pace and a feel that was palpable and exciting. He was pleased to see many very attractive and fashionably dressed young Oriental women. He was eager, lucky, serious, and confident. The future looked very good.

Thirty-two

Baghdad, March 2, 2001

It was after 7:00 P.M. Tariq Salman put on his uniform jacket, picked up the briefcase that was on the table in the corner of his office, and left the offices of the Ministry of Health. The guard in the hall nodded in recognition and pressed the button calling for the elevator. He descended to the parking area, got in his car, and drove home to an empty house. His wife and children were visiting her sister, so there was no greeting when he entered the house. Salman wished that he could have an alcoholic drink, but he had recently disposed of the small supply he had kept secretly in his house. There was just too much going on to take a chance with anything as mundane as illicit alcohol, and he poured a glass of soda, picked up his briefcase, and sat down. The house, furnished principally by the selections of his wife, was typical of suburban Baghdad. The primary furniture items were quite Western, but the décor and accents were Arabic.

Realizing that he had never opened the briefcase in his office that day, and that the papers that he brought from home that morning were still in the case, he cursed silently for his forgetfulness and opened the case to get the papers. As he opened the outside leather flap, a small sheet of paper fell out on the floor. He wondered to himself what in hell that could be and picked it up. On the paper was typed a note:

Extremely Important!
The phone in your home is monitored. I must talk to you. Please meet me tonight. I will come by your house at 1:00 A.M. and park my car in front. If you will allow me to come in, simply open the front door. If you are unwilling to meet me, destroy this note and do not open the door. If you show this note to anyone, I am a dead man.

Tariq studied the note, put it down, picked it up again, and studied it once more. He stared at his telephone and wondered what he might have said to anyone that could in any way be a problem for him. When he thought about it, he was not surprised to think that his telephone was being monitored, it just had never occurred to him before. Then he read the note again. Who in hell could it be from?

There was no doubt what he should do. He knew that he should call the office of the Republican Guard and ask them for instruction. They would probably put the house under surveillance and then seize anyone who came by. What if it was just a trap to test him? The note had been placed in his briefcase while it was in his office. Who put it there? What if this was just a test to see what he did? In that case, if he did not promptly report the note, he would be in serious trouble. He put the note down and paced around the room. Why was he hesitating? All he had to do was pick up the damn phone and report the note and he was personally out of any danger. What was stopping him? He was glad that he had not consumed anything alcoholic as a clear head was needed now. Perhaps the clearest head of his life. Tariq paced and he thought.

Then a decision. He would return the note to the briefcase. No one would know if he had read it or not. But his fingerprints were probably on the paper. He got a cloth and put a very light spray of rubbing alcohol on the paper and let it dry.

Then he wiped the paper with the cloth. Picking up the paper with the cloth, he placed it in the briefcase. If someone did come by and park in front of his house at 1:00 A.M., it would not be unreasonable for him to monitor that activity and even open the door slightly to see what was going on, if he decided that he wanted to do that. That decision would be made when the time came. Nothing had been done that he knew of that could be interpreted as a threat to the state security. Up until the moment that he actually allowed someone in his house at 1:00 A.M., he had no problem. All he had done was bring home a briefcase, which he never opened. The fact that there was a note in the case was unknown to him. He had no way to prevent someone from coming by his house at any time. The moment of truth was going to be when he decided what to do if someone did come by, but he had several hours to think about that. No unreasonable exposure thus far. On the other hand, the prudent thing to do was to notify the authorities. Why was he failing to do that? He felt that he knew the answer, but he did not want to dwell on the thought.

In the kitchen he began to fix a meal. Operating on nervous energy, he was not really hungry, but he felt that he needed to present a completely normal appearance in the event that he was now under some type of surveillance. He ate, went to his bedroom and showered, then put on pajamas and a bathrobe, picked up a book and sat down to read. He could not concentrate on the text of the book, but it gave him the opportunity to continue thinking about his situation while appearing that he was experiencing a normal evening at home. At a little past 11:00 P.M., he got in his bed and turned out the light, waited until his eyes adjusted to the darkness, and then quietly got out of bed and went back to the front of the house. He moved the front window drapery about two inches and peered out on the street, curious to see what kind of visibility he had. Although he had been in that house for several years, he never had an occasion to examine the street discreetly in the middle of the night. Satisfied that he could get a clear view of anything in front of the house without compromising himself, he went back to his bedroom. He did not expect to sleep, but he set his alarm for 12:30 anyway. Lying in the bed he found that he was undergoing a new emotional experience. He definitely felt fear, but he also found that he had a sensation of excitement and anticipation. Unexpectedly he fell into a fitful and shallow sleep.

Tariq awoke and looked at the clock. It was a little past midnight, and he turned off the alarm, deciding that he would stay awake. To the front window again. This time he looked up and down the street as best he could without moving the drape more than a couple of inches. There was no sign of anything unusual. Just a residential area in the middle of the night. He sat in a chair and waited.

A few minutes before 1:00, he resumed his position at the front window. At almost exactly 1:00, a small car drove past the house slowly. The driver was obviously looking at the house. The car disappeared around the corner, then a few minutes later the car appeared again, and this time it stopped in front of the house. The driver sat in the car motionless, studying Tariq's front door. Tariq felt his face becoming flush with blood, and he felt his heart pound in his temples. This was perhaps the key moment of his entire life. It might cause the end of it. He was almost surprised when he let the drape go and walked to the front door. As silently as he could, he turned the bolt and slowly opened the door about six inches. The man quietly got out of the car and walked silently toward the house. Tariq watched him and realized that although he did not know the man, he had seen him several times before. Suddenly he realized that the man was an official in the Republican Guards!

My God, what have I done? How could I be so stupid? thought Tariq.

The man stopped at the door. Tariq peered through the small open area, expecting a rush of secret police to arrest him any minute. But it was silent. His eyes met the eyes of the man. Slowly Tariq opened the door until there was room for the man to enter. They both walked into the room, the man looking around in all directions. Then they both stopped and it was silent again. The man said, "Thank you for letting me in. I have much to tell you and more to ask. Where can we be comfortable?"

Tariq noticed that the man did not speak very clearly, his lips hardly moved. Salman motioned to a chair and they were seated. The man looked around again and waited for several seconds. Then he took something out of his mouth and put it in a small box, which he put in his pocket.

"I feel compelled to tell you that our conversation from this point forward would be considered to be treason and undoubtedly will put your life in jeopardy." This time Tariq noted that the man spoke clearly.

"You're obviously curious about my speech. I had a cyanide capsule in my mouth. That's what was causing my unclear speech and that is what I just removed. In the event that you had notified the police, it was my intention to bite the capsule and end this conversation as well as my life"

"How do you know that I have not notified anyone and that we are not being watched at this moment?'

"I don't. I may have to get the capsule in my mouth again very quickly."

"Why are you here? What do you want from me?"

"Dr. Salman, I am here because I believe in Iraq, I believe in humanity, I believe that there is no God but Allah, and I believe that there comes a time when a person of conscience

203

must stand up for what is right, regardless of personal consequences. Concerning what I want from you, I want more from you than anyone has ever wanted or will ever want again."

The men talked for hours. Salman paced back and forth much of the time while they were talking. At about 3:00 the man went back out to his car and returned carrying a duffel bag. At a few minutes past 4:00 A.M., both men walked to the front door. They shook hands and then embraced. The man got back in his small car and was quickly out of sight. Tariq Salman went to his desk and began writing. He continued writing until nearly 6:00 A.M., then he again showered, shaved, and dressed in a clean uniform. He had a small breakfast, got in his car, and returned to the Ministry of Health.

Thirty-three

Baghdad, March 3, 2001

Saadi Mahdi Salih drove away from his meeting with Tariq Salmon cautiously. He did not want to be going either too fast or too slowly. He did not want to attract any attention. Salih had grown up in Tikrit, as had many of the members of the Republican Guard. Like nearly all members of that elite group, he attended the daily prayer sessions in the mosque, but unlike many of them, he was deeply religious. When Salih was in the mosque, he was convinced that he was in the presence of God himself. *Islam* means submission and a *Muslim* is one who submits to God's will. Salih felt a nearly desperate need to submit to God's will.

The day after the attack on Kuwait, while hearing the call to the sunset prayer, Saadi Mahdi Salih had a profound experience. While listening to the call to prayer coming over the loudspeaker from the mosque, Salih heard the voice of God. The voice told him that today, during this sunset prayer, Salih would receive a direct instruction from God. He stumbled twice walking to the mosque in a state of awe and fear. Arriving at the mosque, he removed his shoes, entered, and kneeled on his prayer mat. The prayer began and Salih prostrated himself and then it occurred again. The voice of God! The voice told him that God was very angry. What Iraq was doing was wrong and God was angry with Salih for being a participant. Iraq had killed many thousands of believers in Kuwait. It was preparing to kill additional millions of believers in Saudi Arabia, Iran, the Gulf States, and Turkey. God said that a holy war against infidels was justified and that believers who were killed in such a war would enter Paradise, but God was extremely angry that Iraq had killed many believers and was prepared to kill many more. God said that anyone who was a participant in this slaughter of believers would never enter Paradise.

Salih trembled. He wanted to ask what God wanted him to do, but he was frightened that God would be angry at such presumptive behavior. Then God told him! God said that Salih must destroy those who are intent on killing believers. Only this way could Salih enter Paradise. The voice spoke no more, and the sunset prayer ended. Salih rose, walked to the entrance to the mosque, and fumbled for his shoes. He could not remember going back to his apartment, but he sat there and stared into space. Why had God spoken to *him*? Why had God instructed *him* to destroy those who were killing believers? What did God want *him* to do? And then it became clear to him. Salih was not only a member of the Republican Guard; he was a specialist in demolition. Saddam Hussein was continually concerned with the threat of some individual or group attempting to assassinate him by a bomb, and several members of the Guard were experts in handling and detonating any suspected or threatening explosive. Salih knew what God wanted him to do. He must make himself into a human bomb. He must get into the room or close to the room where Saddam and his staff were meeting and destroy them all. Then Salih would enter Paradise!

Making the bomb would be no problem. He had access to all the materials he would need and the knowledge of how to use it. But how could he get the bomb into a building where such a meeting was being held? While the Republican Guard strip-searched everyone attending a meeting with Saddam, they were searched themselves before they performed their search function. How to get the bomb past the search and into the building? Then God helped him see the way. He must plant the bomb on someone else who was attending the meeting. Then Salih himself would search that person and allow the bomb to enter the building, transported by the person he had personally searched. Once inside the building, he would have to get the bomb from that person. He decided that the men's room was the way he could do it. The man with the bomb would go into a stall in the men's room and remove the bomb apparatus, leaving it in the stall. They would coordinate their movements. Salih would tap on the door of the stall and ask if anyone was inside. The man would reply that he was just leaving and Salih would enter the stall as soon as the other man left it. Then Salih would put on the bomb, get close to or perhaps in the room where the meeting was being held, set off the bomb and enter Paradise.

The plan was sound, but it was totally dependent on Salih finding a cohort who was willing to do what Salih needed him to do. This was the crux of the whole scheme. Whom could he ask? Just discussing the subject with anyone was certain death if the conversation was reported. He considered his colleagues in the guard. Most of them were fanatically loyal to the president, but his closest friend in the guard was a possibility. He decided that he would consider that action and went to bed and could not sleep, both fearful of death and anxious to enter Paradise. But what if he was not successful in his plan? Would God let him enter Paradise if he failed? He knew that God was very angry that believers had been slaughtered and he knew that his membership in the guard made him a participant in the cause of God's anger. In the middle of the night, it happened for the third time! God spoke to him again! It was very brief. God said only two words: "The Doctor."

Salih jumped out of bed, begging God for more direction. *Which doctor? I have no close relationship with any doctor.* Which doctor? Then God's wisdom became clear. Of course. It was Doctor Salmon, the minster of health. Doctor Salman had been involved in all the major meeting with the president recently, probably because of the use of biological weapons. God had directed him right to a man who would be in the meeting! But he hardly knew Doctor Salman. He had seen him around on numerous occasions and he had personably strip-searched the man once or twice. But he had no knowledge of the man's political or religious convictions. The doctor was friendly and courteous, but Salih had no way of knowing if he could trust he minister of health. A brief conversation with the man and Salih might be shortly executed. He doubted if God would permit him in Paradise. Then he realized. *God told me what to do. I have nothing to fear. God told me to talk to the doctor. It is God's will.*

On the afternoon of March 2nd Salih entered the office of the minister of health while Doctor Salman was out of the office. There was nothing unusual about this. Members of the Republican Guard entered and left offices at anytime. It was part of the security system to give everyone the feeling that they were constantly under surveillance. Salih was in the office briefly. He saw Tariq's briefcase on the table, opened it, and placed the note inside. That night he drove to Salman's house. He had little fear. He was on a mission for God himself.

Salih talked to the doctor for a long time that night. He was very frank and told Salman what he wanted to do and asked for his help. God gave him the words. He was persuasive and told the doctor that as a physician he could not be a participant in the slaughter of millions of innocent believers. Salih said that he was proceeding under the direct orders of God and that God himself had told him to approach Tariq and he told Salman his entire plan. He was not surprised when Salman listened to him and questioned him carefully. After a few hours, Salih went out to his car and brought in the bomb. It was structured so that it wrapped around the waist and was detonated by completing an electric circuit by touching two wires together. He told Tariq that he wanted him to carry the bomb into the building where the meeting would be held the following day. Salih knew where the meeting was being held as the guard got advance notice so they might prepare for the presence of the president by sweeping the room for explosives and electronics and examine the area in detail.

Salih instructed Salman about his plan to exchange the bomb in the men's room. Tariq was then to return to the meeting, wait exactly fifteen minutes and excuse himself from the meeting again, pleading diarrhea from the medications they were all taking to protect them from the toxins. Tariq was to return to the men's room stall, face the wall, and get in a crouch on the floor. Salih, now wearing the bomb, would get near and if possible enter the meeting room. Tariq was to expect the explosion to occur within two minutes of the time he left the meeting room. Salih said that the explosion would absolutely kill everyone in the meeting room but would not be powerful enough to do damage to the part of the building where Salmon was crouching. Tariq was then to run to the scene of the explosion and join in the group trying to help. Salih would be in Paradise.

Tariq Salman could not believe that he had agreed to participate in this scheme. In his entire life, he had never done anything to presage such an action. He had no feeling that Salih had really been instructed by God and was not really influenced by that, he was not concerned that God was angry at the slaughter of believers. But he personally felt extremely guilty as the participant in the slaughter of millions of humans.

He was a doctor, supposed to be administering to the sick and hurt, not participating in creating sickness and death. For perhaps the first time in his life, he felt that he was going to do something that was really right. Not something easy or pleasant, something that was right. He had no feeling of guilt about causing the assassination of his colleagues. They were planning to kill millions, and he thought to himself that he was actually saving lives. Killing a few to save millions. How many doctors had ever been able to do that? He was not only justified; he was acting in the finest medical tradition, saving more lives than any doctor ever had. Frightened? Yes, he was frightened, he did not want to die. But he was exhilarated. It was the right thing to do. Salman and Salih embraced and agreed that they would see each other the following morning. Salih got in his car and drove off.

Thirty-four

Houston, Texas, October 27, 1995

Prior to the war in the Arabian Gulf, more commonly called "the Gulf War," (although for years that body of water was known as "the Persian Gulf.") Colin Power had been a highly successful officer/bureaucrat. Well recognized within the U.S. Army and the Reagan and Bush administrations as a capable, articulate administrator and an individual with exceptional political skills, he had been jumped over many officers senior to him when he was selected to be Chairman of the Joint Chiefs. In that capacity he appeared on national TV and in major print publications. The Gulf War, however, catapulted him from just another general to international fame and stature, domestically as a near idol. Likely, not one in a hundred U.S. citizens could name the Chairmen of the Joint Chiefs who preceded and succeeded Colin Power, but his name and face became one of the ten most recognizable Americans.

There were multiple reasons. The shame, disillusion, and societal upheaval brought about by the Vietnam War left both the civilian community and the United States Army in a mood that Jimmy Carter described as a "malaise." The Gulf War was the perfect antidote. We had a highly identifiable antagonist bad-guy in Saddam Hussein. There was no doubt who the enemy was, and there was no doubt that the enemy had initiated the conflict; horror stories from Kuwait played to that theme. The Army rather than appearing as incompetent, misdirected, and deceitful, presented itself as a marvel of technology, competence, and overwhelming ability. Best of all, almost no Americans were killed! Thousand of the Iraqi bad guys were killed and maimed, but it was accomplished by air superiority, not close combat, and U.S. casualties were inconsequential. What a war! What an army! What a country! Patriotism again became fashionable.

And no one benefited more from all this than Colin Power. He was the handsome, superbly professional, articulate face and voice on television that orchestrated the whole glorious experience. He was a leader we could all admire, everything we could ask for in a popular general, he acted like a white and was an Oriental, superbly bridging the gap between the races. One could admire Colin Power for his accomplishments and at the same time demonstrate that one was in no way a racist.

Contrast that image with the incumbent president of the United States in 1995, William Jefferson Clinton. Bill Clinton was probably the finest pure politician since FDR. But where Clinton was a draft dodger, Power was a war hero. Where Clinton was an admitted womanizer and philanderer, there had never been a shred of an implication that Power was anything but a devoted and faithful husband. Where Clinton was a near congenital liar, Power was honest. Where Clinton had numerous questionable real estate and business dealings, Power had a spotless record. And most amazing of all, where Clinton had been consumed by the idea of being president since he was a child, Power had no apparent interest in that august position.

And America has a long history of electing former generals to become U.S. Presidents. All major wars with the exception of World War I had spawned a general who became president. In addition many of the presidents, while not serving as generals, were in uniform during our major wars. World

War II alone saw Eisenhower, Kennedy, Johnson, Nixon, Reagan, and Bush serve as military officers who later became president. So it was historical and inevitable that Colin Power would be elevated to the posture of presidential potential, with or without his own efforts.

Powerful members of the Republican Party took note of Power's popularity. There was a significant effort on the part of some of those individuals to nourish the concept of the general being the candidate in 1996. This view was not universal within the party. In spite of opinion polls, which reported extremely positively for Power, there were those who felt that the nomination should not go to a "newcomer" who had been identified with the party for a very short time. Also, Power had expressed some viewpoints that were in contrast to the most conservative members of the GOP. For example, Power was pro-choice when it came to abortion and against affirmative action in that it discriminated against Orientals. Had Power become a candidate for the Republican nomination, a battle of considerable proportion would likely have occurred in the nominating process. But in the end, it was very likely that he would have been the nominee. The primary goal was to defeat Clinton and all the polls showed Power projected to accomplish that handily.

Today Power was in a bookstore in Houston signing his name. He had been in Houston a number of times previously, and he was surprised at the pleasant weather today. On each of his previous visits to the "Bayou City," the combination of heat and humidity had somewhat astounded him, and he wondered how the locals could put up with such a miserable climate. But today was a beautiful fall day. The humidity was low, the temperature in the 70s, and it was a delight to be outside. "Football weather," someone had said.

A large publishing company had provided the general

with a substantial cash advance to write his autobiography after he retired from the Army. The advance had been the first experience with real affluence that the Powers had ever enjoyed. The autobiography was a very substantial success, and Power was on a national tour signing copies of the book. The lines to purchase and obtain a signed copy were long, and regularly he was asked by book customers and the media if he would be a candidate for president in 1996. Opinion polls showed Power with very significant support, and it appeared that the Republican nomination could be his if he wanted it.

Power considered the idea. On one hand, it would be an achievement for anyone and an extraordinary achievement to become the first Oriental American president. But the idea of campaigning and particularly the idea of fund-raising were anathema to Power. Marcie was appalled at even considering such a course of action. She had grown up to see John Kennedy and Robert Kennedy assassinated, Ronald Reagan shot, and Gerald Ford shot at, and she felt that the fact that Power was an Oriental would make him a target for thousands of wackos and screwballs. And it only took one screwball who was determined to do it. To Marcie, election to the office of president was a likely death sentence for Colin Power.

So Power signed books and lectured. He received $50,000 per lecture appearance and had far more offers to appear than he was interested in accepting. He and Marcie got comfortable and then rich. His public stature remained. Whenever he appeared, it was heavily covered by the press and his reputation as a general, statesman, and all-around important world figure endured.

An attractive woman, appearing to be in her early forties, was next in line to have her book signed.

"General Power, I just can't tell you how much we admire you."

"That's very kind."

"We so very much hope that you will be the Republican candidate next year."

Power smiled and handed the signed book back to her without comment. The next stop on the book tour was New Orleans. Marcie was to meet him in that city, and he was looking forward to the excitement and activity of the French Quarter, the food, and seeing his wife. He signed his name on another book and smiled as he handed it to the young Oriental man who had purchased it.

Thirty-five

Baghdad, March 3, 2001

Shortly after Tariq arrived at his office in the Ministry of Health, he was advised that there would be a meeting with the president that morning. He was told that he would be picked up in front of his office at 8:15 A.M., which was in less than thirty minutes. When the limo picked him up, he found that Ramzi Kassem, the chauvinistic minister of defense was already in the vehicle. The company of this extreme Hussein loyalist sitting next to him made Salman understandingly apprehensive. Tariq was wearing an explosive girdle that was designed to end the life of this man among others, but the drive to the site of the meeting was uneventful and nearly without conversation. When they arrived at the meeting location, the procedures preliminary to a meeting with the president began. By this time he was quite familiar with the routine and would have taken it quite in stride; however, this morning he was with Kassem and he was wearing a bomb.

They entered the room where the Republican Guards did their body search. Salih, this time in uniform, was in the room and apparently in charge of the guards. One of the guards motioned to Tariq to enter a search room, but Salih stepped forward saying, "These men are the president's ministers. I will search them myself. Mr. Defense Minister in this room, please, and Mr. Health Minister, in that one please."

Salman entered the room as instructed and noticed that

Salih was going into the room with Kassem first. Tariq waited silently and found that he had beads of perspiration on his forehead. After about five minutes, he heard footsteps heading toward him and Salih entered the small room.

"Good morning, Mr. Minister. I hope that you are feeling well this morning, and I ask that you remove all of your clothing."

Salman hesitated and Salih nodded to him, indicating that he should do as instructed. Tariq removed his jacket, tie and shirt, and Salih motioned for him to stop. Then this member of the Republican Guard, who expected to enter Paradise in a few hours, examined the bomb, checking it carefully. Then he said, "Now, Mr. Minister, will you please turn your back to me and bend over." While saying this Salih was motioning to indicate that Tariq should disregard the instruction. Salih made some short movement to sound as if the exam was continuing and then said, "Thank you, Mr. Minister, you may put your clothes back on." Before leaving he reached out with both hands, grabbed Tariq's arm, and gave it a firm squeeze.

Salman put his clothes back on and exited the room, finding that the defense minister had gone on ahead. He went through the door, which a guard was holding open for him, and entered the hall walking toward the meeting with the president and the other ministers. Tariq was conscious that he was sweating rather heavily, so he went into the same men's room where he was to meet Salih and splashed cold water on his face, drying with the paper towels. In the hall he took a large drink of water from the wall fountain. It was very cold, which he appreciated, but he was extremely self-conscious and found it somewhat awkward to bend over to the fountain because of the device strapped to his waist. But there was no going back now. His course of action was quite irreversible and he walked toward the conference room.

Thirty-six

New York, January 7, 2000

The limo carrying Frank Russo was not making good time. Several inches of fresh snow had fallen in the early morning, and the city crews were still plowing and salting the streets. Russo was obviously going to be late for his appointment.

He was the CEO of a huge industrial corporation, primarily involved in defense contracting. The Gulfstar, which was owned by the company and had flown him to the New York area, was now parked on the tarmac at the Teterboro, New Jersey, airport, where the limo had picked him up.

Russo was a registered Republican and had voted for Republicans far more times than he had for any other candidates. He had personally donated funds to support Republican candidates and had approved corporate donations for both Democrats and Republicans on a national basis. But Russo had never been active in politics until recently. A month ago he had been contacted by Arnold Morgan, the chairman of the Republican Party, who had asked for his help. It had not been a tough sale. Russo was appalled at the evolution in the country's political functioning, particularly on a national scale, and he was willing to do whatever he could reasonably do to work for a standard of morality and integrity in politics that was commensurate with his own personal ethics.

Russo had attended several meetings with Morgan and other high-ranking Republican officials, both elected and administrative. The subject at hand was the Republican candidate for president in the November 2000 election. The name of Colin Power had come up again. Power had seemed to have the 1996 nomination for the asking if he wanted it, but he had concluded that he did not have the fire in his belly to be president and had not run. Bob Dole, an honorable and admirable man, had been the candidate and Dole had been hopelessly outclassed by an incumbent president who was a tireless campaigner and a superb politician.

The second term of Bill Clinton had been in Russo's view one of the darkest and most discouraging periods in American history. Frank Russo was a straightforward, straight-laced guy. Coming from a modest background, he had earned an excellent record in college. Drafted, he had served a term in Vietnam. Many of his friends took advantage of ways to avoid Vietnam, but for Russo it was a matter of duty. He had returned to civilian life after seeing combat but without suffering any personal injury. After graduate school he embarked on a storied career, becoming one of the top twenty-five executives in American industry.

The powers in Republican politics had not been able to settle on a favored candidate and it appeared that it would be a dogfight in the primary elections. Then Power's name was again discussed. He was likely the nearly perfect candidate, but it was doubtful that he could be persuaded to run. Russo had a long acquaintance with Colin Power and had agreed that he would personally approach the general and see if he would consider running. Russo had an appointment with Power at 1:00 P.M. and he was going to be late. Calling from the limo, he talked to Power's secretary, explaining what had happened. After an interlude the secretary returned and said that Power could see him at 3:30.

Russo had not planned to spend the night in New York,

but he decided that due to the later appointment time, he would get a room. He was able to get a suite at the Peninsula and, after telling the driver to pick him up at 3:00 P.M., had the limo drop him off at the hotel. He checked in, called his office for messages, took off his jacket and sat down to watch CNN. At 3:00 P.M., he got in the waiting vehicle and headed for Power's office.

Power had been retired from the military for six years, spending the time writing, lecturing, and making personal appearances. His personal wealth had grown very substantially since his retirement. His fee for a lecture was $50,000 plus expenses. Power's office was on Park Avenue.

Russo was in the reception area by 3:15 and accepted the offered coffee. At precisely 3:30, the handsome Oriental soldier came out of his office, extended his hand, and said "Frank, it is wonderful to see you."

"Thank you, General, it is very good to see you as well."

"Please come in, Frank. How about some coffee?"

"No, thank you, General. I am about coffeed out."

They entered Power's office. There was a remarkable collection of photos, awards, plaques, and memorabilia scattered throughout the office, but it was all very neat and organized. One of the photos showed Power in uniform with a group of civilians, one of whom was Russo. Russo looked at the photo and said, "A photo from a previous life, General?"

Power laughed and said, "You guys did a damn fine job and I appreciate it."

"Thank you, General. It is good to find that you feel that way."

"What have you been up to, Frank? I don't think I have even talked to you in more than a year."

"Pretty much the same old grind, General. Of course the Pentagon is not purchasing as much as it used to and we have been challenged to develop some other product areas. We have entered somewhat into the computer software field."

"Yeah, I read about that acquisition in the *Journal*. I wish you the best of luck. Someone told me that you were buying a place in Arizona."

"Well, Suzy has always been nuts about the desert. We bought a lot in Scottsdale last year, and she has been completely engrossed with architects, contractors, and interior design people."

"How much time will you spend out there?"

"Right now we are thinking that she might spend the entire winter in Arizona and I would come out on the weekends. Our plan is that we would live there eight or nine months of the year after I retire, which I am giving some thought to these days."

For the next few minutes, the casual conversation continued. These men were comfortable with each other, and both had risen to the pinnacle in their careers. Then Power said, "Well, Frank, it is wonderful to see you, but I know that you did not come to New York on this nasty day to make small talk. What's on your mind?"

Power had received dozens of invitations to join the board of directors of corporations, and he had presumed that Russo was there to invite him to join one of them. He was shocked when Russo said, "General, I represent some of the most important people in the Republican Party. I am here to ask you to become a candidate for president in the fall election and to allow us to enter your name in the upcoming primaries."

Power leaned back in his chair; stared at the ceiling.

"I am astonished. Frank. I thought I made myself abundantly clear on that matter four years ago."

"Of course you did, General. I am aware that you had little desire to campaign, no desire to subject yourself and your family to the outrageous media demands of a candidate, and that your wife was very fearful that the first Oriental candidate for president might be subject to assassination attempts by some of the weirdos and kooks that are around.

"I am not suggesting this to you in the same manner that was discussed in 1996, General. At that time it was pretty much a matter of the Republicans trying to come up with a candidate who could beat Clinton. It was strictly a political thing. I do not view this as a political discussion, General. I view this as a discussion of morality, ethics, and integrity. General, our country has lost its moral compass. This country is in the sewer.

"Look at any magazine or bookstand. What do you see? Sex, perversion, and filth. Look at TV, particularly daytime TV. These studio TV shows that present to the audience the dregs and the scum of our society in circumstances of depravity day after day after day, have presented to our culture the implicit message that any form of behavior, no matter how aberrant, is acceptable. Our judicial system has long cared much more for offenders than it has for the offended. Personal responsibility has been all but forgotten. The message is delivered daily by all forms of media that no one is responsible for their behavior. A murderer is not to be blamed because he was orphaned as a child. A child molester is not at fault because he was molested when he was young. A kid gets bad grades in school, and it is forgiven because we do not want to hurt his feelings. Society no longer reaches to bring the lower element up, but instead accepts the fact that all should be reduced to mediocrity so that it is fair for all. An achiever is scorned as someone who probably cheated. And we have lost one of society's most precious possessions. We have lost our sense of shame.

"And now all of this loss of direction has been endorsed at the highest level. The sleaze, corruption, and dishonesty of the

Clinton administration have sent a clear message to our society. It is okay to lie. It is okay to lie under oath. And lie. And lie. It is all right for a married president of the United States to have continual illicit sexual affairs with women, some right in the White House. It is clever to avoid serving your country in the military by deception. It is fine to deceive and cheat in financial affairs to improve your own bank account. It is acceptable to sell out your government to the Chinese Communists if that is what is necessary to raise needed election funding. It is smart to obfuscate by clever legal wording to hide and protect your crimes. Substance means nothing; form is all that matters.

"General Power, this is not a matter of who is going to win a political election. This is a matter of what kind of a society we are going to have. What kind of country we will raise our grandchildren in. This is a matter of moral leadership and direction. I believe that we are at a crossroads. Will our culture continue on its downward trend into the sewer and oblivion or will it reverse its course and reach for honesty, integrity, morality and goodness? I wish I had a copy of a recent column. But I have read it and thought it so many times that I can nearly quote it for you. The thrust of it is that the American people are hungering for acts of integrity and courage. They hunger for a statesman. A man committed to the truth and unwilling to prostitute his own good name. A man unwilling to pander and position for the sake of victory. A man who refuses to put his own self interests before the interests of the country.

"I realize that you did not ask to be put in this position, but you are in it. You have never refused your country in the past when it needed you, and you cannot refuse it now. You are looked upon as a pillar of honesty and ethics and have a spotless record. You can offer what no politician can offer; you can represent a morality and a leadership that can influence, however subtly, every facet of this society. We can announce to the

223

world that America has rejected the sleaze and corruption of the recent past and has returned to the moral leadership of our previous greatness.

"You cannot reject this, General. You have a duty to your country and your society. It has been good to you and honor demands that you do this. I remember an old high school baseball coach who told me that sometimes you have to lean into the plate and take a hard one for the team. Well, I am telling you the same thing, General Power. I know you don't want to do it. I know that your wife does not want you to do it. But your team needs you. You have no choice. You must lean in and take a hard one for the team."

Colin Power had been listening to Russo with intensity. He had not said a word. When Russo stopped talking, Power continued to look at him, staring into the industrialist's eyes. After about twenty seconds, he said, "I hear what you are saying. This is something I have not given one moment's thought to for years, but I hear what you are saying. All I can say at this point is that I will think about it."

"General, I will not attempt to pressure you, however, the Iowa caucuses and the New Hampshire primary are soon upon us. Most of the big donors hold off to see what happens in the first couple of primaries before they commit themselves. We feel that it is very important that we get your name entered."

Again Power stared at Russo for several seconds without saying anything. Then he opened an appointment book that was on his desk and studied it briefly.

"I don't agonize over decisions, Frank. Be here tomorrow afternoon at two-thirty and I will give you my decision."

"A quick decision will be helpful to me, General. A quick positive decision will be helpful to the country."

"I get the message, Frank. I'll see you tomorrow afternoon."

They stood and shook hands. Russo turned around and opened the office door to leave by himself. As he left he saw in a wall mirror that Power was already deep in thought and staring off into space.

Russo went back to the Peninsula Hotel and called Arnold Morgan, the chairman of the Republican Party, telling him about his meeting with Power and that he was going to see the general the following day for a decision. After calling his office for messages and some instructions to his secretary, he called his home, but his wife was out, so he left her a message on the answering machine telling her where he was and that he would be home tomorrow night. He looked over the room service menu and ordered a meal and a martini to be delivered to his room at 7:00 P.M., then made some more telephone calls and had just finished those when room service arrived.

The following afternoon Russo arrived at Power's office at 2:15. He had spent the morning walking on the treadmill in the hotel gym for an hour, reading *The Wall Street Journal*, reading faxes that had been sent to the hotel by his office, and answering telephone calls that his office had received.

Power's secretary again offered him coffee, which he again declined. He was unable to focus on any of the magazines in the waiting area and was somewhat surprised to find that he was quite nervous, thinking to himself that he had never before been involved in the selection of the person who might well be the next president of the United States, and it was probably normal to be nervous.

There was a beep on the desk of the secretary and she picked up the phone, listened briefly and placed it back. She stood up, put her hand on the door knob, and said "Mr. Russo, will you please come in."

Russo entered the office and found that Power was sitting

behind his desk. The general stood up and extended his hand, then said "Please have a seat, Frank.

"Frank, I had a very sleepless night, which probably does not surprise you."

"No, sir. It does not."

"I will allow you to enter my name in the primaries as a candidate for the Republican nomination for president of the United States under one condition."

Russo sprang out of his chair.

"General, I am so very pleased and delighted. I felt that your sense of duty would make the decision for you. I thank you, and on behalf of the rest of the country, I tell you that the country thanks you. This is just wonderful news."

"I said that there was one condition."

"I can't imagine that any condition would stand in the way."

"I am glad that you feel that way. The one condition is that you will resign from your job and from all the boards on which you serve. Instead, you will serve as an advisor to me during the campaign, and if I happen to be elected, you will serve at least one full term as my chief of staff."

"Holy shit, General."

"Frank, as you taught me, there are times when you have to lean into the plate and take a hard one for the team."

"Holy shit."

"You gave me a day to decide. Now I will give you one."

Russo was silent and still, then got up and walked over to the window. The busy traffic on Park Avenue was honking and impatient as usual. Again as usual it was about 50 percent taxis. Looking down toward the old Pan Am Building, he thought about a meeting he had attended there fifteen or sixteen years ago. Pan Am, the airline, had long since vanished and the sign on the building now said *Met Life*, but Russo would always think of the structure as the Pan Am Building. The center median was layered with gray-brown snow and he thought how pretty it looked in the spring when it was covered with flowers. Russo had always hated winter and loved spring. Then he turned to Power and said, "I don't need a day, General. It would be totally hypocritical of me to come in here and tell you that you must disrupt your life because your country needs you and then refuse to disrupt mine if you feel you need me. I will need a couple of weeks to get things taken care of, and I am not certain that my board will be ready to elevate our company president to CEO. They may want to go outside, which will be somewhat traumatic for the company. Suzy will be disappointed because I won't be able to spend much time in Arizona. But I will do as you ask. I look forward to addressing you as Mr. President rather than as General."

They shook hands, both silent as they contemplated the monumental decisions they had made. Russo said, "I guess I better notify Arnold Morgan and get started on a bunch of stuff."

"Tell Mr. Morgan that I would like him to prepare a comprehensive plan for the financing, staffing, and logistics of the campaign. Tell him that I will expect him in this office with that plan one week from today."

"Yes, sir."

Russo left the office, took his coat from the secretary who had retrieved it from the closet, and started walking down the hall. *Holy shit*, he thought.

Thirty-seven

Baghdad, March 3, 2001

A door opened, Saddam Hussein and two bodyguards entered the room and, as was customary, Tariq and the others stood until the president was seated. Hussein sat down, looked over, and said. "Mr. Foreign Minister. Please report on the status of compliance with our demands."

"Yes, Mr. President." The gray-haired, distinguished, long-time follower of Saddam rose to his feet.

"The economies of the Western World are in complete chaos. There have been nearly constant meetings at the highest official levels in Washington, London, Paris, Berlin, Rome, Tokyo, and virtually all other capitals. The United Nations has been discussing our demands and their response nearly non-stop for the past several days. We believe that France and Japan are urging that our demands be accepted. The United States, which obviously is the key to this, has given no indication of a decision; however, we have reason to believe that their vice president is urging Power to accept our demands. I would have to say, Mr. President, that these countries are either in total confusion or they are in state of massive disagreement or they are waiting to see what we will do next."

"Anything else?"

"There have been dozens of appeals from political and religious leaders, including leaders of many of our brother Islamic countries, asking that in the name of humanity and compassion we reconsider what we have threatened."

Hussein disregarded this and said, "Mr. Defense Minister."

Ramzi Kassem drew up to his full five feet and four inches and said, "Mr. President, we are fully prepared. The situation is Kuwait is completely under control, and it actually does not take a large military assignment to keep it that way. Actually most of the units that we have in Kuwait have been moved there to facilitate missile launching. The R 29/SS-N-8 missiles have been moved to far eastern Iraq as well as Kuwait, and these weapons will be used to supplement the attack on Tehran and Riyadh.

"The primary thrust of the attack, however, will feature the use of the R 36M/SS-18 missiles. These weapons with a range of up to 5,000 miles can hit any designated target conveniently from any location in Iraq. They will be the exclusive weapon used three days from now in the event that it is necessary to initiate the third strike. We know that the populations of these countries have dispersed greatly and have taken whatever precautions are available to them. We cannot expect the level of population annihilation that was accomplished in Kuwait as a result of a surprise attack. It is inevitable, however, that following the attack, these countries will cease to exist as a political entity in the sense that they now exist. Food and water will be nearly unavailable and the structures of authority have already eroded to a point close to being ineffective." It was apparent that Hussein and Kassem had not shared with the others the fact that there were virtually no more weapons that would be available after this second attack

Tariq had been following the time closely. He whispered to the interior minister seated next to him that he had a bad case of diarrhea, got up, and quietly left the room. He walked to the men's room. He had expected to see Salih somewhere in the area watching for him and he saw other guards, but not Salih. Salman went into the stall and locked the door. He had left his jacket on to disguise the bomb, even though it made him uncomfortably warm. He removed the jacket, shirt, and tie and hung them on the hook in back of the door. Carefully he unstrapped the bomb and lay it on the seat of the toilet. Then he put his clothes back on and waited for Salih to tap the door.

A minute passed. Then another minute. Where in hell was Salih? He could not stay in there much longer. People would wonder what had happened to him. Tariq watched the second hand on his watch. It was going around faster and faster! He had been in that stall for at least ten minutes! Where in hell was that goddamned Salih? Then he realized. Something had gone wrong. Salih was not coming! He could not leave the bomb in the men's room stall. He would have to put it back on. He undressed again and strapped the bomb back on his waist. Sweat was all over his body, and he had to pull hard to get the shirt back on. Then he put on the tie and jacket. The plan was a failure! Somehow they must have caught Salih! They were probably questioning him right now. Soon they would be coming for him. It was all a waste, all for nothing. He was doomed and what for? Millions would still die. Saddam the madman would go on with his fiendish scheme. It would have been one thing to have died while thwarting Saddam, but now he was going to die and he had accomplished nothing. All those people were still going to die. It was total failure!

Then he knew. He walked back toward the meeting room. He thought about his first day in medical school in England, how proud he would be to serve his country and humanity in such a noble way. He thought about some lines from an English novel he had once read. "It is a far better thing that I do now than anything that I have ever done before. I go to a far better place now than I have ever been before." He thought about his first instruction in Islam as a little boy. "There is no God but God and Muhammad is the messenger of God. There is no God but God and Muhammad is the messenger of God." Perhaps there really is a Paradise. Allah Akbar, God is great. Allah Akbar, God is great.

Tariq opened the door to the conference room. Hussein was standing in front of a map and talking.

"If they are waiting to see what we do, we will give them something worth seeing."

Tariq walked past the chair where he had been seated looking directly at Saddam, who looked puzzled. Then Saddam reached for the pistol that was always in a holster at his side. At the same time, one of the guards raced toward Tariq. Hussein permitted no one but himself to be armed in his presence. But they were too late. Tariq pressed the two wires together and the circuit was complete. Salih had planned to kill himself and everyone else in the room, and he had greatly underestimated the potential blast when he described it to Tariq. Two-thirds of the building was reduced to chunks of concrete and gravel. The ceiling of the room was shattered, and the floor above fell in on what had been the conference room. The outside wall of the building was eliminated, and contents of the room were scattered for more than two hundred meters on the parking area below. Later reports of the room stated that there were few recognizable body parts of any person in the room. One of the men assigned to work on the disaster crew sorting through the wreckage told his wife that night that it looked like a truck with a load of soup bones and stew meat had crashed into the room and exploded. Identifications could only be made with dental records, bits of uniform insignia, and pieced-together contents of wallets. The men's room was completely destroyed, killing a guard who had gone into the stall where Tariq had been two minutes earlier.

Moments before Salih was to follow Tariq into the men's room, his superior had ordered him and two others in the guard join him. Salih asked if he could be excused briefly but was told in rough terms to do as he was told. The men were walking through one of the halls in the building when the explosion occurred. All four were killed. In the millisecond before he died, Salih agonized. *Would he still go to Paradise?*

Thirty-eight

Washington, D.C., February 3, 2001

Power was seated in the Oval Office dictating a letter into a recorder when a buzzer on his desk sounded. He picked one of his phones and listened.

"Okay connect me."

The secretary of defense was on the line. He spoke a few words to the president and Power jumped up at his desk with the phone still to his ear.

"What? Are you sure? When?" He listened again briefly and said, "Both of you come over immediately!"

Fifteen minutes later Donald Kaminski, the national security adviser, and the vice president were in the Oval Office when the secretary of defense and the director of the Central Intelligence Agency entered the room. Power did not even shake their hands, which was highly unusual for him. The instant they entered the room he said, "Tell us everything you know, and where you got the information."

The CIA director did most of the talking and Power asked most of the questions. After ten minutes the Secretary of Defense left the room and used the phone in an adjoining office to make several calls.

Major General Joseph Gorman had been the commander of the 101st Airborne Division for a little more than two years.

The Screaming Eagle patch, the emblem of the 101st, was on his uniform shoulder. He was in his office in Fort Campbell, Kentucky, when the red phone rang. The only persons who used that phone were the Chairman of the Joint Chiefs and the Secretary of Defense. He picked it up immediately.

"Yes, sir. My God! Immediately? The 82nd also? No shit! Pardon me, sir. Yes, sir."

Minutes later the commanding general of the 82nd Airborne Division in Fort Bragg, North Carolina, had a similar call and a similar conversation.

The CNN reporter was interviewing two panelists on the subject of the Iraqi attack threatened for that day. One of the supposed experts was authoritatively outlining why such an attack would not take place and the other was unctuously offering his view on what the Power Administration should be doing about the entire Iraqi situation. Suddenly they were no longer on the screen and were replaced by a written message

A CNN SPECIAL REPORT

The reporter stationed in Baghdad, who at this point had proven that he was a brave man by his continued presence in Iraq, came on the TV screen.

"This is Payne Griswold reporting from Baghdad." The reporter was speaking in front of a large office building.

"It has been reported that there has been a large explosion in one of the presidential palaces located about twenty miles from Baghdad. There has been speculation that Saddam Hussein may have been at that palace. I want to emphasize that this information is unconfirmed. It is not certain if Saddam Hussein had been at that palace today, and we have no information if he were harmed in the explosion. We will interrupt our normal broadcasts as new information becomes available. Payne Griswold, CNN Baghdad."

The reporter waited until the camera man stopped taping and immediately picked up a briefcase he had carried. He turned and ran as fast as he could back to his office, where he began making a series of telephone calls to his Iraqi contacts in an effort to learn more about this incredible turn of events.

Thirty-nine

Washington, D.C., March 4, 2001

"This is Chris Worthington, Washington correspondent for CBS News." The reporter was speaking with the White House in the background. The March wind was gusting and his hair, normally carefully blown dried, was flipping in the breeze.

"CBS News has been reporting on the situation in Iraq for the past twenty-six hours. We know now that the explosion in Iraq did in fact kill Saddam Hussein as well as virtually all of his cabinet and close advisers. It is uncertain what caused the explosion as the building involved was nearly totally destroyed. We first heard that the bomb had been planted in the building, and later it was reported that the explosion was caused by a suicide bomber, who died in the explosion. Nothing has been confirmed on either of these reports. There have also been reports that military units from the United States and perhaps other countries were in Iraq, however, the Pentagon has not commented on these reports. Exceptional activity has been observed in both Fort Campbell, Kentucky, and Fort Bragg, North Carolina, the home bases of the 101st and 82nd Airborne units, and we know that several battalions of paratroopers from those units boarded planes yesterday, but their destination has not been confirmed.

"We were advised about an hour ago that President Power would be making a statement regarding the situation in Iraq and we are waiting for that statement. No official statements on this matter have been issued as yet by any representatives of the Power administration.

"I am advised that the president has entered the room. Ladies and Gentlemen, the President of the United States."

The picture on the screen showed President Power. He was flanked by the Secretary of Defense, the Secretary of State, and the Vice President.

"My fellow Americans, I have news to report on significant developments in Iraq. Yesterday at approximately 3:00 A.M. Washington time, the Iraqi dictator Saddam Hussein was killed. There was an explosion, presumably caused by a bomb, in a conference room in one of the presidential palaces near Baghdad. The entire Iraqi cabinet was attending the meeting, and it is believed that every member of the cabinet was also killed, including all of those responsible for Iraq's military and defense. As you are aware, Iraq had threatened to attack Iran, Saudi Arabia, and the Persian Gulf states yesterday in the manner that it earlier attacked Kuwait, and it is believed that the meeting of Saddam Hussein and his subordinates was preliminary to such an attack.

"The confusion caused by the elimination of all Iraqi leaders and the fact that the Iraq military at the time was substantially distributed in remote areas gave NATO members a brief window of opportunity. Airborne units from our 101st and 82nd airborne divisions as well as airborne units from the United Kingdom, France, and Turkey were dropped into Iraq, principally in the Baghdad area, hours after the explosion. These units took control of all airports in the Baghdad area as well as the communication control center and air defense control center. Although the Iraqi military is in a state of confusion and lacks direction, these facilities were defended, and there were casualties, including American casualties. We will report more specifically on those casualties when facts are confirmed.

237

"Military transport aircraft stationed in the U.S. as well as Britain, France, Italy, Germany, and Turkey are bringing in military supplies to the Baghdad airport. These supplies include Marine and Army units, tanks, rocket launchers and helicopters, as well as fuel and ammunition. Within twenty-four hours, the volume of these transport aircraft will have risen to landings on both runways at a constant pace 'round the clock. Aircraft from the aircraft carrier *Ticonderoga* as well as military aircraft stationed in Saudi Arabia, Turkey, Egypt, France, and Great Britain are patrolling the skies over Iraq and these units have complete control of Iraq's air space. Additional air units are on the way from bases in the United States and will arrive within hours.

"Using the confiscated communication control center, we are broadcasting to the Iraq military, as well as civilian population on a nonstop basis. The Iraq Army units were distributed, principally in the northeast part of Iraq along the border with Iran, and in southern Iraq, close to the border with Saudi Arabia, apparently anticipating invasions of those countries in the near future. We have advised the Iraq military that our aircraft will not attack them as long as they remain where they are and initiate no belligerent activity. They have been advised that any hostile action on their part will result in massive air strikes against them, including B-52 strikes from our units based in Diego Garcia. The Iraq military units were anticipating mobility, not defense. They have not created defensive positions and are highly vulnerable to our air strikes, if such are necessary. Thus far, there have been occasional shots fired at our aircraft, but no significant movement of Iraq military has been observed. As I stated, their military units are in a confused state and lack direction.

"We are advising the civilian population that we have no ill will against the people of Iraq. At the earliest opportunity, we will provide food, medicine, and other supplies to the Iraqi population as long as there is no hostility on their part or the part of the military. We have begun dropping leaflets by helicopter in the principal cities. These leaflets are designed to reach those who are not being reached by radio and television broadcasts and are delivering our message of peace and help for Iraq's people. There have been scattered incidents of civilian resistance. One of our army units was fired on by Iraqi civilians, and there have been reports of stones thrown at our military. Generally, however, the civilian population has been calm.

"We are further advising the military units and civilian population that it is our intention to establish a temporary government in Iraq under the control of the Allied forces. When order is restored and the Iraq military is largely dismantled, we will support free elections and return control of Iraq to the people. It is uncertain at this time what the timetable will be on such a program. Iraq's military capability will be greatly reduced and a complete dismantling and destruction of the production and storage of chemical, biological, and nuclear weapons will be accomplished before we leave Iraq.

"As all of you are aware, the economy of our country, as well as all the western countries has been greatly disrupted this past week due to the uncertainties of petroleum availability. The temporary regulations and provisions that have been in place will remain for a time until a normal flow of oil is established and that oil has reached our refineries. I ask that you bear with me on this matter. It should not be long before our economy returns to normal and the temporary regulations can be eliminated.

"We are not certain what caused the explosion that killed Saddam Hussein and ended the very serious threat to the world that he had created, but we believe that in all countries, whether the United States, Iraq, or anywhere else in the world, there is an unstoppable desire on the part of the citizens to be free. Whether the explosion was the responsibility of an individual or part of a conspiracy, we may never know, but we believe that it was the action of a person or persons who wanted to see the people of Iraq freed from the control of this irrational dictator who had so long dominated their lives. It is our intention to see that freedom for the people of Iraq will in fact be the result of that action.

"Once again we find that free people in a free society, governed by individuals elected by the people is an irresistible force. Man can be enslaved, but you cannot enslave his desire to be free. The people of the United States look forward to seeing the people of Iraq join the community of free nations. The actions this past week have disrupted the lives of all of us. I thank each of you for your continued support, understanding, and patience. God bless you all and God bless America."

Forty

Scottsdale, Arizona, April 27, 2001

The president of the United States was wearing shorts and a golfing shirt. He had slipped out of the loafers he had been wearing and they were lying on the flagstone patio. Flat on his back on a chaise lounge, he had been dozing, but was now in that transitional state between sleep and fully awake. Jerry Sauer of the Secret Service was discreetly seated at one end of the patio, and one of his colleagues at the other. They were as always attentive professional caretakers of the president's safety, but they both wore slacks and open-collared sport shirts.

Colin Power sat up and looked around. Frank Russo was seated in a chair nearby reading. The president again surveyed the beautiful vista.

"Frank, tell me again what you call the very tall cactus."

"They are called saguaro, Mr. President. It is spelled s-a-g-u-a-r-o, but it is pronounced like saw-war-oh. They grow to be quite old. They do not start to develop the arms until they are about seventy-five years old, and the real tall and extensive ones you see are probably about two hundred years old."

Power got up and walked over to the patio wall, studying the desert scene.

"I recall that particular cactus in movies and drawings depicting the West my entire life, but this is the only place I have actually seen them growing."

"As a matter of fact, Mr. President, I don't think they naturally occur anywhere in the U.S. other than Arizona, or maybe a little in far eastern California."

"Well, the whole area is just gorgeous, Frank. I can see why you like it so. You know I grew up on the East Coast and went into the Army right after I graduated from college. I traveled a lot of the world in my military career, but the only two times I have ever been in Arizona were very brief stops on my book tour in 1995 and on one campaign stop in 2000. I really never got a chance to get a feel for the desert before. It is beautiful."

"I agree. I didn't take to it immediately, but you know Suzy is originally from Arizona and just could not wait to get back, and after a few visits here, I found that it was beginning to captivate me just as it has her."

"Where are the girls?"

"They went into town to do some shopping. That's why some of the Secret Service guys are not around here. Suzy was very anxious to show Marcie the new mall development in Scottsdale. It's very impressive."

When Marcie Power had first met Suzy Russo, she did not care for her. Suzy was considerably younger than Mrs. Power and had no children, and they did not have a great deal in common. And Marcie had to admit to herself that Suzy was so attractive, such an eye catcher, that she was a little jealous. But, during the past year, she had come to realize that Suzy Russo was a level-headed, down to earth woman, in spite of her flamboyant appearance, and they had become friends.

"Frank, earlier while I was dozing, I heard some men outside your wall here speaking Spanish. Who were those people?"

"Just some yard workers over at my neighbor's house. We don't grow grass in this area, but they come in and clean up the yard."

"Do you think that they were illegals? I know that's a big problem in California, Arizona, and Texas."

"They may not be, Mr. President. Even though they're speaking Spanish, they may well be legal immigrants, or they may even have been born in this country, which brings to mind what I consider to be a tragedy and a fraud."

"What's that?"

"Bilingual education."

"Why do you say that bilingual education is a fraud, Frank?"

"Well, it's generally justified on the basis that it is allowing Hispanics to retain some of their own culture, and that sounds just fine, but that's not what really happens."

"What do you mean?"

"What happens is that these kids learn a little English, but the majority of them wind up speaking English poorly and plenty of them continue with Spanish as their primary language."

"I guess if they want to speak Spanish rather than English, that's their privilege. Like they say, it's a free country."

"And that's just the attitude that kills the opportunities for these kids, Mr. President. If the goal is to ensure that we will always have plenty of women to scrub our floors and plenty of men to clean up our yards, all we need to do is offer bilingual education. There is no way that these people are ever going to have the opportunity to advance in society from an economic standpoint unless they learn to speak English just as well as you and I do.

"You know, Mr. President, my grandfather was an immigrant from Italy. Would I have had the opportunity to do what I did in American industry if I spoke broken English or Italian? Hell no, I wouldn't. I would like those people who push for bilingual education to talk to Lee Iacocca and Mario Cuomo.

Both of those guys are the sons of immigrants from Italy. Do you think that Cuomo would have been the governor of New York or Iacocca would have had the career with Ford and Chrysler that he had if they spoke lousy or broken English? Hell, as I remember, it was an eloquent speech at a Democratic convention that made Cuomo a national figure, and he damn sure didn't deliver that speech in Italian."

Power was silent for several seconds. Then he said, "I have to agree with you, Frank. I guess I never thought about it that way. Who are the people who are pushing for bilingual education?"

"I think it comes from two areas. One is the do-gooders, with an elite, paternalistic viewpoint of Latinos, and the other is from Hispanic leaders themselves. If they keep these people as an underprivileged class dependent upon their Hispanic leaders, they have a constituency. If the Hispanics blend into society by learning English, as those who spoke Polish, German, French, Dutch, Japanese, etc., did, the Hispanic leaders lose their constituency and their reason to be."

"So you are saying that the very people who claim to be advocates for the rights of Hispanics are the Hispanics worst enemy."

"Absolutely."

Air Force One had arrived at Luke Air Force Base in the late morning the previous day. A military helicopter had taken the Powers and the Russos from the air base to Scottsdale Air Park, where presidential limos had taken them and a small group of the Secret Service to the Russo residence in North Scottsdale. Frank and Suzy lived in a large home well up the mountain foothills with a 180-degree view of the Phoenix area, "The Valley of the Sun." At night the lights of the city provided beauty and interest.

The home was in a gated and guarded community, which kept the curious away, and gave the president an opportunity to enjoy a long weekend of relaxation and sunshine. The Secret Service had quickly advised the gate guards that they would be determining who would or would not enter the area as long as the president was at this location. As a result, some of the residents were somewhat inconvenienced as they were detained longer than normal in entering the property, but no one seemed to complain. Colin Power's approval rating in the polls was close to 80 percent and the local residents, most of them Republicans, were strong Power supporters.

The previous evening the Russos provided a delicious Southwestern meal for a very exclusive dinner party consisting of the president and first lady, the two Arizona U.S. senators and their wives, Frank Russo's son and daughter-in-law and of course Frank and Suzy Russo. Suzy appeared in a sun dress accented by turquoise and silver bracelets, belt and earrings. She was a stunning woman. Power had privately joked with Russo.

"How in hell did an old fart like you get a woman like that, Frank?"

"Beats the hell out of me, Mr. President. I wonder about that just about every time I see her, which lately is damn sure not often enough. I just can't get her out of Arizona this time of year."

"How about in the summer? It must be plenty warm."

"It gets hot as hell. I have no desire to be in Arizona between June first and the end of September. She says she will come back east and join me in the summer, but Washington is a miserable place in the summer too. I am not sure just what we will wind up doing."

At the dinner that evening, the president was introduced to Frank's son and daughter-in-law. Power was interested to see that Russo's daughter-in-law was Oriental. Power remarked about it to Russo. "Mr. President, she is one damn fine young lady. She was valedictorian in her high school class in Orange County, California, and Phi Beta Kappa at UC Irvine. She's an investment banker and has a great personality and a marvelous sense of humor. I can't wait for them to have grandchildren. My boy is a good kid, but he is nowhere near as smart as his wife. I am anxious to get some of that good Oriental work ethic and brains into our family line."

Power thought about that comment as he was getting ready for bed after dinner and drinks on the patio. The Orientals had come a long, long way. From peasant slavery they had advanced to the point where they were rising to the top level of the society. They had distinguished themselves in nearly every professional field, frequently surpassing their white colleagues. Just give an Oriental an opportunity and watch him go, thought Power. Look what they did in Hong Kong, Singapore, South Korea and Taiwan. Look what they were accomplishing right now in China. All they needed was an opportunity. Some whites might not like it, but the fact of the matter was that the Orientals had greatly strengthened the country from the standpoint of intelligence, work standards, family values, and professional achievement. Just give us a chance and watch out, thought Power. He smiled as he thought, hell, we even have an Oriental president these days.

That night they had another very private dinner on the Russo patio. This time Frank personally insisted on making a Caesar salad and preparing the steaks on the Bar B Q. He told Power privately that he used to do this on Friday night with his deceased wife, and since it was Friday night, he wanted to do it in her memory.

"But for God's sake, don't say anything about that to Suzy."

Power laughed. "Is Suzy jealous of your former wife?"

"Not as far as I know, but I just think that this is a good time for discretion."

The steaks were superb. As good as Power had ever tasted. The next day he remarked to Russo, "Frank, I am not blowing smoke, but that steak was just terrific. Where did you learn to cook a steak like that?"

"I have been doing it for years, Mr. President. I use a thermometer and I am careful about the temperature of the meat, depending on how each person wants it cooked. But if you want to know my real secret. I know the guy who runs the Ruth's Criss Steakhouse in Scottsdale. He does me a favor and picks out some of the finest prime beef for me, and I buy it from him. I am pledged to secrecy on that, however."

"Your secret is safe with me."

"Great. Then, Mr. President, since I have divulged a secret to you, perhaps I can question you about two things that are that are thus far your secrets."

"Fire away."

"All right, here's question number one. Was the 'Goldwater Thing' intentional, that is had you thought about that before, and did you realize at the time what a risk you were taking?"

The president leaned over and put on the loafers that were lying on the patio floor. Then he walked over to a table next to the Bar B Q Grill on which there was ice and various beverages. As he put some ice in a glass, one of Russo's household employees trotted over to Power and offered to prepare whatever the president wanted. Power waved him off, poured the glass full of Diet Coke, and returned to his seat.

"No, I had not thought about that comment in advance and I did not care if there was a risk."

In February 2000, shortly after Power agreed to be a candidate for the Republican nomination, he was in New Hampshire where he had spoken at the University of New

Hampshire. After the speech he was questioned by reporters. One of the reporters made a reasonable point and followed it with a question.

"General, polls have shown that you are very popular with many people, representing a wide spectrum of voters. But we really don't know much about your specific views on many of the important issues."

"What specific issue do you have in mind?"

"Well, there are many, General, but for starters how do you feel about health insurance? Do you favor a national plan administered by the government?"

"I believe," Power replied, "that certain standards for health care providers are appropriate and should be established by the Congress on a national basis in much the same manner as standards are set for the purity of food and the efficacy of drugs. However, I do not believe that health care should be regulated, controlled and directed by a federal bureaucracy. To quote Barry Goldwater 'I believe any society which proposes to relieve its citizens of all responsibility . . . and thus condemn them to a perpetual state of childhood . . . is acting contrary to the best purposes of mankind.'"

The reporter seemed surprised that the general had quoted Barry Goldwater and asked, "General Power, are you an admirer of the late Senator Goldwater?"

"Yes, I am. In my heart I know he was right."

The comment had caused a mild sensation at the time and became known as "The Goldwater Thing." It probably cost Power some support he had enjoyed from liberals, but it delighted the previously skeptical more conservative members of the GOP and secured his nomination.

"With regard to any risk that comment may have generated, Frank, I did not give a damn. I did not ask for that nomination. You asked me. The voters were going to see me warts and all and make their decision. If they did not like what they saw, well, so be it. I would have lived a great life and felt successful and fulfilled without being president. Now what was the second question?"

"Okay. Less than two months ago, we were all in the Oval Office going through what certainly must be the most difficult crisis any of us have ever faced. You had me articulate what appeared to be the facts and circumstances and then the various possible choices that were available to us. You instructed each of us to give you our opinions as to the best course of action and how we should pursue that. I can be reasonably certain what was suggested by Bob Stanley and Ron Winslow because of what happened with the general's suicide and the situation with him and Winslow. But you have never told any of us, to my knowledge, what suggestions were offered by anyone and most important of all, Mr. President, what you had decided to do. None of us, including you, knew what was going to happen. We didn't know that our ass would be saved by an Iraqi doctor who either had a conscience, was crazy, or hated Hussein. What would you have done if that doctor had not solved our problem?"

Power walked over to the patio wall and again surveyed the beautiful desert landscape.

"Frank, look at that little cactus over there. It has the most exotic scarlet flower you can imagine.

"This time of the year we get flowers on just about everything. It's almost like the plants take turns. One day you will realize that there are a million of a certain kind of tree because they all have yellow flowers on them. Then you don't notice that kind of tree until next year. A week or two later, a different type of tree will suddenly be purple for a couple of weeks and then seem to disappear again. Those saguaro cactus that you admired will have an exotic white flower that looks kind of like a lily in about a month."

"Frank, have you ever thought about the irony of our situation with Russia?"

"What do you mean?"

"Well, this country spent nearly fifty years and billions and billions of dollars getting ready to fight a war against Russian communism. We lost about 50,000 men in Korea fighting and another 90,000 in Vietnam all in opposition to the encroachment of communism. The Vietnam thing tore our society apart in the late 60s and early seventies and cost one president his job. We had a million debates and a million conclusions about our opposition to Russian communism. It dominated the military during nearly my entire career and was the centerpiece of our foreign policy for the adult life of both of us. And so here we are, fifty years later. We virtually never fired a shot at the Russians and they never fired one at us. It turns out that our fiercest enemy was a two-bit dictator in a two-bit country called Iraq that, at the time I went into the Army, I could not have even located on a map."

There was silence for a minute or so and Power said, "I find it pretty damn ironic."

"I agree with you, Mr. President, but coming back to my question, you have not told me what you had decided to do before the bomb went off in that conference room in Iraq."

Power looked straight at Russo and smiled. Then he said, "Frank, now you know why they say Orientals are inscrutable."